"Every cop ~~i~~ "

Lauren told D[...]e library door. S[...]

Her hand was [...]rrow struck.

Fury replaced anger and she turned on him. "Who do you think you are, shooting arrows at people?" She pulled the arrow from the door with a mighty jerk and snapped it in two over her knee. "I've half a mind to call the cops and tell them you're here."

She had no chance to argue further. His grip on her arms was not gentle, and she was suddenly aware of the pressure of his body against hers. It was insane, stupid, irrational—but she couldn't resist him.

"What's the matter?" he asked, reading the shift of emotions in her eyes. "Second thoughts about dallying with a criminal?"

ABOUT THE AUTHOR

Growing up in a small Mississippi town with plenty of woods around, Caroline Burnes often played Robin Hood with her brothers and friends. A figure of justice and romanticism, Robin Hood seemed to be the perfect man for a mystery set in the beautiful town of Natchez, Mississippi—a place with its own romantic past and present. The book also contains a small dose of humor, which adds to the element of legendary hero and river town.

Books by Caroline Burnes

HARLEQUIN INTRIGUE

86–A DEADLY BREED
100–MEASURE OF DECEIT
115–PHANTOM FILLY
134–FEAR FAMILIAR*
154–THE JAGUAR'S EYE
186–DEADLY CURRENTS
204–FATAL INGREDIENTS
215–TOO FAMILIAR*

*FEAR FAMILIAR series

Hoodwinked
Caroline Burnes

Harlequin Books

TORONTO • NEW YORK • LONDON
AMSTERDAM • PARIS • SYDNEY • HAMBURG
STOCKHOLM • ATHENS • TOKYO • MILAN
MADRID • WARSAW • BUDAPEST • AUCKLAND

To my wonderful friends and fellow writers—
Rebecca Barrett, Reneé Stuart and Jan Zimlich.
Their comments and criticism have been
invaluable.

Harlequin Intrigue edition published June 1993

ISBN 0-373-22229-7

HOODWINKED

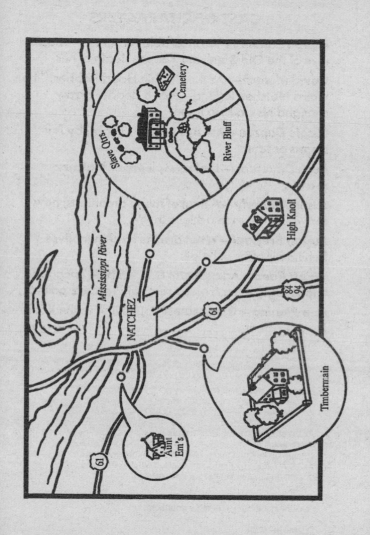

CAST OF CHARACTERS

Lauren Sanders—An incurable romantic—whose love of the Old South may be the death of her.

David Malachi—As the "Robin Hood Robber," he was a Natchez legend—until a deadly arrow changed his claim to fame.

Nicole Dupree—Always willing to fight, by fair means or foul.

Rene Devereau—He knew plenty of Natchez secrets.

Jason Amberly—A man of many ambitions; how far would he go to achieve them?

Burton Brecktel—What are the hidden motives behind his offer of help?

Wyatt Reed—An assistant D.A. with an uncanny knowledge of the crosscurrents of Natchez politics.

Lem Pinning—The greatest opposition to the Robin Hood Robber.

Chapter One

Lauren Sanders pushed her glasses up on her nose and stared at the quiver of arrows that landed with a plop on her paper-shrouded desk.

"I hope you haven't decided to take justice into your own hands," she commented wryly as she looked up at her boss, District Attorney Jason Amberly. "I don't trust your aim. It seems all too often that I'm the target."

"Whining will get you nowhere," Amberly said, sitting on the one clean corner of her desk. "Since you're so determined to make sure this office doesn't prosecute any mentally defective criminals, I bring you this case with complete delight." He grinned at her, and there was something of a hungry wolf in his eyes.

"I can't wait." Lauren didn't bother to hide the sarcasm. Since her job with the Adams County District Attorney's Office had begun two weeks before, she'd met with resistance and resentment at every turn. Jason Amberly didn't personally dislike her—he had nothing but contempt for her profession as a criminal psychologist.

"You won't have to wait to meet this crackpot," Jason said, standing. He turned to the door he'd left open. "Bring him in!" he called.

Lauren readjusted her glasses as she focused on the tall, lean man who entered her office, hands behind his back in handcuffs. As a trained observer of human nature, she appreciated first impressions—she let her gaze wander over the man, taking in his straight posture and the barely concealed amusement in his light gray eyes. His hair, a shade of light brown with golden highlights, was well cut, though tousled at the moment. Even with handcuffs, he exuded a certain ease that Lauren registered as "privileged."

"Ms. Sanders, this is David Malachi. We've charged him with the Robin Hood robberies. Judge Clinton has ordered that he be given a mental evaluation."

Lauren could hear the sneer in Jason's voice, but she didn't interrupt.

"It appears that Mr. Malachi has refused to enter a plea of any type."

The two men's gazes locked in fierce combat. David finally broke the standoff.

"Jason, you of all people should know there's no law that requires an accused person to enter a plea." David Malachi's voice was low and pleasant.

Lauren didn't allow her surprise at the men's familiarity with each other to register on her face or in her voice. Instead she, too, addressed Jason. "Please remove the handcuffs, unless you think Mr. Malachi is dangerous." She let the word linger a moment, allowing both men to understand how ridiculous she found it. "I'd like to speak with him alone."

Jason signaled the deputy to remove the cuffs, but he turned hard eyes toward the man standing before him. "You, of all people, should know better than to play these games, David. You've had every opportunity—education, family, wealth. You're thumbing your nose at all of us, and you're going to pay." He slammed the door as he left.

Folding her hands in her lap, Lauren looked at the prisoner. He was unperturbed by Amberly's threats. He was either very confident of his position, or a fool.

David rubbed his right wrist gently, then pointed to a chair opposite her desk. "May I?" he asked. "Or do you intend to perform the interrogation while I stand. Usually, at least from a psychological standpoint, it's the person standing who has the advantage. Isn't that true?"

"Supposedly," she said. "Please take a seat." Every one of her senses was completely alert. Professionally, David Malachi was the challenge she'd been waiting for. "Exactly what are you doing in my office?" she asked as he eased his lean frame into the chair.

"It would seem I've been ordered here." He lifted one brow. "Our state's tax dollars at work."

"Why hasn't your attorney ordered a private examination?" Malachi was obviously well educated, and Jason had referred to his wealth—most people in similar circumstances demanded private psychiatric evaluation.

"I have no attorney."

She raised her own eyebrows. "Why not?"

"I have a small problem, Ms. Sanders. I have absolutely no belief in the judicial system. Therefore I refuse to participate in this ruse that we now call a trial."

Lauren picked up the folder that Amberly had dropped beneath the quiver of arrows. "Let's see. They have you charged with seven counts of breaking and entering, armed robbery, destruction of private property, the list goes on and on."

"They may charge me with whatever they wish." David crossed his legs. "It doesn't mean I'm guilty."

"And are you innocent?"

His smile hinted at a sudden desire to make trouble. "Now that would be too easy entirely. You're supposed to force me to confront my own actions, aren't you? I have to assume responsibility for my acts, and then I'm ready to stand trial."

"Why did Jason call you the Robin Hood Robber?"

He shrugged. "Some foolishness about robbing the rich and giving to the poor. Remember the legend?"

"I do. Very well." Lauren had been a devotee of Robin Hood as a young girl. She and her brothers had played in the woods behind their family home, reenacting the legend over and over again. Then as she'd matured, she'd graduated to a different type of romantic fiction. *Gone with the Wind* had opened the door to the Old South to her—and even though she didn't want to admit it, Lauren knew that books had influenced her decision to take the job in Natchez, Mississippi.

David leaned forward. "What are *you* doing here, Ms. Sanders? The last thing the state of Mississippi needs is to spend tax dollars on someone who justifies their existence by playing sixty questions with a criminal."

"The state has seen the need for evaluation of criminals, Mr. Malachi, whether you like it or not. Too many mentally disturbed people are prosecuted—and sentenced. They aren't criminals, they're people with emotional or mental problems. I'm here as their advocate." Her face was flushed with anger. Why was she justifying herself to a man who allegedly ran around in tights with a bow and arrow?

"Jason wrote the governor about you. I fear he wasn't overjoyed to find you on his payroll. He needs prosecutors, not someone to take up for accused criminals, you know."

"He finds my salary a total waste," Lauren concurred. "And I value his opinion almost as much as yours." She let the barb sink in before she continued. "How do you know so much about Mr. Amberly and his business?"

"I used to work in the courthouse, before I . . . retired." He grinned again, and the imp of trouble sparked.

Lauren saw the mischief in his eyes, and she couldn't resist asking, "Aren't you a bit young for retirement?" He couldn't be over forty. Her best guess was thirty-nine.

"Well, you caught me, that is a bit of an exaggeration. I gave up law and involved myself in an old, substantial commodity. One that is often abused but never fails to yield a profit. A commodity that some men die for and others sell without a twinge of conscience."

"What is that?" Lauren asked. She found herself enjoying his dry humor.

"Dirt."

"Dirt?"

"Land, soil, sod, loam."

"You farm?" Lauren looked quickly at his hands. The fingers were long, artistic, but his palms were calloused. His

face had the tan of someone who spent plenty of time out-
doors.

"In a manner of speaking. I landscape."

"You gave up a legal practice to landscape?"

"Why do you find that hard to believe? There's honor in
growing things, which is more than I can say for the legal
profession."

Beneath the amused smile, Lauren sensed real anger. David Malachi was exhibiting the first symptoms that might
indicate some emotional turmoil—or malfunction.

"Tell me about Robin Hood," she said, changing the
subject.

"I'll be glad to lend you my library card, Ms. Sanders.
They have a copy of the book."

"Tell me about your family," she countered. He was very
quick—like a cat, he landed on his feet no matter how she
tried to unbalance him.

"Jason said it all. Wealthy, privileged. I think he forgot
to mention that my parents are dead. My sister lives in West
Palm Beach. She's married, with the obligatory two children. I believe Mr. Amberly would describe her life as in-
dolent." He practically dared her to comment.

Against all of her training, Lauren felt her own anger begin to rise. David Malachi was so damned smug and arrogant. So he'd grown up privileged. He was intelligent
enough to realize that he shouldn't run around rubbing
people's noses in it.

She hit the button on her telephone to signal the deputy
to return. "I'll set up some tests for you in the morning,"
she said. "I'm sure you'll want to make bail. Just be here by
ten. We'll get the scores in and evaluated so that Judge
Clinton can do whatever he thinks is best."

David watched as she shuffled his file into order on her
desk. With her honey-blond hair in a neat French braid and
her horn-rimmed glasses, Lauren Sanders looked a bit severe. But her brown eyes were quick to sympathy—and anger. She was one smart and extremely sensitive woman.

"I've lost your sympathy, haven't I?" he asked. The arrogance was gone from his features.

"You never had it. It isn't my job to be sympathetic."

"But you were with all the kids in juvenile hall when you were evaluating their ability to stand trial."

His words were spoken softly, but they carried a knowledge that Lauren hadn't expected. He knew plenty about her background. How? And more importantly, why? "People who are caught in situations they can't help elicit my sympathy. Some of those kids never knew anything except violence and abuse." She gave him an assessing look. "I don't believe that's the case with you."

"I've had something far more important stolen from me." His eyes were unreadable, all emotion concealed.

"And what might that be?" Lauren checked the door. She suddenly disliked the verbal cat and mouse game she was playing. She was ready to end the interview.

"My ideals. My beliefs."

The office door swung open and a deputy entered.

"I believe Mr. Malachi is ready to leave," Lauren said stiffly.

"Would you speak to the prosecutor on my behalf, Ms. Sanders?"

Lauren couldn't conceal the shock. "For what purpose?"

"Until you determine that I'm not going to rush out into the streets and commit mayhem, they're holding me in jail. It's an excuse, as you well know, for Jason to extract his pound of flesh. I don't mind, actually, but I have some young saplings that have to be planted or their roots will die. I need to get back to work."

"Many of your legal problems seem to be of your own making," Lauren observed sharply. "If you hired a lawyer..."

"That's not very objective."

Lauren stilled the flip retort that came to her lips. She knew that where David was concerned, she was going to find it very difficult to be objective.

"I don't see that you're a menace to society," she said. "I'll speak with Judge Clinton."

"You might try Jason first," David suggested, gray eyes wide with innocence. "Judge Clinton is an old family friend. It will only irritate Jason more if the judge steps in and overrides him."

"Thanks," Lauren said. Of all the things she didn't need, it was Jason Amberly down her back any harder because she'd bucked his authority.

"Thank you," David said. "I owe you one."

"No MATTER WHAT your prejudices, the man is certainly capable of signing his own bond," Lauren argued. She leaned forward on her boss's desk.

"How long did it take him to charm you?" Jason Amberly stacked the empty plastic coffee cups on his desk.

"I resent that." Lauren felt her face flush, and that made her resentment even stronger.

"I apologize," Jason said. "That was uncalled for. It's just that Malachi is such a . . ."

"You don't have to say it, I know exactly what you mean. He's intolerable." And charming, she could have added, when he wanted to be.

"Is he competent to stand trial?" Jason asked.

Lauren framed a careful reply. "He appears perfectly competent, but I've set up some tests tomorrow. I want to be certain he's aware of what he's doing, and the consequences."

"Watch out for him—he's a smart man."

"So I've noticed." Lauren stood. "I'd better read his file and prepare. See you later." She hurried out of his office and down the hall to the front door.

The March afternoon was dazzling in its brilliance. The first tinges of green were in the trees, and in seven days, the annual Spring Pilgrimage of Homes would begin. It was something she'd dreamed of, growing up in the flat stretches of the sun-baked Midwest. The South—in full bloom and played out in the antebellum mansions that were as magnificent as she'd imagined them.

The day was still chilly, but her brisk walk kept her warm as she hurried to the daily newspaper office. She wanted to do some research on the Malachi family before she met David again for his tests. He knew about her and her business, and it was a distinct disadvantage. Well, she had a remedy for that.

The _Natchez Democrat_ had an extensive file on the comings and goings of one of the most prominent families in the South. The family history dated back to pre-Civil War times, when Belton Malachi founded River Bluff plantation, renowned for its production of crops, especially cotton. Throughout the war, the Malachis played prominent roles as statesmen, military figures and ministers, with a dedication to community and family—if the flowery newspaper articles were to be believed.

Lauren read, taking notes on pertinent facts with a cynical flip of her pen. When a family owned the only cotton gin in town—and the general store—and included the local minister and doctor—only the most daring newspaper would print anything but glowing, positive reports.

She read through the years that saw the family rise out of the terrors of the Civil War and move into the new century with continued prominence and public service. The 1920s saw the Malachis prospering and thriving.

"Eccentric Sarah Malachi-Lee Shot Seven Times In Gloomy Mansion." The headline stopped Lauren dead.

If the press had handled the Malachi family with kid gloves for the past seven decades, those gloves were off and bare knuckles were flailing. The newspaper account of the murder of the middle-aged woman was vivid in detail and speculation. Even over a distance of sixty-odd years, Lauren felt the horror of the events of April 10, 1932.

Scanning the daily stories that pumped the murder on the front page, Lauren saw the public conviction of Sarah Malachi-Lee's cousin, Darcy Woodson, before any formal charges were even made. On April 15, Woodson was charged with the crime, and on August 1, he hung himself in his jail cell—but not before the press had dug into his bare and eccentric existence in the slave quarters next door to his first cousin's palatial home and the reported incestuous relationship the two cousins had shared before the murder.

The forties, fifties, sixties, seventies and eighties yielded little press coverage of the family. Their sun had descended in the public eye.

Until David was arrested for armed robbery.

The article on David was brief and to the point. She gleaned no new information there, except that he was a Rhodes scholar and a graduate of Harvard Law School. Not exactly a member of the Good Ole Boys network. Money and privilege. Opportunity and means. With a sigh, she closed the file and returned it. No wonder Jason Amberly was out to get him. For a guy like Jason, who'd worked and scraped and fought and struggled to get where he was, David was a slap in the face.

To her surprise when she exited the newspaper, she found the better part of the afternoon was gone. The clean smell of spring swept off the Mississippi River and tempted Lauren to play hooky from the courthouse. There was a pretour of some of the more famous homes, and she wanted to get to know the town where she'd put down her roots only three weeks before.

A tiny voice in the back of her head warned her that reading the history of the Malachi family had tweaked her curiosity about some of the aristocracy that had once ruled the social scene—and probably still did.

On the other hand, duty called. She'd taken the job knowing full well that Jason resented her presence and the fact that her salary came from his already inadequate budget. If he caught her larking about town, visiting historical homes during working hours, he'd have plenty of grist for his complaint mill.

It was Thursday, almost the weekend, she consoled herself as she took the several blocks back to the stately old courthouse. This weekend, she'd tour a few homes, check out bookstores, libraries and specialty shops. For now, though, she had to go back to work.

"Lauren!"

She looked up, surprised to hear her name called in a city where she knew only six people at best.

"Burton." She smiled at the assistant district attorney who was waiting for her on the courthouse steps. "What's going on?"

"Jason said he delivered David Malachi into your hands. What do you think?"

"I'll know more tomorrow." As much as Lauren liked Burton Brecktel, she had no intention of discussing her client with him.

"Malachi has a long reputation for eccentricity." He lifted an eyebrow in a leering gaze. "It runs in his family."

"So I discovered at the local newspaper." She started to say something about journalistic ethics in past decades but held back. She had the odd sensation that the information she'd gathered on David was somehow... too personal.

"How about a drink tonight after work? There's a great jazz band at Riverbend."

"Sounds like fun," Lauren agreed. "Six-thirty?"

"That's fine." Burton laughed and chucked her under the chin in a casual gesture. "Don't work too hard, though, or Jason will begin to think you're the better investment, after all."

Lauren was still chuckling as she entered the courthouse and hurried up the three flights of steps to her cubbyhole of an office. The rest of the D.A.'s office was on the second floor. There had been no room for her there, so they'd renovated a broom closet on the third floor. Renovated was a highly flattering word to describe the fact that they'd taken out the pails and mops and installed a desk and a telephone.

As she pushed open her door and entered, she was thankful that at least she had a window. It was the golden shaft of light streaming in from the west that first caught her attention. For a moment she failed to see the arrow that was standing up on her desk. When she did see it, she approached slowly, cautiously.

Sure enough, the arrow pinned a small, handwritten note to the wood of the desk. Very gently she pulled the note from the arrow, creating the unmistakable sound of paper separated by a sharp blade.

When a system becomes unjust, it is up to the individual to see that justice is not thwarted. There's not a buffalo alive on the range today. No hidebound judge can prevent a just man from a just cause. Tonight at nine.

The note was signed "Robin." "Damn his soul," Lauren muttered as she crumpled it into the pocket of her skirt. With a swift jerk, she unlodged the arrow and examined it. The shaft was finely carved, the feathers handmade. The tip had been fitted with a razor-sharp hunting blade in contrast to the target arrows she was familiar with.

She tore out of her office and ran down the stairs to the district attorney's office. When she rushed in the door, she suddenly stopped as eight pairs of eyes looked up at her with amusement.

"Where's Amberly?" she asked, finding his desk empty.

One of the young D.A.s tapped his watch. "I'd say popping his dinner in the microwave and getting ready to take his shoes off."

Lauren checked her own watch. It was twenty minutes after five. She looked around the room, hoping to see Burton Brecktel among the ambitious young lawyers who worked as prosecutors. He was absent. Probably waiting for her at Riverbend.

"Can we help you?" Wyatt Reed asked. "You look like something terrible has happened."

Lauren shook her head. If what she suspected was true, David Malachi had decided to don quiver and leggings again that night. If so, he could jeopardize his future—and hers, as well. She was the one who'd asked that he be released on his signature. She was the one who'd vouched for him.

She was the one who'd been hoodwinked by a rascal. And before he ruined himself and her, she intended to figure out his cryptic little note and stop him.

Chapter Two

Lauren's scribblings ran halfway down the third page of her notepad. She'd pulled the words *buffalo* and *hidebound* out, following her intuition that those were the keys to the puzzle. But what she was supposed to learn from Robin's little note was more than she could figure out.

She checked her watch once again. Seven-thirty. She'd left a message for Burton at Riverbend, apologizing for having to break their date. When she saw him in the morning, she'd give an explanation in full. Right now, though, she had less than an hour to solve Robin's riddle if she was going to arrive at the scene at 9:00 p.m. to stop him from committing a new felony.

Where? That was the question she had to answer.

She went back to the case files on the seven robberies that had preceded David's arrest. All were prominent families. All were old Natchez families. All were businessmen. Some lived in old homes, some new.

System of justice. That phrase ran through her mind and she tried to forge a political link in the robberies. There was none she could find. Of course the structure of Natchez politics would run much deeper than what met the eye. Still, there was no clear line of thought she could follow.

Her eyes were burning, and she took her glasses off to rub them. She checked her watch. Seven forty-five. Time was slipping away.

On a whim, she picked up the Natchez phone book and began running through the Yellow Pages. It was relatively small, so she started at the beginning, trying to find a name or business that triggered some link. Page after page, she ran down the listings. Her finger never paused.

She was almost at the end when she came to Tanner Mercantile. It was one of the largest—and oldest—stores in Natchez. Local stories said that Bedford Tanner, one in a long line of wealthy and colorful Bedford Tanners, had melted door fittings down for the Rebel forces to use for bullets when Natchez was under attack by Union forces. There was also the grim rumor that he'd charged double for the fittings.

There was a tiny click in the back of Lauren's head. Buffalo. Hidebound. Tanner. Was it possible?

Judging from the other Robin Hood victims, Bedford Nathan Tanner the Thirty-fourth or whatever numerical title of descent he held was the perfect candidate for a visit from the Sherwood Forest burglar.

Lauren's heartbeat increased. If she was right, she might be able to prevent David from committing a serious crime. If she was wrong, she'd simply have a long drive out to the country and wind up looking a fool on the doorstep of Nathan Tanner's home.

She picked up her car keys, glasses and purse and ran down the steps to her car. Night had settled over the small city, and the evening breeze coming off the river invited fancies.

Lauren didn't have time for the romantic thoughts that the Mississippi evoked. Brushing away images of dark-eyed gamblers, she aimed her car for the highway that led north, and she put her concentration into driving. She'd never been to the Tanner plantation. She didn't, in point of fact, even know if Nathan Tanner actually lived on the property any longer. It wasn't exactly possible to call up and ask. She silently cursed David Malachi as she drove. When she got her hands on him, she'd see that he was safely locked up in some institution where he couldn't do himself, or her reputation, any further harm.

Once clear of the city, the highway was dark. There was no traffic and Lauren contrasted the piney Mississippi highway to the long stretches of Kansas interstate that cut across the rich grain fields. Her ambitions had carried her far from home, and during her years as a criminal psychologist she'd found a world that was often ugly and mean. Her recent move to Natchez had been fed by romantic dreams—and books. At least she could live in a beautiful setting.

Was that why she was chasing a crazy man around the Mississippi landscape? She thought about that question as she drove. There was something about David that caught at her. He didn't steal for himself, if the charges were true. He really gave it to people who were less fortunate than he. His angry accusations about the justice system were ideas she'd often thought, too. Sometimes "justice" was awarded to the highest bidder. There had been times when she was tempted to take justice into her own hands, like the bandit of Sherwood Forest.

Robin Hood, indeed, she almost snorted. Was she still some teenager caught in the raptures of a legend? Yes, she'd read too many books, too many works of *fiction* where noble impulses were real.

She was ten miles out of town when she saw the High Knoll sign. She slowed as she took the gravel road that led to the Tanner estate. She was still on public property, but she felt as if she was trespassing.

The road narrowed as thick hardwoods and the ever-present pines crowded closer and closer. Even the clear light of the moon was blocked as Lauren drove forward. She checked her watch in the glow of the dash. Eight-forty.

When she saw the small fairy lights that outlined the drive, she pulled her car to the side of the public road and got out. No sign of another vehicle. In fact, she couldn't be certain that another car had passed that way in the past week, or month. Apparently the Tanner estate was the only

home on the entire road. At least wealth could buy soli-
tude.

Feeling like a criminal, she changed from her working
pumps to a pair of tennis shoes she carried in her trunk, and
started down the drive. In the distance she could see the
lights of the house, a big, two-story Colonial. Perfect for
Robin Hood. Judging by his rap sheet, he had a fondness
for works of art, silver and, most especially, jewels.

Lauren jogged toward the house. She had no game plan.
And there wasn't time to devise one. She'd circle the house
to see if she could find signs of activity within. If she saw a
member of the Tanner family, she'd ring the bell and rouse
the household on the pretext of...something. That should
be sufficient to discourage Robin. He wouldn't willingly
walk into a trap.

Would he?

The front of the house was shut up tight. Thick curtains
prevented Lauren from gaining a view of the inside. Stepping over as many plants as possible, she moved around the
east wing and toward the back.

The house was big. Wicker furniture crowded a covered
porch that would be too inviting to resist on spring morn-
ings. A crystal pool with Moroccan tiles glistened in the
moonlight. The gentle tinkling of three fountains could be
heard scattered about the garden, which dropped away
down the gentle slope of the yard. High Knoll was a beautifully maintained estate.

She found the kitchen windows, but there was no sign of
life in the lower floors. She hurried around the bay window
and stopped. French doors were open wide. White lace curtains drifted in and out on an uneven breeze that chilled her.

Taking care not to make a noise, she moved forward. If
she caught David in the act of a robbery, as an officer of the
court, she'd have to turn him in. She'd hoped to prevent this
very thing from happening. And what a bold felon he was,
walking in through the—she peeped inside—library doors.

"David." She whispered his name. "David." She tried
louder.

When there was no answer, she stepped into the house. "David, don't do this. Get out of here," she whispered.

If he would only run. But he wouldn't. Not the man she'd met in her office.

The only light in the library came from a lamp in another room. Lauren tiptoed forward. She couldn't give up now. She'd come too far. If David Malachi was in the house, she intended to confront him. He'd left the note, so that was what he'd wanted.

She was almost at the door when her foot snagged on something. She went down on one knee, barely catching herself before she pitched face-first onto the floor. Groping in the dark, she searched for the large object that had snared her. Her hand closed around something cloth-covered and firm. She put both hands on it, feeling a moment before it registered.

She was holding a human leg.

A leg that did not move.

She froze, a scream caught in the back of her throat. Her fingers gently moved up the body, stopping at the chest. A slender wooden stick had pierced the man's heart. Sticky blood coated her fingers. Even though she knew it was futile, she felt his neck. There was no pulse.

Lauren let her training kick in. She shut off the personal side of her brain and simply began to register facts. The material she felt was suit, expensive cloth, starched shirt. The body was still warm. Whoever had shot the man could still be in the house. She wanted to turn on a light, but she was afraid. Afraid of what she might see, and afraid of who might see her.

The victim had been shot with an arrow. She had seriously misjudged David.

Lauren rocked back on her heels and began to retreat from the body. The first order of business was to get out of the house, back to her car, to a telephone and call the police. She was in a jam, that was for sure. She'd broken into a home and come upon a murder. A mental image of Jason Amberly's face when he heard that bit of news floated before her. Well, that was too bad. She could take losing her job—but not her life.

Step by painful step, she inched out of the room and back to the beautifully drifting curtains.

The pattern of moonlight on the polished oak floor was what she concentrated on. Seven steps, six, five. She moved cautiously toward the door. If she made it outside, she'd be safe. Four, three, two. She was almost there. The toe of her Nike edged on the threshold. A sudden gust of wind blew a curtain around her face.

She fought the sensation of choking that came when the material wrapped around her. When the hand gripped her shoulder, she almost died.

"Hold!" A masculine voice ordered her. "So the riddle I posed gave you no quarrel. Now you'll pay the consequences." The voice was a strange blend of accents and diction.

She snatched the curtain from around her face and threw it over her assailant's head. Surprised, he loosened his grip on her shoulder. Lauren bolted. She hurled herself down the gentle slope of the lawn and into the gardens. The tall camellias and azaleas gave cover, and she darted among them, following her instincts.

"Lauren!"

She heard him calling her. As if he didn't know why she was running from him! What kind of monster was he? Panting, face torn and scratched from the branches of the shrubs she hid among, she tried to think. Where was he parked? How long had he been there? Had he robbed the house already? Could she get back to her car? Or should she wait for daylight?

One wrong step might cost her her life.

Perhaps she could circle the house, staying well within the woods. If she moved cautiously, and slowly, she could negotiate the circle and get back to her car. Just to get behind the wheel and lock the doors—if she could make it that far, she knew she could get away.

Ears alert for any sound, she began to creep forward. She realized for the first time that there were statues in the garden. Life-size figures that seemed to loom out of the darkness, catching the moonlight almost like flesh. She gritted her teeth and pushed on.

The gardens ran for what seemed half a mile. There was a low stone wall, which she easily climbed. Perched on the solid bricks, she had a better view. Her breath caught as she saw a tall, lean figure silhouetted by the lights of the house. She recognized David's athletic form as he slipped from shadow to shadow. He was headed away from the house. Toward her.

She leapt to the ground, scrabbling and running. The surrounding woods were thicker than she'd anticipated, but she plunged into them, getting her bearings from the stars that shone so brightly through the leafy canopy of the trees.

If she'd never appreciated the time her older brother had spent teaching her sports and camping skills, she did now. She should have paid more attention. She walked deeper into the woods and turned left. She had no idea about compass points, but she knew she had to keep an eye on the stars she'd picked out as her guideposts. The three bright ones set in a triangular pattern were over her left shoulder—the way to her car, if her calculations were correct.

Branches slapped at her face and caught at the tweed of her jacket. Her legs, once silk clad, were essentially bare and bleeding from a million little scratches. She trudged on, trying to be as quiet as possible.

Her gaze was focused on the ground in front of her when she heard the soft chuckle. Like a deer, she froze, one foot poised to step. The whoosh of the arrow passed just below her right ear. It pierced the trunk of a nearby tree, vibrating with the force of the arm that sent it.

Lauren dropped to the ground, ears straining. Once again, the soft chuckle reached her ears. The bastard was playing with her! Stalking her like some prey. She crept forward, wondering where he was and if he could see her. Nothing in her initial interview with David had prepared her for such a vicious, gleeful assault. Nothing! He'd hidden his nature quite well—too well to be sane. And she was the one who had unleashed him on society. Nathan Bedford Tanner was dead because of her.

"David, they're going to execute you for this," she said out loud. "You'll never get away with it."

The laugh came again, confident and easy. "Such dire threats from a maiden on the verge of death."

The accent was a twist of Old English and Southern drawl, making it impossible for her to identify the voice as his. He was using a fake tone.

"You lured me here to kill me? Why?"

"She poseth the acute question. For justice, my love. Pure justice."

Lauren rose slowly to her feet. If she was going to die, it wouldn't be groveling in the dirt. She brushed the leaves from her jacket and skirt. "Step over here by me," she challenged. "Let me see your face."

Her answer was the soft twang of the bow, immediately followed by the arrow. The sharp blade bit into her arm just below the shoulder, shredding her jacket, shirt, and her flesh as it passed through. Lauren couldn't suppress the cry of pain and shock. She looked down at her arm and saw the fresh flow of blood that had begun to soak through her jacket.

She turned and ran. All sense of direction was lost as she crashed through the underbrush, intent only on getting away from David. Her pounding heart and crashing body covered any sounds of pursuit, and she didn't try to listen for her hunter. She merely ran. Sweat trickled down her body and her lungs burned with the effort. One foot before the other, she trudged on. When she could finally run no more, she sank against a tree trunk and panted harshly in the brisk night.

"Lauren!"

David's voice whispered her name through the darkness.

She started forward again, her body rebelling, but her will to live forcing her on.

"Lauren!"

He was closer now. This time he'd finish her off. He was tired of cat and mouse. Tired of the chase. He couldn't afford to let her live because she knew he'd killed Bedford Tanner.

"Lauren!"

His voice was right on her, but she was too tired to tell where it came from. Even the trees whispered her name. They leaned toward her, black branches plucking at her face and clothes. She put her hands up to fight, and a searing pain rushed through her arm.

"Lauren!" Strong arms grabbed her and pulled her to a broad chest. "What the hell happened? You're bleeding!"

Lauren refused to faint. She looked up at the man who held her. The amusement was gone from his gray eyes. Lodged there instead was worry and puzzlement. "You won't get away with this," she whispered.

Her honey-blond hair was a tangle in her frightened eyes, and he could feel the tension vibrating through her. "What happened to your arm?" he asked again. "We'd better get you to a doctor. I saw you climb the garden wall and take off into the woods, but I lost you. You were running like the hound of the Baskervilles was on your heels. What happened?"

"You'd run, too, if you tripped over a dead man with an arrow in his chest." She hurled the words through clenched teeth. "Why did you kill him, David? Why don't you just go ahead and finish me here?"

She twisted free of him and staggered forward a few feet. A root snagged the toe of her shoe, and only David's quick grip on the back of her jacket kept her from crashing to the ground.

"Quit acting like a fool and let's get out of these woods," he said harshly. All tones of sympathy were gone from his voice. "I won't have to kill you, you'll bleed to death if you don't take care of that arm." With more roughness than kindness, he shoved her forward.

Lauren never had another chance to check her position against the stars in the sky. David pushed her relentlessly forward. Whenever she paused, his firm hand caught at her uninjured arm and propelled her on.

"You could have killed me, too. Why didn't you?" she finally asked, playing for a moment to catch her breath. Her arm was throbbing with a fiery pain.

"There's someone in these woods who might take you up on that offer," David said in a harsh whisper. "Now shut up and walk. Unless you want to see both of us dead."

"I'm not an idiot, David. I saw you. Clearly. I can identify you."

"Good for you, Sally Sharp Eyes. Now walk."

Lauren stumbled under the roughness of the thrust he gave her. Her legs weighed a thousand pounds. The entire right side of her body was on fire. Why didn't he go on and kill her? Surely she wasn't much sport in her sorry condition.

A branch slapped her face, cutting across her nose and knocking her glasses off. She couldn't suppress her cry. David's hand shot across her mouth, firm and constricting. His other arm circled her waist and pulled her back against him in a grip so tight she felt as if her ribs would crack. Her first impulse, to struggle, was quickly squashed. The harder she fought, the harder David held her until she was sure he meant to crush the life from her.

"I'll let you go if you promise to keep very quiet."

David's voice was a whisper at her ear. He spoke so softly and with such gentleness that for a moment Lauren didn't comprehend his words. When she did, she nodded slowly. Immediately she felt the pressure lessen.

"Someone is following us," David whispered. "Be very still."

His arms released her, and Lauren gulped a draft of air. She sank quietly to the ground, wanting only to breathe and sit still for the rest of her life.

When she knew she wasn't going to die from lack of oxygen, Lauren began to listen to the woods. There was no sound to indicate anyone else was around. She looked at David as he stood only three feet away, his body taut with listening.

It was a ruse. He was trying to make her believe there was someone else involved, someone who might have shot her and killed Bedford Tanner. He was a clever man. For some hidden reason, he didn't want her dead, at least not yet.

She eased up to her knees, watching to see if he'd notice. He didn't shift his stance a hair, but he spoke softly.

"If you dare go running off through those woods, I'll leave you to him. After all, you're the only person who can positively identify me, as you so succinctly put it."

Lauren tried to read the intent in his eyes, but without her glasses she couldn't see clearly. She'd been ready to bolt, but she hesitated. The impulse to run faltered and she sank back onto her heels. In the stillness of the night, she forced herself to listen. If someone else was out there, she would hear him.

David eased over to her side and squatted so that his lips brushed against her ear. "We're about a hundred yards from your car." He nodded through the woods. "Straight through there. Now, creep. Go slowly, and don't make any noise. When you get to your car, get in the passenger side and put the key in the ignition. I'll be right behind you."

"And if you're not?" she asked.

"You don't have to worry about that. I'll be there."

"I don't believe you," she hissed.

"I don't care what you believe." David's intense gaze locked with hers. "I did trick you into coming here. Therefore I'm responsible for you. But if you choose to act like a pigheaded fool, then I wash my hands of you. Now get up and try to make it to your car before you faint from blood loss or I lose my patience and leave you here."

Something in his voice made Lauren rise. She'd never been one to take orders from anyone. But there was an edge to David's tone that warned her to obey. Still, there was plenty he wasn't telling her, and she had to know.

"Why did you want me here?" she asked. That was the question that bothered her most. If he'd intended to murder Tanner, why had he asked her along as a witness?

"There's no time now." He nodded toward her car. "Go! I'll make sure he doesn't get you from behind."

"Tell me why," she insisted.

"Lauren, there was something I wanted to show you. Now it doesn't matter. Getting out of here alive is what matters, now move it."

Lauren turned in the direction he'd indicated and stepped among the trees. She felt in front of her with her hands. She was near-sighted, but she could see well enough to make her way home—if she could get to her car.

She heard a limb crack behind her, but she kept on moving toward the car. Following as straight a line as she could, she finally burst through the trees and onto the road. She'd missed the target by twenty-five yards, but she could see her little car parked almost in the ditch. With a small cry of relief she ran toward it, pulling the keys from her skirt pocket as she stumbled forward.

She was about to slide into the driver's seat when she was grabbed from behind and pulled back.

"Passenger side," David reminded her.

"Get away from me," she replied.

"Your arm, remember? Your car's a straight shift. You'd better let me." Without another word, he slid behind the wheel and cranked the engine.

Lauren hurried to the passenger side and got in, not knowing whether she was more afraid of riding with him or being left behind.

When her door was closed, he reversed and spun out of the sand.

"Where are we going?" she asked. The trees were a blur in her unfocused vision.

"To a safe place where we can talk. And where I can take a look at that arm."

"Mercy Hospital will do fine," she said.

"Oh, no, my fair-haired maiden. Your fate is sealed with mine now."

Lauren felt her blood chill.

Chapter Three

Pressed against the kitchen table in the old house where he'd taken her, Lauren glared at David as he advanced. She had no idea where she was. They were in an older residential part of town, with large houses, lots of trees and lawns—and no near neighbors.

"Scream, if you want," he said, as if reading her mind. "There's no one to hear. Now take off that jacket."

She could feel a fresh stream of blood oozing down her arm. When David had attempted to examine it, she'd jerked away roughly. The sudden jolt of pain had almost dropped her to her knees.

"Take me to a doctor," she said.

"I'll make that decision once I've seen the damage." He took two steps closer. "Take off your jacket and blouse, or I'll do it for you."

The cool threat in his voice made Lauren even more afraid. Reluctantly she unbuttoned the jacket and carefully shrugged out of it. Even the smallest motion made her arm throb. She looked at what had once been her best white silk blouse. The right arm was saturated with blood, and it was shredded from the shoulder and hanging loose. She forced herself to look at the wound. The muscle was neatly sliced and lying open. The sight of it made her dizzy.

Before she could object, David helped her into a chair. His fingers found the small buttons on her blouse and moved from chin to waist with amazing speed. He eased the material down her arms so that the wound on her shoulder was accessible.

For the moment, the pain was too intense to allow for any embarrassment on Lauren's part.

Without a word, David went to the sink and began running hot water. He rummaged through several drawers until he found three clean dishcloths.

"I'm going to the bathroom for some disinfectant. Stay still and don't move. The muscle is cut and it's going to require some stitches. We'd better get it wrapped before you go anywhere, though. There's no point risking permanent damage, and if you keep twisting around, that could happen."

Lauren nodded. Nothing else he'd said could have made her sit still. She dared a look at the wound again and felt her head begin to swim. Too many horrible things had happened.

To keep her mind off the growing pain in her arm, she examined the room. It was an old-fashioned kitchen. High ceilings. Big cupboards painted a clean white. One large white sink. Gas stove and gently humming refrigerator. The room was big and dominated by the large table that seated eight. White curtains hung at the windows and for the first time Lauren noticed the immaculate cooking utensils hanging around the room.

"This was my aunt's home. I spent a lot of happy days here as a child." David stood in the doorway, his arms filled with bottles and bandages.

"I have the feeling that there was . . . happiness in this room." For some crazy reason, Lauren had been about to say love.

"Aunt Em was a special lady. I stayed here whenever I could wrangle my parents into it. Em had her own children, all older than me, so she welcomed the chance for another baby, I suppose."

There was none of the arrogant tension in David's body that she'd seen before. Lauren saw what a real smile could do to his face, and she wondered why he didn't smile more often. There was something childlike and open in his face now, and she instinctively knew that it was a rare moment. David Malachi had more defenses than an armed camp.

He looked at her arm as he stepped forward, and Lauren followed his gaze. She felt a hot flush touch her face as she realized that her blouse was hanging. Blood had soaked the white fabric of her bra, and there was nothing she could do about it. Any of it. When he pulled up a chair next to hers and lifted her arm, she looked away.

"You're a tough woman," he said matter-of-factly. "This must hurt like hell."

"It does." She gritted her teeth as sweat popped out on her forehead.

"Why don't you ask me some questions, to take your mind off what I'm about to do?"

She tried to think of something important, but her mind was hazed with pain. "I thought Robin Hood wore tights," she managed. David was wearing jeans, tall boots and a long-sleeved, dark green shirt. Only his leather jerkin suggested the Sherwood bandit.

"If you're trying to see my legs, you're going to have to do better than that," he answered. He worked quickly and efficiently, cleaning the wound and surrounding area.

Lauren smiled just as he swabbed the wound with iodine. Lights exploded behind her eyes from the pain. She felt herself slipping from the chair, but he held her, pulling her into his arms.

"That's the worst of it," he said, supporting her in a grip that was as gentle as his last had been harsh. "You're very brave, Lauren Sanders."

The pain blocked out all logical thoughts for several moments, and Lauren yielded to it, allowing herself to lean on David so that she wouldn't faint. As the fiery tentacles began to release her, cold reality returned. She was sitting at a strange kitchen table letting a murderer give her comfort and support. Her spine tightened and she started to sit up.

David released her, sensing by the sudden rigidity of her body where her thoughts had gone.

"Why did you kill Bedford Tanner?" she asked, turning so that she could stare into his gray eyes.

"I didn't."

She gave him an A for not flinching or looking away. Some liars were very good at direct eye contact while they twisted the truth to suit the purpose of the moment. Was he a sociopath? She'd never have thought so. She'd always been able to rely on her intuition, and David Malachi hadn't struck her as a liar. Then again, he could be so deeply disturbed that he hid it very well.

"So, you're innocent. I suppose there are two Robin Hoods running through the streets of Natchez. Is this a town idiosyncrasy no one told me about?"

"I like you much better when you're swooning with pain." He stood and began to pick up the medicines. "There's something you should remember for future reference." He looked fully at her, his mouth quirking at one corner. "It's hard to have a serious conversation with you when you're only half dressed."

Anger rushed to Lauren's brain. "You..." There was no word to describe what he was. "Creep."

David laughed. "Let's get with the right period. How about 'churl' or 'knave'?"

"It's a pity they don't hang common thieves," she said. She tried to struggle into her blouse, but it was still tucked into the waistband of her skirt. She saw David make a step to help her and she lifted her chin. "Touch me again and I'll hurt you."

He tried not to laugh, but he couldn't help the grin. "Beneath that cool exterior beats the heart of a person who likes mayhem," he said dryly. "Even after your own blood has been spilled, still a lust to see other's."

"Take me home," Lauren demanded. Her outburst had reignited the pain in her arm, but she was determined not to show her weakness. David was a dangerous man. One moment kind and tender, the next a fiend...and what else? She had to admit it, she was baffled by him. His touch, the way he looked at her, all spoke of a man with deep compassion and kindness. Yet he robbed people. And he had been at the site of a gruesome murder. "Please take me home." She calmed her thoughts and her voice as she spoke.

"I can't. Not yet."

"What are you doing, David? I could have helped you before. I would have—I'd have done everything in my power because I think I understand about the failures of the justice system. But this has gone too far. If you didn't kill Tanner, who did?"

"I don't know."

"But you have an idea!" She leaned forward. "Tell me."

David stared at her. "It all happened a long time ago—" Abruptly he broke off. "I'm taking you to see a friend. That arm needs stitches, and though you may accuse me of murder, you won't be able to say that I allowed you to cripple yourself."

"Why did you leave me that riddle, David?" she pressed. "You wanted me to know something."

All humor left his face and tension returned to his eyes. "I made a mistake. A serious one. I never intended to involve you in anything like this. We're all victims of the past, Lauren, but I more than others. The past is the key."

"You wanted my help and not for a robbery. What was I supposed to find?"

"It won't do any good to talk about it now."

She could actually see the muscles in his jaw bunch as he continued to talk.

"There was something in that house I thought might explain my actions." He turned away, walking to the kitchen window above the sink.

With his gaze diverted, Lauren was able to struggle into her blouse and pull her jacket over her shoulders. The house was cold, and she hadn't even noticed it until now.

"We'd better hurry," David said. "We haven't much time."

"David, I have to call the police about Bedford Tanner."

He didn't even stop to look at her. "We'll discuss that after your arm is stitched and we've both had a few hours' sleep."

"David..." She was on the verge of telling him that she wanted to help him. He was so torn. It wasn't possible that he was a cold-blooded killer.

He grasped her good arm in fingers of iron and pushed her forward out of the house.

"David..." She planted her feet and balked.

"Walk along on your own, or I'll carry you—after you're gagged," he warned her.

She saw the icy glint of determination in his eyes. He'd do it, she knew. Once again, he was a man who frightened her.

"ARE YOU A REAL doctor?" Lauren eyed the older man with suspicion. He handled her arm like a doctor, and the syringe filled with Novocain looked real enough.

"I'm a dinosaur." The man chuckled. "A family practitioner. You know, the kind of doctor who makes house calls, has a cup of coffee in the kitchen and delivers babies without the benefit of hospitals." He raised her arm. "I retired two years ago. This is going to sting a little at first."

"Dr. Smith was set up by someone," David interjected, his voice sharp with anger. "It was either retire or see everything he'd worked to save taken from him."

Lauren didn't flinch at the prick of the needle. In only a few moments the Novocain went to work. She tried to avoid watching as Dr. Alan Smith prepared the needle and thread. Somehow, in all of her thirty-three years, she'd managed to avoid stitches of any kind. She wasn't looking forward to the experience.

"That's right," the doctor said as he began to draw the needle in and out of the muscle, making neat, small stitches. "If it hadn't been for David, I would have lost everything, anyway."

"How's that?" Lauren asked, looking everywhere but at her arm. The tug of the needle and thread was not pleasant, but it didn't actually hurt. Her gaze settled on David.

He was leaning against the doorway, watching the doctor work. She pulled the exam gown closer at her breasts.

"It doesn't matter," David answered before the doctor could. "All that matters is that Alan's still here in Natchez, and a lot of people benefit from that fact. If it weren't for him, many of the indigent or homeless wouldn't have any medical attention at all."

"If it weren't for...Robin Hood, I wouldn't have a building to practice in," Alan insisted.

"There's no justification for breaking the law." Lauren caught David's gaze and held it three seconds before she continued, "Especially not when a man dies."

Alan looked up abruptly. "What's this?"

David shook his head. "Something you don't want to be involved in, my friend."

"David, you don't need trouble now." Alan tied off the last stitch and began bandaging Lauren's arm. "Especially not now..."

"Well, he's got it. A man I'm certain is Bedford Tanner is dead. Shot through the heart with an arrow. David was at the scene..."

"And so was Ms. Sanders," David said smoothly.

"Tanner is dead!" Alan Smith's hands trembled for the first time as he put on the last piece of tape. "What happened?"

"I wish I knew," David said. "Someone found out where I was going. They got there before me. By the time I arrived, I saw Ms. Sanders dashing across the lawn in an obvious state of terror. I never even made it inside the house. But now I'm going to have to go back."

"Why?" Alan and Lauren asked in chorus.

"To make sure nothing was planted there to frame me for murder."

"I'll call..."

"No!" David's sharp voice cut Alan off before he could finish. He nodded to Lauren. "Don't mention any names in front of her. She isn't exactly a friend. Ms. Sanders is on the D.A.'s payroll."

"Sweet saints," Alan said, leaning against the edge of his examining table. "What are you going to do?"

"Leave Ms. Sanders in your tender care while I go back. Don't let her near a telephone. Once I've made a check to be sure there's no physical evidence, you can let her go. She can call the police or do anything else she feels like."

"Once you've changed the evidence," she said angrily, her suspicions mounting again. "You're a lawyer. You know what to move and what to leave alone. Maybe you're going to plant something that incriminates me."

David raised an eyebrow. "Now that would be one way to insure your cooperation."

"As soon as I get back to work tomorrow, I'm going straight to Judge Clinton and tell him I was crazy to talk Jason into letting you out on bail. You're going to be locked up so fast—"

"That's assuming you get to work tomorrow, Lauren. If I'm such a rogue and criminal, maybe I'll just keep you tucked away for a few days. After all, the scuttlebutt down at the courthouse is that Jason would be relieved to see you gone. He might not even bother to mention that fact for several days."

Lauren backed down. She couldn't be sure by David's tone if he was serious or deviling her. As miserable as it was, what David said was true. When Tanner's body was discovered, and it would be soon, Amberly would probably pray she was dead. She *was* the one who'd talked him into letting David go free.

"You can't keep me here against my will," she insisted, but even she could hear that her voice wasn't as firm as it should have been.

"Watch me," David answered. "Treatment Room B, Alan."

The doctor nodded, then turned to Lauren. "Please don't make this difficult for me. I'm an old man, but I've had a lot of practice with frightened and fighting patients. Please come along."

"Great," Lauren shot over her shoulder as the old doctor led her away, "If I fight, you'll probably drug me. You are a vile, dastardly criminal," she called out.

"Alan, if you have to sedate her, could you see about clipping that tongue while she's out?" David asked quietly.

"Certainly, David, if you desire."

They both laughed at the shocked and horrified expression on Lauren's face.

"A joke, my dear," David said. "But then it might not be." He turned around and left.

IT WAS FIVE A.M. before David returned. He was tired and upset, if the expression on his face was any reflection. He spoke little as he bundled Lauren into her car and drove to the address she gave him.

"Was it Tanner?"

"Yes," he admitted. "Shot through the heart with an arrow identical to mine."

"But it wasn't yours?" She couldn't figure David out. He was taking her home. After leaving her in an examining room with a bed, lamp, several novels and a door that bolted on the outside, he'd come back for her hours later, more tired and drawn and uncommunicative than when he'd left. She knew nothing of what he'd found or what he was looking for. But his behavior wasn't that of a killer. Unless he was a split personality.

"I didn't shoot it," David said. "And I don't know who could have gotten my arrows. I keep them locked away." He pulled her car into the drive and when she started to get out, his hand restrained her. "Who did you tell about the riddle I left you?"

"No one."

"Are you certain?"

"Absolutely." She hesitated, and then decided to tell him. "I was careful not to mention it because I didn't want Jason to know I planned to meet you. I had every intention of talking some sense into you, and I knew that if Jason found out about it, he'd either fire me or try to set a trap to catch you in the act."

"Do you keep your office door locked?"

"Not all of the time," Lauren admitted. "Or how else could you have gotten in to deliver the riddle."

"Good point. What about the quiver of arrows? Was it left on your desk?"

"Yes." Lauren could see where he was going. Whoever had read the riddle could have taken some of his arrows and used one to kill Bedford Tanner and two to shoot at her. "How many were supposed to be in that quiver?"

"Fifteen."

"I'll count them when I make it in to work."

"Lauren, I'm going to be the prime suspect in this murder. If I were you, I'd call in an anonymous tip about Tanner. I know you have to report it, but if you can keep yourself out of this, all the better." He got out of the driver's side and walked around the car to hand her the keys. "This could become very sticky for you, and I'm sorry for that. I never intended to drag you into a mess like this."

"What did you intend, David?"

"That's a moot issue now." He stared at her, noting the dark circles under her brown eyes—eyes that showed a simple willingness to believe in him. "I'm going into hiding. I'll be in touch." He started down the drive to the oak-lined street of the old residential neighborhood.

Lauren watched as he disappeared under the streetlights. It was five in the morning and her arm was beginning to throb. She looked down at her clothes and realized that if one of the neighbors should happen out for the early morning paper and saw her in such a bedraggled condition, he'd very likely call the police.

She ran up the steps and into the house, stopping only long enough to pet her cat Gumbo. "Long night and no party," she whispered as she scratched under the cat's chin and brought forth a purr.

She headed straight for the bathroom and the big old clawfoot tub that was one of her favorite things about the

Creole cottage she'd put a downpayment on. Great! If her job fell through, how would she pay for it? She shed that thought along with her clothes and began to prepare a story to tell her co-workers.

How did she injure her arm? She settled on a bad bruise and decided to wear long sleeves for the rest of her life. Or at least until she could tell how badly she'd scar.

As she slipped into the hot water, careful not to soak her dressing, she thought of David. Why had she gone to meet him at the Tanner place? It was against all reason and logic. In a patient she'd classify such behavior as subconsciously self-destructive. Was it?

She couldn't believe so. There was something about David that made him worth the risk. He believed in what he was doing, and Dr. Alan Smith was her first evidence that Robin Hood actually gave the money to the poor. But it was still wrong. Wasn't it?

And if David didn't kill Bedford Tanner, who did?

Could it be someone who'd been in her office? Not even the hot water could counteract the chill that came with that thought.

Chapter Four

Lauren concentrated on the stack of work on her desk, but the words were meaningless. It was almost a relief when the door flew open and an angry Jason Amberly glowered at her as he strode into the room.

"'He's not a menace to society,'" he mimicked her earlier words. "Ask Bedford Tanner about that."

Lauren wanted to crawl into a hole. She'd lost all moral fiber and called in Tanner's murder anonymously, as David had suggested. She'd never dreamed the day would come when she'd see herself as a cowardly snitch.

"Jason, calm down," she said, her own voice barely audible. She started to reach for her coffee and winced.

"What the hell happened to you?" Jason asked, noticing the multiple scrapes on her face and the pain in her eyes. "Where are your other glasses? You look like a hippie."

The granny glasses she wore—a backup emergency pair—were a holdover from her college days. Not only were they old, scratched and the wrong prescription, when worn with her rumpled hair and scratches, she looked pitiful.

"I, uh, lost them," she said. The deal she'd made with herself was that she wouldn't lie—directly. She just wouldn't volunteer any information. "Has anyone seen Mr. Malachi at all? Anywhere? Maybe at his business?"

"No one's seen him, but he did pay a call on his competitor."

Lauren felt her scalp tighten. What had he done now?

"Malachi and Lem Pinning have been . . . antagonists for several years now. It goes back to an issue involving the free flow of a stream."

Lauren realized that Jason was enjoying himself, drawing it out as long as possible. "Get to the point," she snapped. "What did he do?"

Jason chuckled. "You're a little edgy where Malachi is concerned. Feeling the weight of your bad decision?"

"You don't have a shred of proof that David Malachi killed Bedford Tanner. It's an assumption on your part, and I think it only fair to point out that your personal dislike of Mr. Malachi has colored your ability to think clearly and fairly."

"A handmade arrow is circumstantial, but it's a pretty good signature, Lauren. Not to mention the fact that the house was robbed of only the items the Robin Hood Robber takes."

"What about a note? Robin always leaves a note." Lauren couldn't believe that David had gone back to actually rob the house, but he certainly hadn't taken anything when he was with her. Had he been stupid enough to leave a note, too?

"There was no note." Jason lost interest in tormenting her. "What I was going to tell you was that Malachi took all his saplings and left them in Pinning's driveway."

"He *gave* them to his competitor?"

"Right," Jason said. "Maybe he is crazy, after all." He caught Lauren's startled look. "Crazy like a fox. He only did that to make us believe he left town."

"Maybe he did," she said, shrugging before she remembered her injured arm.

"What's wrong with you?" Jason asked again. "Get in a bar fight?"

"Something like that." Lauren picked up a file on her desk.

"Your personal life is your business, but let me say that I wouldn't recommend making a habit of coming to work looking as if someone beat you up." His voice softened. "If you have a problem, Lauren, you can approach me with it. I'm not quite the ogre I pretend to be.''

Unexpected tears stung Lauren's eyes, but she blinked them back, glad for even the little privacy the round lenses of her glasses gave her. "Thanks, Jason. I ran into some trees and things. It's not a big deal, and I don't plan on making a habit of it.''

"Okay," he said. "If you aren't sick, then I want you to put everything else on hold and find Malachi. I don't believe for a minute he's left Natchez. He's got a home here, plus his aunt's rambling place out on Three Dog Trace, plus a cousin's boarding house down by the bank, and friends who would find it a great game to hide him from the law.'' From the depth of his pants' pocket he pulled a list and tossed it on her desk.

"I gather the philosophy behind this is that I lost him so I can find him?''

"Something like that." Jason grinned, but there was an edge to it. "Just remember, Lauren, when I let you talk me into agreeing to bail, it put me on the line, too.''

"I know that, and I'm sorry. More sorry than you'll ever know.''

"See what you can turn up. Until Malachi's formally charged with murder, the sheriff doesn't want to waste his manpower on hunting him. As much as I dislike Malachi, it would be better for him, and you and me, if he gave himself up.''

Lauren stood, determined not to show any pain. "I'll get after it now." She hesitated. "Jason, did you remove the arrows from my desk?''

Jason looked blank a moment. "Oh, yeah," he said. "I had them taken to evidence for safekeeping." He frowned. "You thought maybe someone took one of those arrows and killed Tanner?''

"It did cross my mind.''

"Forget it. There were fifteen in the quiver when we found it, and there were fifteen locked in the evidence room.''

Lauren felt her hopes sink well past her knees. "Thanks." She picked up her purse with her good hand and started out the door.

"Where are you going to look?" Jason asked.

"His family. Those friends you mentioned. Those are the logical places. If nothing turns up there, then I'll try another tact."

"I'm not a man to say I told you so, Lauren . . ."

"Yeah, but you told me so," she said as she brushed past him.

"Take Brecktel or Reed with you."

"I thought you said everyone was too busy," she called over her shoulder as she started to descend the steps.

"All of the sheriff's deputies are busy. Both of those guys are pining for a chance to be with you. Might as well make. one of them happy and get them off their butts."

"Thanks, Jason," Lauren called, "but I don't want their help. Or ridicule." She didn't want their interference, either. She had to find David, but she had to do it alone.

"Take one," Jason called down. "That's an order. You might not think Malachi is a menace to society, but he sure as hell killed Bedford Tanner. Take Brecktel or Reed as protection. I mean it."

"Yes, sir." Lauren turned right at the second floor and hurried into the D.A.'s office. Brecktel's desk was empty, but Reed was watching her with open interest.

"Grab a coat and let's go," Lauren said irritably.

"Is this a lunch invitation?"

"This is a follow-your-boss's-command."

"You're looking for David Malachi," Wyatt Reed said as he slipped into his suit jacket. "I always wanted to play Dick Tracy."

NICOLE STERLING lifted the heavy silver teapot and poured three cups. "I find your questions very unsettling, Ms. Sanders. My friends and I aren't the caliber of people who run afoul of the law. Furthermore, I'm certain if David were in trouble, I'd be the first person he called. We are . . . very close." Her hand fluttered at the button of her coral silk blouse.

Nicole's blouse and cream silk slacks, brightened with gold earrings, chains and bracelets, perfectly matched the cool interior of the sunroom where they were sitting. The room was exquisite. Paisley cushions blended with striped curtains, colors picked up by the wool rug on the parquet floor. Large windows ran the length of the room, from ceiling to floor, and a gentle breeze billowed the sheers and Nicole's striking black curls. Lauren felt mauled, bulky, and distinctly unfeminine in her business suit.

"You're saying you're involved with Mr. Malachi?" Wyatt asked helpfully. It was his first question.

"David is a special man." Nicole handed a teacup to Lauren. Her green gaze lingered on the scratches on Lauren's face. "You know you shouldn't claw at yourself like that, dear. You'll permanently scar your face, and even though your complexion isn't the best, it is all you have. I have a wonderful dermatologist. I could make an appointment for you."

"Thanks, but that won't be necessary." Lauren placed her untouched tea on the table and opened her notepad. "Would you consider Mr. Malachi a man capable of murder?" Lauren asked. She adopted her most professional tone.

"Oh, absolutely. Every Southern gentleman is. There's a time when violence is the only honorable solution, you know. Some folks just need killin'."

"Ms. Sterling, surely you don't believe David Malachi killed Bedford Tanner?" Lauren's voice showed her disbelief.

Nicole's shrug was thoughtful. "There are plenty of folks who wouldn't mind seeing old man Tanner six feet under. I'm one of 'em."

"And why is that?" Lauren leaned back into her overstuffed chair.

"The Tanners are an old family around these parts." Nicole arched her brows at Lauren. "You don't know what that means, but those of us with deep roots here are all knotted together. Family and tradition are the core of Natchez. Newcomers never seem to be able to grasp that fact. Especially women like yourself who think a career is an entrée into the social world. You have no name, no money, no breeding, but you think the little shred of power you've gained by working in the D.A.'s office will be an acceptable substitute. Well, you're wrong."

"Ms. Sterling, a person couldn't spend ten minutes in this town without realizing that the past is the most important thing that ever happened here." Lauren held her notepad to keep from slapping Nicole's perfectly made-up face. There were just some people who needed slapping.

"Isn't it interesting how those without a past are always contemptuous of those who have one. A reputable past, that is." Nicole smiled.

"Have you heard from Mr. Malachi?" Lauren decided to ignore her. If this society barracuda wanted to show her teeth, Lauren would let her. Nicole might reveal something useful. Out of the corner of her eye, Lauren could see that Wyatt was enjoying the show. Lauren rapped his shin sharply with her toe and was rewarded by a look of pain. "If you've had any contact with Mr. Malachi, we'd like to know," she continued in a pleasant voice.

"Not direct contact. Not the physical kind I need."

"Indirectly?"

"There was a note, uh, pinned to my front door this morning."

"With an arrow?" Lauren asked.

"Yes, as a matter of fact. David always was so elegant and creative in his . . . communications."

"What did the note say?" Wyatt asked. "Where is it?"

"Oh, it was merely a threat. He warned me to keep my mouth shut if I valued the ability to speak, among other things. And as to the second question—" she pointed across the room to the fireplace "—I burned it. No point in leaving evidence lying carelessly about the house."

Lauren was furious. "If you knew it was evidence, then you shouldn't have destroyed it."

Nicole's look was smug. "Are you sure you aren't the spirit of schoolmarm Lydia Parks come back to haunt and taunt me into insanity? Give you another ten years and you'll be a regular harpy. You can't come into my home and tell me what to do and not to do."

"Ms. Sterling," Wyatt interrupted smoothly, "we'd appreciate it very much if you could tell us what the note said. I'd consider it a personal favor."

Rolling her eyes at Lauren, Nicole directed her answer at Wyatt. "The note said to destroy it, so I did. I only thought just this minute that it might be evidence." She sighed. "This is all very trying for me. You come here and tell me David's in trouble, and then this...woman tried to trick me into saying something I don't mean."

"I never—" Lauren was cut short by a stern look.

"What things would David not want you to tell?" Wyatt asked sharply.

"Why, now if I told, that wouldn't be exactly proper, would it?" Nicole actually looked shocked. "Anyway, it was nothing important."

"It would be best if the D.A.'s office made that decision," Lauren gritted through her teeth.

"Ms., uh, Sanders, I'm going to have to ask you to leave my home. I don't believe I can stand another minute of your rude behavior. Your tone is completely unacceptable, and you've interrupted my discussion with the gentleman. Now, Mr. Reed is welcome to stay and ask me any questions he chooses. But you must leave." Nicole turned to the assistant D.A. "You do understand that I can't allow her to treat me in this fashion, don't you?"

Wyatt turned to Lauren, his gaze asking how she wanted to handle the situation.

"Stay," she said. "I'll be more than happy to vacate the premises. I hope you don't die of overexposure to saccharin." She picked up her purse and walked out of the room without looking back. When she closed the front door, she slapped her purse against one of the white columns.

"What a witch," she exclaimed under her breath. And Wyatt had sat there and made cow eyes at her. She hurried down the steps and through the front garden where a white gazebo glistened in the midday sun. To the left of the house was a postcard view of the Mississippi River. The grounds were perfection, and the interior of the house had been decorated in classic good taste. Nicole Sterling was an interior designer, and she was obviously a professional at her trade.

Lauren held on to her anger, knowing that when it began to dissipate she'd have to confront the insinuations that Nicole had made about a relationship with David. Why did the idea that the two of them were lovers bother Lauren so?

Because she'd thought there was more to him than that? Because she wanted there to be more to him than that? Because she'd sensed for a moment that he felt something for her, an interest of some kind, a mutual recognition of intelligence?

Well, Nicole was intelligent enough, she was also vain and stupid and pretentious and cruel. If that was the kind of woman David Malachi went for, maybe his motives weren't as pure... Good grief, she was trying to rationalize her attraction to a possible murderer! She was in deep trouble.

Lauren found herself at the river, though she'd had no intention of going there. The slow-moving water was mesmerizing. There were riverboats—tourist attractions but interesting ones—that paddled up and down the river on tours with dining and dancing. It was something out of a historical romance.

Leaning against a willow tree that grew out from the bank at an angle, Lauren let her body relax.

Her arm was throbbing. Her head was pounding, and she felt suddenly close to tears again. She hadn't even lasted a month in her new job before she'd messed up big time. What would she do when she was fired? She didn't want to go back to Kingston, Kansas. She couldn't stay in Natchez. What would she do?

"Get off my butt and find that criminal David Malachi," she said out loud. She pushed off the tree with her good arm and pulled Jason's list from her pocket. René Devereau was the next name. "'David's boyhood chum, ladies' man and avid traveler,'" she read Jason's description aloud. Well, old René might be able to turn up some new sod on David, and at least she'd shaken Wyatt Reed. She hoped Nicole didn't cocoon him before he could escape alive. But then, that was Wyatt's problem. She had enough of her own.

"DAVID HAS ALWAYS BEEN—how should I say this without sounding like some demented poet?—a dreamer, I guess. Even in grammar school he always believed that justice won out. Even when Clyde Dunaway beat him up every Thursday on the way home from school, David would never vary his route. He believed that one day he'd thrash the fool out of Clyde."

"And did he?" Lauren leaned forward on the French brocade sofa in René's posh sitting room. Glancing around she recognized the touches of Nicole's taste. So, she'd redone Timbermain House for René. She was a *busy* woman.

"Not to my memory," René said, then crossed one leg elegantly over the other and laughed. "But David never gave up. He went home the same way every Thursday with the sure idea that one day he'd be able to win. It was resolved, as I recall, when Clyde Dunaway robbed the local drugstore, taking only prophylactics, Neapolitan ice cream, Spiderman comic books and acne medication. He was sent off to reform school, and David survived junior high."

Lauren laughed despite herself. René was a fascinating conversationalist, even though he was skirting the topic she'd come to discuss.

René leaned forward in his chair and refilled her coffee cup. "If you've been by Nicole's, I know you had that wretched tea she insists on serving. Some pretentious effort to appear genteel. You know she's River Road white trash who married a bit of money and parlayed it into a good business.''

Lauren almost choked on her coffee. "Excuse me?"

"Oh, Nicole was playing the grand lady? Talked about her roots, did she?'' René laughed. "Her roots go deep in Natchez, but not in the rich cotton field soil. More like the river mud.'' He laughed again. "I love Nicole, and I firmly believe that if you stripped away the artifice and makeup, there might be the core of a real person there. David's stripped off more than artifice, I understand.'' He raised his eyebrows.

"You were telling me about David's idealism." Just at this moment, Lauren didn't want to talk about Nicole. Particularly not Nicole and David.

"Of course,'' René said, his mouth drooping into an apologetic frown. "David is where your interest lies, not Nicole. It's just that we're all such old, dear friends. Anyway, I wasn't a bit shocked when David was accused of being the Robin Hood Robber. I thought it fit him perfectly. He would do something that bizarre.''

"How do you mean?"

"Go to the trouble of stealing something just to give it away. I mean, really, if I put my neck on the line to steal beautiful jewelry or paintings, I'd keep the proceeds for myself. Or at least use them to win the affections of some beautiful woman.''

Lauren felt his gaze warm upon her, and she hid her confusion by touching the cloth napkin to her lips.

"Like you," he concluded.

Her only hope was to ignore the personal remark. "Mr. Devereau, why do you think David is doing this? If he is doing it. I mean, he hasn't been convicted, and he never actually said whether he was Robin Hood or not."

"It's David," René said quickly. "As I said earlier, it bears his twin trademark—idealism and romanticism. When we were young, we often played in the woods around Natchez. Guess who was always Robin Hood?''

Lauren didn't have to guess. "And you? What role did you play?"

A wicked light touched René's hazel eyes. "Guess?"

"Will Scarlett, though you are dark and don't seem to be the type to assume a secondary role."

"The Sheriff of Nottingham," René said. "I must admit that I had a flair for the role. Especially when it came to pursuing Maid Marion."

Lauren joined in his laughter. René plainly enjoyed the spice of notoriety. "And did you win the fair maid's heart?" Lauren asked.

"That remains to be seen," René answered, his eyes on hers. He stood up. "You asked me why David does what he does. What can he gain? Well, immediate justice, by his own standards, for one thing. A sense of control, as if he could make a difference. When he went to law school, he wanted to come home and open a free clinic. He said he wanted to make a difference in people's lives."

"What about money?" Lauren watched René pace the room. "I mean, a free clinic isn't exactly the most lucrative practice a man with David's intelligence could have."

"Money has never meant anything to David."

"Because he's always had plenty," Lauren commented dryly.

"Yes, and no." René settled on the arm of the sofa, his thigh very close to Lauren's arm. "David's family had money." He held both hands out in front of him, palms up. "Before you ask, I have no idea what his financial status is now. I don't know if he chooses to live at his aunt's old barn of a house for sentimental reasons, if he works out in the sun like a farmer because he enjoys it, or if he has no other option. All I can say is that the young *GQ* man I went to college with has completely disappeared." René leaned forward so he was only inches from Lauren's face. "Maybe he isn't stable."

Shaken by his comment, Lauren's next question held a fragment of concern. "Would he kill someone?"

René pursed his lips in thought. "If he felt they deserved it, maybe."

"Did Bedford Tanner deserve it?"

"Without a doubt," René answered without turning a hair.

"Why?"

"Now that's a long, long Natchez story. It goes back to 1932 when David's relatives were involved in a local scandal. The Tanners were powerful and wealthy, and my understanding is that they were instrumental in making trouble for David's family. They've maintained that practice of profit before anything else ever since."

"Was there something personal between David and Tanner?"

"My goodness, look at the time," René said as he stood in one fluid motion, tapping his expensive wristwatch. "I'm afraid I'm going to have to conclude our little chat, Ms. Sanders."

"Certainly. I should have called before I dropped in." René had suddenly grown reticent. Why? "Could we schedule another time?"

"How about tonight? Over dinner?"

She looked into his hazel eyes and saw more than interest in her range of questions. Dinner would not be a good idea. "Perhaps at the office tomorrow?"

"I'm afraid I'm leaving early in the morning, and I have business appointments the rest of today. It's either tonight or not for the next two weeks."

"Tonight would be fine," she capitulated. He was manipulating her sinfully, but she had to go along.

René's smile held a victory she didn't understand until he spoke. "I hope David is in town. This will stick in his craw."

"Why should it?" she asked.

"Oh, David hates it whenever anyone talks about his family. He'll know we're doing exactly that."

Lauren felt her heartbeat increase. "Why would you want to make David angry?"

René's smile was suddenly secret. "The roles we play in childhood aren't always left behind. We take them up again. Sometimes in sport." He boldly traced a scratch on her cheek with his finger. "And sometimes in deadly earnest."

Chapter Five

The third-floor patio garden of Timbermain provided a beautiful view of the Mississippi River. Three glasses of wine had mellowed Lauren to the point that she could sit back in her chair and relax, but René Devereau still made her uncomfortable. He was a master gamesman, and she wasn't certain what rules he played by, or what he called a win. There was definitely competition between him and David, though. A serious, long-standing battle.

Dinner at Timbermain had taken her aback. She'd expected a restaurant. But René had picked her up and driven her back to his home. The barbecue catfish had melted in her mouth with a delicious tang. Sweet potato pone and corn pudding were Southern delicacies she found irresistible. She felt disgustingly stuffed and lazy. But not too somnolent to keep a watchful eye on René. He'd skirted all around the subject of David. It was her curse, having to deal with men who knew exactly what she wanted, yet refused to give it.

"You know about the murder of David's Great-Aunt Sarah?"

Lauren snapped to attention even though she kept her body comfortably tilted back in the chair. "I read an account in the newspaper."

"Darcy Woodson didn't do it. Everyone in Natchez knew it, but no one would step up and say so."

"They let an innocent man die?"

"By his own hand." René filled their wineglasses. "Allegedly."

"Are you saying Darcy Woodson was murdered, too?" The question was academic. The Lee-Woodson murder-suicide was sixty years old and nothing could be done about it now. But it was at least closer to David than any topic they'd discussed.

"Some say he was. There's a story that's been circulating about town that Sarah and Darcy wound up with a great deal of money." He took a bite of the fish but his gaze never wavered from hers. "That money maybe wasn't theirs. Anyway, the story goes that Sarah and Darcy wouldn't tell where they'd hidden the treasure, so someone killed her and framed him. When he wouldn't talk, he was killed before he could sway public opinion his way."

"The newspaper accounts made him seem like he was . . . not in his right mind."

"He was a recluse, true enough. And he lived like a monk, without electricity or any modern luxury. He said the Malachi money was tainted by blood, and he wanted no part of it." René smoothly signaled his housekeeper for coffee and an after-dinner drink. "I'm not positive that makes him crazy."

"And Sarah? There was an implication of incest."

René shook his head. "Who knows. My father spoke of it, but with no real conviction. Sarah and Darcy courted at one time. Remember, marriages between cousins were part of the natural order of things at one time. Look at European royalty."

"Did David ever speak of . . . this family tragedy?"

René took a decanter from the maid and poured two measures of some amber liqueur that Lauren couldn't readily identify. He handed her a glass before he spoke. "Of course he never knew either Darcy or Sarah. They were dead long before his time. But it affected his Aunt Em a great deal. He spoke of the murder only once, and it was to repeat something Em had told him."

"What?"

René held up his glass and sipped. Lauren followed suit, allowing the delicious liquid to burn slowly down her throat.

"He never told me. He only said that he would one day find the answer to their deaths. And when he did, whoever was responsible would pay dearly."

"Could it..." Lauren hesitated. "Could it have been Bedford Tanner?"

"That thought has crossed my mind. And Nicole's. The entire Robin Hood scheme could have been a setup to kill Tanner."

"But David was already arrested! That doesn't make a bit of sense. To kill Tanner dressed as Robin Hood after he was just arrested is stupid, and David Malachi is not a stupid man."

René's level gaze assessed her. "You're the psychologist. What if we substitute the word 'unbalanced', or 'irrational'?"

Deflated, Lauren sat back in her chair. "I see your point."

"It is only an opinion," René said. "I haven't really talked with David in years. Like Darcy, he began to develop a distaste for his inherited wealth. When he moved from his family's main estate at River Bluff to his Aunt Em's house, I knew he had changed radically."

"Did you ever question why?" Lauren sipped her liqueur to counteract the bitter taste of disappointment. René's assessment of David was damning.

"The schism between us was gradual, but relentless. David found less and less time to spend with his old friend. I didn't try to cling." He drained his glass and signaled for more hot coffee. "I should have asked, but I didn't."

"Was there anyone David was close to?"

"You won't find him with a friend or relative. He wouldn't endanger either."

"Any suggestions?"

"Try Dr. Smith at the free clinic. And there's a rumor that Robin Hood funded a new food co-op on Westwood. The bookmobile got an unexpected 'grant' a few months ago.

Check with Tom Shaw, the hospital administrator. There's probably a million places to look, but no matter, you won't find him. When David wants to disappear, he does. He wouldn't endanger anyone he really cared about.''

The liqueur glass was slowly lowered to the table and Lauren straightened her back. ''No, he isn't the kind of man who would endanger...a friend.'' She pushed the implications of that statement to the very back of her mind. Later, when she was alone, she'd deal with it. ''I have a list of everyone Robin Hood has robbed. All are old Natchez families.'' She paused. ''In fact, there are nine families whose ancestors lived in Natchez before or during the Civil War period.'' She paused again, but René only sipped his drink. ''All of those families except two have been robbed by Robin Hood.''

''How fascinating. Who are the families that are left?''

''Yours and David Malachi's.''

''So,'' René said with a smile, ''you have drawn a conclusion.''

''Several.''

''And they are?'' René finally put his empty glass down, wiped his lips with his napkin and sat forward.

''There is a deliberate pattern to the robberies. Robin Hood is avenging the past, for whatever reason, and I'm not sure yet what it is. But I suspect you might be able to tell me.'' She waited.

''I can tell you that you are a very beautiful woman with a quick mind.'' He rose and walked around the small table to assist her from her chair. ''I can also tell that you have a personal interest in David's safety.''

''I have an interest in saving my job, Mr. Devereau. Since I pushed for David's release, my boss is holding me responsible.''

''And are you holding me responsible?''

''It seems strangely coincidental that you and David are friends, and that Timbermain has not been robbed.''

''Perhaps David hasn't had time to get here yet.''

''You don't seem overly concerned.''

"It isn't in my nature to worry about such things. I have staff. The house is never left empty. And I have other interests to pursue. I'll gladly take the risk of losing a few paintings for the pleasure of a beautiful woman's company. How about dinner tomorrow?"

"I thought you were going out of town?" Lauren felt René's fingers close on her elbow.

"My plans were canceled at the last minute. I find myself with time on my hands and a desire for the pleasure of your company."

"I'm afraid I won't be staying in Natchez very long if I don't find Mr. Malachi and convince him to turn himself in. Jason will fire me," Lauren said bluntly. "He's as much as told me so. I'd better put my efforts into searching for our elusive bandit, but thanks for the offer. Dinner was wonderful. You must compliment your cook."

"Another time, then." René raised her hand to his lips and kissed it a brief second longer than was necessary. "Take care of yourself, Lauren. Jumping to conclusions can be a risky pastime."

"So I've discovered," she said quickly as she picked up her purse and followed René out the front door to his waiting car.

THE SMALL THUMP ECHOED eerily through the house again, and Lauren snapped completely awake. She was used to the nocturnal ramblings of Gumbo, Cat from Hell. The little stray had come with the house when she'd purchased it. Lauren had been unable to turn away from the liquid green eyes and the pitiful, scruffy body that showed an immediate need for attention.

Now, only two weeks later, Gumbo was running the house. And Lauren was learning the role of cat master— doing whatever the five-pound creature demanded.

Throwing back the covers, she went to the kitchen and snapped on the light. From the back of the refrigerator she took out the cream that had once gone in her coffee. She poured the last in Gumbo's dish and looked around for the feline. She could have sworn she'd heard her flying around the kitchen.

"Kitty, kitty," she called softly. She stepped on a catnip mouse with her bare foot and stumbled in the near darkness. Damn! Where had she put those horrible glasses? No matter what else she did, she was going to have to buy some new glasses. Her hand patted along the island counter where she last recalled putting the spectacles. In a moment she fumbled into them. With a sigh she put them on. Suddenly the room was in focus again, but Gumbo was nowhere to be found.

"Well, get me up for a snack a_d then run off," she said as she nudged the bowl of cream closer to the counter. She pushed her glasses up on her nose and froze.

Very, very slowly she took the glasses off and looked at them. They were the same horn-rimmed frames she'd worn the night she'd been shot. Goose bumps crawled up her bare legs, across her stomach and along her upper torso and arms. The jungle-print nightshirt did nothing to ease the chill.

"I thought you might want your glasses back."

David's soft voice came from a chair in a darkened corner of the room.

Lauren forced her body forward. At the wall switch, she hit the light. Dressed in black jeans and a dark pullover, David Malachi sat, legs casually crossed.

"I'd appreciate it if you turned off the light. Your neighbors are probably asleep, but I don't really want to take the chance of being seen. It wouldn't do much for you, either."

"I'm calling Jason." Lauren went to the telephone.

"Don't do it, Lauren. If I'm ever going to clear my name, I must have the freedom to do it."

"What are you doing in my house?" She could hear her voice rising out of control.

"I came to return your glasses . . . and to talk with you. I know you've been to see Nicole and René. I have to find out what they told you."

"David, you've risked my entire future. The stunt you pulled is going to get me fired. Not to mention that my sanity is now in question. If Jason knew I'd been running all over the woods with you, and now entertaining you in my kitchen, he'd have me committed."

"I am sorry, Lauren. You can believe it or not. I never intended to draw you into this."

"I *don't* believe you," she snapped. "You deliberately lured me to Bedford Tanner's home—"

"True enough," David interrupted. "But not for a murder."

"I suppose Mr. Tanner offered some objection to your presence on his property, so you shot him. With an arrow, no less." She pushed her hair out of her eyes.

"I did not kill Bedford Tanner." David's voice was tight. "I'm not a murderer."

"Then who did?" Lauren ran her hands down her hips, realizing how short her shirt was.

"Your scratches are healing nicely," David said, his gaze moving along her exposed legs. "I was worried about that one on your right thigh. How's your arm?"

"Fine, perfectly wonderful. Much better now that it's been ventilated with an arrow." She backed to the counter and put it between herself and David's direct gaze. "What *are* you doing here?" Her voice changed slightly, softening.

"Someone set me up. I have to find out who, and I was hoping you might be able to tell me something useful."

"Such as?" she prompted.

"Did René say anything about his family business?"

"No. I did point out that he hadn't been robbed, though."

David's face showed a moment of concern. "Be careful, Lauren."

"Why?" Her heart began to pound. She'd felt a tension with René, a competition between the two men. Could it have been more than that? "Are you saying René might hurt me?"

"He's very smart. And he likes his life just the way it is. He won't allow you or anyone else to upset his apple cart. Some of your questions and observations may reflect poorly on him."

"And would he kill to prevent disruption in his life?" Lauren found herself staring at David's gray eyes. There was quicksilver in their depths as his emotions shifted.

"I don't know," David said slowly. "I honestly can't imagine René harming anyone. But to protect his way of life..."

"That's almost exactly what René and Nicole both said about you. That you were capable of murder for the right reasons." A chill touched her legs, moving over her entire body. Was everyone in this old Southern town touched by violence?

"That's a universal truth, Lauren. Almost every man has a point beyond which he can't tolerate. Take a mother protecting her child. She can be driven to acts that normally would never cross her mind."

David's voice was low and reasonable. Lauren recognized the truth in what he was saying, but she held onto her fear. "Protecting a child and protecting a life-style are two very different things, David."

"Agreed. But that's René's concept, not mine."

"That's true," she conceded. "He said your value system was justice, that you were capable of taking justice into your own hands." She gave him time to answer, but he said nothing. The old grandfather clock on the mantel ticked away, and Gumbo finally made an appearance in the kitchen, moving unerringly to David's legs to rub up against them.

Lauren watched as the tall man bent over to scratch the cat on the head and lift her into his lap. Gumbo purred contentedly, rubbing her whiskers on his chin.

"She hates strangers," Lauren said.

"Cats always take to me. Dogs and children, too."

"When you take justice into your own hands, David, that's nothing more than vigilantism."

"Or real justice." David's tone was firm. Still stroking the cat, he looked at her. "There are people in this town who've made a fortune injuring other people. It seems a fair system that the rich should give a little back to the community."

"That's why there are charities."

"Not everyone has a generous streak—except at the end of a gun, or long bow, as the case may be."

"I didn't realize that you had been appointed to play God."

David rose, gently settling Gumbo on the floor before he advanced on Lauren. His strides were long, and his gaze never left hers.

"I don't think I'm God. But I can see injustice. For generations a few families have become richer and richer and richer. They've had ample time to assume the role of generous patron to the less fortunate in this town. And they've done nothing."

"As is their right." Lauren tilted up her chin, her own gaze defiant.

David captured her left arm, his fingers digging into the muscle above the elbow. "I watched a friend of mine die because he didn't have the money to go to a hospital."

"That's ridiculous. A hospital wouldn't turn a dying man away."

"Tell that to Jimmy Freeman." David's eyes blazed.

"Then why didn't you take some of the Malachi family money and see that your friend got medical care?"

Lauren realized she'd gone too far when she saw the skin whiten around his eyes. His grip on her arm became more than just unpleasant. He was hurting her.

"He wouldn't take it. For personal reasons." He dropped her arm and turned away.

Lauren took two steps toward him before she stopped herself. She'd seen rage in his eyes, anger and disappointment. It was as if he'd expected more of her.

"I believe you've spent your own money," she said softly. And she did. There was that about David. He wouldn't take from anyone more than he was willing to give himself.

When he turned back, his face had settled. The whiteness was gone from his eyes, and he watched from a safe distance as Lauren unconsciously reached up to rub her arm.

"I'm sorry," he said. "I didn't mean to hurt you."

Lauren didn't answer. She stopped the rubbing motion and stared at him. He seemed perched on the edge of flight, as if he'd disappear at any moment.

"What are you going to do, David?" she asked softly. "They're hunting for you everywhere. It might be better if you gave yourself up."

He shook his head. "No. If I don't find out who killed Bedford Tanner, no one else will make the effort. Too many people would rather believe that it was me." He didn't break the gaze they shared. "Even you."

The resignation in his voice was harder to take than the anger. "I don't know," she said. "I don't believe either way."

"And what would it take to convince you?" he asked. He stepped forward, as if his body moved without conscious thought. "What if I can't produce another murderer?"

"Then another motive, perhaps." She took a deep breath, and he moved closer still. "I think Tanner was murdered to frame you. But why? And who?"

"Will you help me find out the answers to those questions?"

Lauren's own smile held a twist of irony. "David, if I don't convince you to turn yourself in, Jason's going to nail my hide to the courthouse wall."

David's laugh was warm. "I don't think so. Though you've probably given him cause."

"Thanks," she said dryly. "But let's say I agree to help you. Who hates you enough to want to frame you for murder?"

The easy smile left David's face and a mask of no emotion fell into place. "There are a number of people."

"You'll have to do better than that if I'm going to help."

"You might try René as one suspect. Or Nicole."

"Nicole?" Lauren couldn't hide her surprise. "She said you were..." She left the sentence unfinished.

"Lovers?" David supplied, one eyebrow lifting.

"Well, she as much as said that."

"We were. But it's been a while. The interesting thing about Nicole is that she has the ability to twist time to suit her needs. Question her tomorrow, and you might find that she insists we were little more than high school sweethearts."

"And why would she hate you enough to frame you for murder? Besides, I don't think Nicole could draw a bow hard enough to kill a man. I think it takes considerable strength."

"A point well taken, madam psychologist." David pointed to the coffeemaker. "If we're going to have a 2:00 a.m. discussion on all the people who would like to see me behind bars, maybe we could have a cup of coffee. I'll bet the blend René served you was Southern pecan."

Lauren looked up, startled. "How did you know I had dinner with René?"

"I made it my business to know."

"But why?"

"I'm not certain. Maybe to be sure you were okay." He leaned his arms on the counter as he took a seat on a stool.

A rush of warmth touched Lauren's chest and moved up her face. It was a pleasant sensation. She dropped her gaze from David's and turned to make the coffee. Only then did she remember her short nightshirt. She wanted to tug at it, but that would only draw attention to her lack of appropriate dress. She hurriedly measured the coffee, turned on the pot, and faced David.

"Let me go change into something else."

"I was admiring your legs," he said without hesitation. "The first time I saw you in a suit, I thought you'd look better in a T-shirt." His eyes were alive with mischief. "In fact, I think I'll send Jason a note telling him that the district attorney's office could be vastly improved by a change in the dress code."

"Jason already admonished me about coming to work with my face scratched." Lauren couldn't help but laugh. "He thought I made the office look bad."

"That would be impossible. You're a lovely woman, Lauren. Thank you for taking time to help me."

"I haven't done anything yet." Behind her, the coffee hissed and gurgled.

"By the way, you'd better consider the possibility that Jason Amberly might be the man who set me up. He hates me enough."

"Jason?" Lauren forgot all about her appearance and slid down on a stool beside David's. "Jason does dislike you. He doesn't even try to hide it. But he's an honorable man, David. I can't believe he'd kill an innocent human being just to extract revenge."

"He had access to my note. And motive."

"But he's the district attorney."

"And power," David added.

"I can't believe that he would—"

David's hand slipped to her mouth and he pressed her lips gently shut.

"Shush." He put his arms around her and drew her against him as he slowly slipped from the stool and stood. "There's someone outside."

Lauren froze. She allowed David to ease her to the floor, her breath coming in painful gulps. The terror of the night in the woods came back to her. Her ears strained for the noises that David seemed to hear so easily. There was only silence.

"Where?" she whispered against his loosened hand.

David nodded to the windows that ran along the kitchen. "Out there. I heard them."

"Who?"

He shrugged. "Give me a moment and I'll surprise them."

"No!" Lauren used her good arm to grab hold of his arm. He was solid, a real man who could be injured. She was afraid for him. "Get out of here while you can!"

He shook his head. "No." Her willingness to help him to safety caught him by surprise. She was trying to get him to save himself. Lauren Sanders was a remarkable woman.

Huddled together, they fell silent as they strained to listen. Lauren was ready to give up when she heard a light tread on the small porch outside the kitchen. It was followed by the sound of a side window lifting in the cool night.

Chapter Six

"Lauren!" A female voice called through the night. "I know David is there. I must see him."

David lifted Lauren's chin with his hand and gently kissed her forehead. "Thanks for helping me," he whispered. "You're a good friend, Lauren. That's a special thing." A mischievous smile touched his eyes and lips. "And you have great legs."

Before she could say anything, he was across the kitchen and departing from a back window.

"Lauren Sanders! Let me in this minute or I'm going to beat on your door like a Texas tornado!"

"Wait," Lauren whispered to David, grabbing his disappearing shirt as he pushed his torso out the window. "It's Nicole."

"I know," he said as one long leg disappeared. There was a jaunty jiggle of his remaining foot and he was gone.

"Lauren! Let me in!"

"Great," Lauren mumbled under her breath as she unbolted the side door. "My home has become the unofficial meeting place of the Clandestine Society of Natchez. What is it, Nicole?" she asked, exasperated.

"Where's David?" Nicole breezed into the room. "I have news for him."

"As you can plainly see, he isn't here."

"The bedroom!" Nicole half ran down the hallway before Lauren could grab her. She returned to the kitchen several moments later. "He isn't here."

"I believe I told you that, unless I was talking to someone else who just barged into my house." Lauren went to the door. "You've had the pleasure of putting me out of your home, now I'm doing the same. Get out, Nicole. Now."

"I'm not leaving until you tell me where David is." Nicole leaned against the kitchen counter with a smile that dared Lauren to move her. "You could not only lose your job, you could go to prison for aiding and abetting."

"You must have slept with some lawyers to pick up that much legalese." Lauren watched the color rise to Nicole's face with a sense of real satisfaction.

"David's a lawyer," Nicole countered.

"Not when he was in high school."

"That only proves two things." Nicole straightened and took a step in Lauren's direction. "You have seen David, and he continues to lie. David uses women, Lauren. That's his stock and trade. Some of us find the compensation worth the use." She laughed.

"Get out." Lauren was too angry to even consider a retort. "Get out now before I throw you out."

"There's a time for violence in each person's life. I dare say that throwing someone out of your home is tantamount to murder in your tight little framework." Nicole sauntered toward the door. "Just tell David I have some information for him about Bedford Tanner. This will be a true test of your feelings for him, won't it? Will you tell him and risk sending him to my bed? Or will you not tell him, and possibly risk his neck?" Nicole paused in the doorway and took a look around. "You could do with a little decorating advice, Lauren. Because you're a friend of David's, I'll give you a discount."

Nicole jumped back before Lauren could slam the door in her face.

Cheeks red with fury, Lauren went to the telephone and picked up the receiver. Her finger had dialed the first three digits of the Natchez police before she paused. She should report David's visit. It might be the only thing that saved her job. But could she do it? Even after Nicole's visit, she could not. She put the phone down and slumped at the counter.

She felt the cat brush against her legs and she automatically picked Gumbo up. "What should I do?"

Gumbo leapt from her lap and went to the refrigerator where she clawed at the door.

"Good advice. Eat!" Lauren found a piece of cold chicken for Gumbo and some cappuccino-and-fudge-swirled frozen yogurt for herself. She curled in an armchair in her den and waited for Gumbo to join her as she ate.

She had to tell David what Nicole said. If there was some clue about Bedford Tanner, David had to know. She could only hope that as soon as Nicole spit it out, she'd choke on her own venom. What could the decorator know? Did David truly consider Nicole as a potential murderer? Or was that a lie, too? A new awareness dawned slowly. Was it possible that Nicole had been trying to goad Lauren into calling the police? So many questions, so few answers.

"SO YOU FOUND your glasses." Burton Brecktel stuck his head in the door of her office. "I warned you not to look too efficient. Jason's going to expect all of us to show up for work at six-thirty."

"I couldn't sleep." Lauren knew the remark was unnecessary. She looked as if she'd been run over by a truck.

"Taking this Malachi case pretty hard, huh?" Burton asked. "I heard Jason was leaning on you heavy."

"He is, but I deserve it." She sighed and pushed her glasses up on her nose.

"How about some brunch?"

"I had a bowl of yogurt for breakfast at five. I guess it's close to lunchtime by that standard."

"Great. I have something you might be interested in."

Burton refused to answer her questions until they were sitting at the Magnolia Café over a hot breakfast of eggs, bacon, grits, biscuits, coffee and scuppernong jelly.

"What's the news?" she asked. She felt as if tiny little pins were under her eyelids.

"There was an attempted break-in at Timbermain, the Devereau home, early this morning." Burton's eyes were alive. "Malachi's still in town, so there's hope the police may catch him."

"Attempted?"

"Yes, René Devereau was supposed to be in New York on a business trip. He'd told several people about it because he was very excited about finding an international exporter for certain products. His plans changed and his trip was delayed until later this week."

Lauren started to say something about René's changeable plans, but decided against it. "Go on."

"Devereau was in his library. He said he was thinking about a woman he'd just met and he couldn't sleep. He was lying on the sofa when he heard someone at the French doors. He kept very still until the door opened, and then he rose and confronted the robber—"

"Who was dressed like Robin Hood," Lauren interrupted.

"Exactly."

"Did Devereau see the man's face? Can he positively identify David Malachi?"

"No, but that isn't important. Everyone knows it had to be David, he hasn't denied a single charge. What is important is that Malachi hasn't left town. If we can find him, we can save your job. Otherwise, Jason is going to be forced to fire you."

"I know that," Lauren said slowly. "It will jeopardize the validity of criminal psychologists in a lot of other cities, too." She felt the full weight of what her failure would cost. "But what if Malachi is innocent of murder? What if he feels he's been framed and has to find the real killer?"

"Then he should turn himself in and let the legal system work. That's why we have law officers and courts, Lauren. He can't take justice into his own hands. That's what got him into trouble in the first place."

But he doesn't trust the system, Lauren wanted to say. She sipped her coffee instead. The warm food had at least made her feel as though she could survive the day.

"Thanks for the tip, Burton. How'd you hear about this?"

"Wyatt Reed's cousin is dispatcher at the sheriff's office. He told Wyatt all the details, and Wyatt told me this morning. He wanted to tell you himself, but I stole his thunder."

"He'll survive," Lauren said, "but I'll make it a point to thank him, anyway. How come the two of you are trying to help me keep my job? I thought the entire prosecuting staff hated me."

"Hell, Wyatt and I aren't blind. You're the classiest thing that ever walked into the D.A.'s office. We'd be a fool to let Jason run you off."

Lauren laughed for what seemed like the first time in weeks. "Thanks, Burt, I needed that. Just goes to show that a little bit of flattery is a wonder drug for a tired and beaten female."

"What did happen to your face?" Burt asked. "You have a few cuts and bruises. And I'm no doctor, but your right arm seems a bit stiff."

"I got lost in some woods. I panicked a bit and wasn't careful where I was going."

"Next time you want to go hiking, call me. I'm an official Eagle Scout, and I grew up around these parts. There are some beautiful places, but you don't have to lose forty percent of your skin to see them."

"I'll keep that in mind. And thanks for the breakfast, Burt. Now I'd better go make a report to Jason. I'm sure he's in his office doing the fee-fie-foe-fum number."

They parted at the steps of the café. Burt had a witness to run down and Lauren opted to walk. The morning was brilliant with the promise of spring. She hurried to the courthouse, and instead of going inside, she got in her car.

The drive to Timbermain was a fairyland trip of white dogwoods and the first buds of the riotous azaleas. Natchez in the spring was one of the most beautiful places she'd ever been. She was reminded of a scene in a book when—

She pushed the memory out of her mind. She was in hot water with her job and her future. Now wasn't the time for fantasies.

The gates of Timbermain were locked, and there was no one about to open them. Undaunted, Lauren parked and circled the enclosure until she found a vine-covered gate. She no more believed that René Devereau had been robbed than she believed she could fly. The suspicion she'd pointed out to him—that only he and David had *not* been robbed—had provoked this immediate action. He wanted no smoking gun pointed in his direction, so he'd staged an aborted self-robbery. Attempted robbery! Ha! If David had chosen to rob Timbermain, it would have been an accomplished fact, not a feeble attempt.

She paused beneath a sweet smelling mimosa to contemplate her line of thinking. Great. Now she was championing David's robbery expertise. Where had her principles gone? She didn't wait for an answer to that question as she pushed the recalcitrant gate open and stepped onto the estate. René Devereau couldn't hide in his house. He was going to have to confront her.

Timbermain seemed to frown at her intrusion as she crouched in the azaleas up against the brick privacy wall. She'd thought of walking up to the front door and demanding entry, but the foreboding stance of the huge house intimidated her. Perhaps it would be better to sneak around to see if she couldn't find René without going through the staff.

She wasn't completely familiar with René's home, but she could easily identify the kitchen door and the double-wide library doors that seemed to be so much a part of the traditional Southern estate. An enclosed patio was marked with a twelve-foot-high wall with windows covered in wrought iron. Peeping through, Lauren found a jungle of lush vegetation around a crystal pool. She circled the house twice, seeking the best point of entry. She finally decided on the front door. After all, she had professional business with Devereau. She shouldn't be slinking around like some cheap private detective.

She banged the lion's head knocker on the door to no avail. The sound echoed hollowly, but no one answered. Pushing down on the heavy handle, Lauren almost cried out when the door swung open. The large foyer, immaculate in black-and-white tile, was empty. In two steps she was inside, closing the door silently behind her. Perhaps she could find some clues.

The house was impressive. Not a magazine was out of place. According to Wyatt's cousin, the robber had entered through French doors and René had been drowsing on the sofa.

Dreaming about some woman he just met.

Lauren pushed her glasses up on her nose. René, Nicole—they were both treacherous. How would it look to Jason if he found out she had dinner at the next house on Robin's hit list? And the assumption *was* that Robin had struck. Well, her credibility would sink another few notches. At this point she was barely above sea level.

She went to the library. The beautiful room, filled with leather-covered volumes, looked as if each shelf had just been dusted. If someone had attempted to take anything, there was no evidence of it.

She went to the sofa that fronted a fireplace and examined it. Yes, René could have been dozing here when the doors opened. It would, or at least could, be an exact reenactment of what had happened at the Bedford Tanner home.

A shiver of nerves made the hair on her arms stand on end. She went to the sofa and laid down on it, careful to keep her feet on the ground. Lying thus, a person could easily sit up and surprise an intruder... Her thoughts were at the Tanner estate rather than Timbermain. Was that why Tanner was dead? Because he'd suddenly sat up on the sofa and alarmed the burglar?

She suddenly swung up off the sofa and turned around. Her breath caught in her throat and she almost choked. "David!" She stared at the man in leather jerkin, black pants and green shirt, a quiver on his back and a bow fitted into his hand.

"Lauren! What are you doing here?"

"The better question is, what are you doing here? Every cop in Natchez is after you." The conversation was stupid, inane, but the best she could manage. Her heart was trip-hammering.

"I came to show that clown René that I don't fool around with attempted robberies. If I'd wanted something from Timbermain, I would have taken it."

"David, please, don't compound your problems." Lauren took a step toward him.

"Oh, I'm not going to steal from René." There was a coldness in David's voice. "I didn't realize you were such good friends that you would come over to his library for a nap."

His tone and accusation were maddening. "There are lots of things you don't know about me, David Malachi. My business with René is *my* business. And by the way, Nicole said she had something important to tell you. Something about Bedford Tanner. She wants to see you."

Lauren stalked toward the library door. She had to get out of the room, off the emotional roller coaster with David. She'd delivered Nicole's message, and that was all she could do. Her hand was on the wooden frame of the door when the arrow struck. The vibration of the wood rattled the delicate French door, and Lauren let go as the tremor passed to her arm. The arrow was a good six inches from her, yet it made her go cold with fear.

"Wait a minute, Lauren. I want to talk with you."

Fury replaced anger and she turned on him. "You can go to hell. Who do you think you are, shooting arrows at people? You're worse than a kid."

"Lauren!"

She ignored him. "I'm tired of it."

"Lauren!"

She pulled the arrow out of the door with a mighty jerk and snapped it over her knee. She was breathing hard. "That's what I think of your foolish behavior. I've half a mind to call the cops and tell them you're here. If you're going to risk your hide with such a wanton display of stupidity, maybe I should make it easy for you to self-destruct."

"Hush," David said softly as he approached her.

"I won't." She glared at him, her chest rising and falling in the rapid rhythm of anger.

"You will," he said, his voice a harsh command. The expression on his face changed instantly to one of alertness. "Listen."

"Don't try this on me again, David. I'm not a fool."

She had no chance to argue further. His grip on her arms was not gentle, and his lips covered hers completely to stop any sound she tried to make.

His arms were strong and held her steady. As she struggled to free her head, his hand clutched her hair and held. Shock immobilized her for an instant, and then anger flashed through her like a potent jolt of lightning. Her body coiled, preparing for a deadly strike. But when she attempted to deliver, she found that David still held her with ease. His only response was to deepen the kiss.

Without warning, his grip on her loosened. She found that only the pressure of his lips on hers held her—that and the sensations he had stirred. The urge to cease struggling came over her like a soothing whisper. His arms held her, but they didn't hurt her, and his lips on hers was an insistent pressure, not an act of domination. Something in Lauren responded to the feel of him.

She slowed her efforts to resist, and was suddenly aware of the pressure of his body against hers. Warmth crept over her skin. Her hands, pressed hard against his chest to ward him off, released their tension and Lauren opened her mouth to his kiss. It was insane, stupid, an act of irrational behavior, but one she couldn't resist. She wanted to kiss him, had wanted to for some time, she realized.

His hold on her became gentler as he freed her body and her lips. Softly he explored, giving her time to acknowledge and respond. At last he drew back. "There's someone outside," he said softly. "You'd better get out of here."

"And you?" she asked.

"When you're safe, I'll follow."

"David, give yourself up. Please." The thought that he might actually be killed if he was seen trying to escape the police made her physically ill.

"I can't. There's more at stake here than just me." He brushed her lips lightly again. "I never meant to kiss you. At least not by force."

"I never meant to let you," she said, shrugging. She knew she had to get away from Timbermain, but for one second more she wanted to look into his eyes. Was he a killer? No, that wasn't possible.

"Second thoughts about dallying with a criminal?" he asked, reading the shift of emotions in her eyes.

"Yes," she admitted candidly. "It is a touchy situation for someone who should know better. We have to talk, David. Meet me tonight."

"Where?"

"Wherever you say."

"There's a backwash that makes a natural port just north of town. Old Dockery Road. Outlaws used the area for robbing riverboats and hiding the goods. Under the bridge near the river," he whispered. "At ten."

"Wait for me," she answered as she looked out the library door. "Who's out here?"

"I'd say the sheriff's men. They're probably coming for fingerprints, that kind of thing."

Lauren looked at his bare hands. "You deliberately..."

"Go, Lauren, before they come back here. They'll wait only so long at the front door."

"They'll know you were here, David."

"I want them to know." He drew another arrow from his quiver, one with a note attached. "Go!" he ordered, "or I won't have a chance of escape."

Lauren bolted out the door, moving across the lawn toward the mimosa tree that marked the gate.

"Lauren!"

She heard her name, but it wasn't David's voice. She started to turn around, but something warned her to keep running.

"Lauren! Wait up!"

She cursed her slowness and her clumsiness, but she halted her dead run and slowly settled to a stop. When she turned around, Wyatt Reed was running across the grounds after her, his suit coat flapping in the gentle breeze.

"Wyatt, what are you doing here?" She was confused, and flustered. Now the fat was in the fire for sure.

"Does Jason know you're here?" Wyatt's face was red with exertion, and possibly anger.

"Mr. Devereau is a friend of mine. I can pay a call without Jason's permission."

Wyatt's hands were on her shoulders, shaking her lightly. "Don't you know your job is in jeopardy already? Lauren—" he pushed her behind a clump of willow tree "—get out of here. If the deputies see you they're going to make hash out of you."

"I didn't do anything wrong," Lauren insisted, but the expression on Wyatt's face let her know how much trouble she was in.

"We'll talk about this back at the office. Now, however you got over this wall, go back the way you came. And pray I can divert those deputies until you're out of sight."

"Thanks, Wyatt," she said humbly as she slipped deeper into the willows and began looking for a chance to dash to the wall. Wyatt hurried across the yard without turning back. Hidden among the trees, she saw him motioning to two sheriff's deputies in their olive brown uniforms. Together, all three men went back into the house.

Spying her moment, Lauren sprinted the last twenty yards to the wall. With concerted effort, she pushed at the rusty gate. When it refused to open, she had to use her body to slam against it again and again. At last the hinges moved and the gate opened far enough to allow her to slip out. She looked down at her skirt—a shambles, not to mention the three hideous runs that had crept up her hose. Another day of humiliation, but she had to get back to the office. She had to talk with Wyatt before he went to Jason.

Chapter Seven

Unable to concentrate in the stuffiness of her small office, Lauren shut the file on a young man accused of repeated shoplifting charges. He came from an affluent family, good education, plenty of spending money. The items he had taken were nonessential "toys." She read the list again: several CDs, a portable cassette player, sunglasses, a silk scarf—which he gave his mother, very expensive after-shave. It went on for another page. Hypochondria? A cry for attention? Or something darker? It was a case that should have held Lauren's interest, but at the moment did not. Everytime there was a creak on the stairs, or the door of her office rattled, she looked up expecting to see Wyatt Reed's angry face.

After an hour to think over the situation at Timbermain, she had to agree that Wyatt had taken a terrible risk to protect her. A long sigh escaped her compressed lips. How was it that both Burton and Wyatt, two men who were known to go for the throat on an accused criminal, had put themselves on the line to help her?

And David?

What had he done except put her career at risk?

When her door opened and Wyatt stepped into the room, she felt a sense of relief that her well-deserved dressing down had arrived at last.

"Have a seat," she said, indicating the chair in front of her desk. "Wyatt, I'm sorry about today."

He waved a hand in dismissal, and then leaned forward. "I overreacted. It's just that we've heard the talk about you and Malachi."

"What talk?" Lauren felt a pulse of unpleasant warmth on her face.

"That you talked Jason into letting him out of jail. Poor judgment—" he gave an apologetic smile "—that kind of thing. I was afraid if you were caught at Timbermain, Jason would view it as another bad decision on your part."

"As well he might," Lauren said. "As I mentioned, I am friends with Mr. Devereau, and I had stopped by to talk with him about Mr. Malachi's background, and also about the attempted robbery. It would greatly behoove me to find David."

"Watch out for Devereau, and Malachi," Wyatt said slowly. "Their families have run this town for generations. They both have the idea they're above the law."

"I got that impression," Lauren agreed. "And are they?"

"Let's just say that if I did some of the things René has done, I'd be breaking rocks in the state prison."

Lauren hadn't anticipated such a wealth of information from Wyatt. He was a man much like herself. Ambition had brought him to Natchez from his hometown of St. Paul. Single, he was known as a loner with a dry wit. He'd only been in Natchez for a year, yet he'd made it his business to learn the political structure of the town. It was a side to him she'd never seen before, and her estimation of him rose accordingly.

"You've done some research into this, haven't you?"

"Enough to know that this business with Malachi is more than just a struggle about robbery."

"I know—it's murder now," Lauren said darkly.

"It's even more than that. It's the old order trying to hang on, Lauren. Politically, Natchez has been strangled by families like Malachi and Devereau and Tanner. They kept each other's secrets, and they turned their backs when one committed a criminal act. They knew enough to all stick together. Now, that unity is shattered."

Lauren listened with intense interest. She could see by the passion on Wyatt's face that he was very involved.

"What do you project will happen?"

"The old order will fall and a new, progressive leadership will evolve. And I intend to be part of that, along with Jason and a few others."

"I've never underestimated Jason's ambitions," Lauren said.

"Well, don't get in the way of them. That's really all I had to say to you. Watch your step. Burton and I, along with some of the other prosecutors, really believe in the job you were hired to do. But we can't help if you're determined to shoot yourself in the foot."

"I understand that, Wyatt, and I thank you for all you've done already. I never intended to be a liability to this office."

"Once Malachi is behind bars and paying for the crimes he committed, things will ease up on you." He smiled. "Until then, I'll do whatever I can."

"Thanks." She swallowed a lump of emotion.

"Just to make sure you're not in any danger, how about dinner tonight?" There was a teasing glint in his dark eyes.

Lauren hadn't anticipated the question, and she felt a sudden apprehension. She liked Wyatt, as a friend, and she sincerely appreciated his efforts in her behalf, but..., "I have plans for this evening. Maybe another time."

"Are you having dinner with René Devereau again?" he asked.

"You are well informed." Lauren forced herself to smile. "I didn't know anyone was interested enough in my social calendar to know where I dined." She was also sick and tired of people poking into her personal business. Now wasn't the time, though, to argue that point with Wyatt.

"René can be very charming, Lauren. He's also been through every woman in Natchez. Let's just say he's a bit on the fickle side."

"Thanks for the tip." Lauren rose. "I have to go down to the docket room and get some information. Then I'm going over to the library. Can I get anything there for you?"

"No thanks." Wyatt walked to the door and held it open for her. "I do have one other question."

Lauren halted, her hand on the doorframe. She looked over her shoulder. "Yes?"

"Devereau wasn't at home. The staff was gone. How did you get inside Timbermain?"

Lauren sensed there was more behind the question than a request for simple facts. "I never said I went inside."

Wyatt grinned suddenly. "You're plenty smart. That takes a load off my mind." His hand touched her shoulder as he helped her out the door.

SOME OF THE BOOKS Lauren had taken from the library were so old that she worried she might damage them by turning the pages. But she read on nonetheless, engrossed in the story of a small river town that defied the force of the Mississippi River, and for a while, the Union Army.

Of many wild river towns, Natchez was known as one of the wildest. The city's history included figures of national prominence—and notoriety. The Natchez Trace, the overland road between Natchez and Nashville, Tennessee, was one of the most crime-ridden stretches of road in the history of the United States.

Lauren read with fascination the material covering the mound-building Indians of the Creek Indian Nation and the arrival of the white settlers.

As more and more pioneers began to emigrate from east to west, and north to south, Natchez played a crucial role. The river port was the loading zone for many travelers who came overland from Memphis to Natchez and then decided to ride the wide Mississippi the rest of the way to New Orleans.

During the Civil War, Natchez had been spared much of the destruction that laid waste to Vicksburg, another historic town up-river from Natchez. Although Natchez was under Union occupation near the close of the war, it was not decimated to the extent that Vicksburg suffered.

Throughout the history of the town, Lauren read again and again the names of David Malachi's ancestors. Lawrence Malachi was a general of great standing in the Confederate cavalry. He was killed in action at the siege of Vicksburg. Dr. Archwell Malachi was the ordained minister of the Natchez Episcopal Church in 1912, and Dr. James Malachi was the town's only doctor for some twenty years.

An interesting aside to James Malachi was his alleged membership in a band of outlaws who robbed the travelers on the Natchez Trace.

The book Lauren was reading was printed in the 1890s, and tracked the Trace Gang back to several of the more prominent Natchez families. James Malachi was the gang's physician, according to the text. No charges were ever brought against him, and when the local sheriff made a small effort to do so, the town rose in defense of the medical man.

There was some doubt that James Malachi had ever ridden with the gang, but he did patch their wounded on a number of occasions, and the leader of the outlaws, one Joshua Denton, had publicly acclaimed James Malachi's healing abilities from the gallows.

Lauren read the quote again. "'Hang me and be damned to you. Just see that James Malachi gets my corpse before it's cold. He's patched many of my men and I believe he can raise the dead.'" Upon that macabre note, the hangman dropped the floor out from under the convicted outlaw and he died in the town square of Natchez.

Lauren shut the book with a glance at her watch. It was time for the library to close. She had plenty of time to warm something for dinner and make it to the rendezvous point to meet David.

WHEN SHE'D FINISHED a microwave dinner, which Gumbo had declined to share any part of, she tugged on a pair of jeans, sneakers and a sweatshirt. If she was going to play games in the woods with Robin Hood, she was damn well going to be dressed for the occasion. She couldn't stand to destroy any more of her suits.

Although she wasn't completely familiar with the Natchez terrain, she found the road that led down beside the old backwater bridge. Interstate 84, spanning the wide river, was visible in the distance, but all traffic noises were muted. The weed-choked path spiraled toward the river, and Lauren put her car in first gear. David had found seclusion!

Signs warned all trespassers away, but Lauren worked the clutch and brake, and drove on. Bushes closed in on the road and made it a narrow tunnel; a very uncomfortable sensation assailed her.

When she reached the bluff that marked the drop down to the mighty Mississippi, she felt her heart sink. There was no sign of David. Her watch said ten o'clock exactly. Killing her lights, she turned off the motor and sat back to wait. She'd give him fifteen minutes. There was the chance he'd been detained. At Nicole's. She clamped that thought out of her mind. She couldn't afford to care what David did with his free time.

The sounds of a spring night drifted through her open window. Crickets chirred and the spooky call of a lone owl was magnified by the water that gurgled some fifty feet below her. Somewhere the wind picked up the perfume of wisteria. Lauren tilted her head back on the seat, shut her eyes and allowed her senses to experience the richness of the night. She didn't want to think, not for a few moments. Everything was too confusing.

The owl called again, and Lauren wondered if the nest was somewhere in the girders of the rusty bridge. It was pointless to look, so she kept her eyes closed.

The gentle brush on her cheek felt like an insect, and she lifted her hand to rub her face. The breeze stirred her hair and she inhaled deeply. Once again the tickle came, just below her ear.

She brushed it away again.

"You look almost like a child when you're relaxed."

David's voice startled her, but she didn't move. She opened her eyes and found him crouched at her car window, his gaze level with hers.

"I didn't hear you drive up."

"I've been here. I wanted to make sure you weren't followed."

"I'm not stupid," she answered irritably.

"That's a debatable question. You are meeting me here, and I'm certain that Jason Amberly would consider this the height of stupidity."

"Point well taken," she said, straightening her posture in the car seat.

"I avoided the three deputies at Timbermain, but I saw that Wyatt caught up with you. Any trouble?"

"Not yet. Wyatt and a few of the other prosecutors seem to have taken me under their wings. He pretended not to see me." She felt her anger returning as she talked. She had put her co-workers in a bad situation, and she was doing it again.

"Nicole's information was worthless," he said. "But she made me pay dearly for it, anyway."

"I don't want to hear this." Lauren couldn't help the edge of jealousy that crept into her voice.

"Lauren, can you go over the evidence that was taken from Bedford Tanner's?"

The question brought her back to the immediate problem at hand. "Maybe. I don't really know. It's down in the evidence room in the basement."

"Would it put you in a bad position to ask?"

"Possibly. Why? You went back to the Tanner home and took whatever you wanted. I figured you cleaned up everything except the corpse. That would be a little difficult."

"What are you talking about? I went back and found your glasses and made certain that nothing was amiss. Whoever killed Tanner intended to frame me, so I wanted to make sure there really was no concrete evidence. Lucky for me I went back. Someone had penned a note that took credit for the murder and signed the name Robin. Except for the fake note, I didn't take a thing."

"You swear?" Lauren couldn't believe what he was saying. "The house was robbed. Some jewelry, silver, paintings and an original Picasso were taken. It was exactly the type of loot Robin Hood always took."

"Not Picasso—too hard to fence."

"Excuse me," Lauren said. "Not having a criminal background, I suppose I overlooked that small complication."

David shrugged. "It happens."

"I love the way you show regret."

"If we're through needling each other, maybe you would like to hear about Bedford?"

"I thought Nicole didn't have anything to tell you?" Lauren asked.

"She had plenty to show me, though."

Even in the darkness, Lauren could see the imp sparkling in David's eyes. "I'll bet she did."

"Very interesting, too."

"I'm sure it was complete with a decorator's touch."

David laughed. "It's good to see your sense of humor is still holding up."

"We aim to please." Lauren's anger dissipated slowly. "What did you learn?"

"Tanner was expecting a visitor that evening. He'd been in Jackson on a business trip that day and wasn't expected to return. That's why I selected that night to rob his home. See, he hardly ever left the estate. That was one reason I was so desperate to get out of Jason's clutches. I knew I wouldn't have another chance at Tanner's home—his empty home—for another nine months at least."

"You said you had saplings that were dying," she accused.

"That was true enough. It just wasn't the entire truth. I left them for my old pal Lem to take care of."

"Go on about Tanner. So you didn't think he'd be home?"

"Nicole said that he had called her that afternoon and made an appointment with her to come out the next day. He wanted some guest rooms renovated. He said he was meeting with someone that evening, and that he'd soon have houseguests and he wanted to know how quickly she could fit two guest rooms with antique furnishings. Something about the antiques seemed very important."

"What?"

"Nicole specified he wanted Ballard beds."

"So? Natchez is rife with that brand of antique, isn't it?"

"Yes, that's what Nicole found so interesting. Bedford was acting as if he would be the only person to own a Ballard antique bed. He said he'd purchased two and wanted to know if Nicole could locate any others in the area for sale."

"Some of the brochures for the tour homes point out the Ballard design in a lot of the furniture," Lauren mused. "I saw a table at a plantation called Rosemont. It was magnificent, but why would Tanner be so obsessed by that particular type of antique?"

"Good question."

"And you think there might be a clue in the evidence that was collected?"

"If there was a letter or something . . . some paper with names or dates or places. Maybe Tanner had a list of people he wanted Nicole to buy antiques from. I don't know! But there's something here. I can sense it. Something that might give us a clue where to look!"

Lauren watched the way his eyes dropped for a fraction of a second. "David, what are you hunting for? You were at Bedford Tanner's looking for something specific."

He looked up, his expression carefully designed to give nothing away. "You have a good memory."

"You said you wanted me to meet you there to show me something. I'm assuming it was something that would make me understand why you do what you do. What was it?"

"I was looking for something specific." He stood up, effectively ending the conversation.

"If I knew what it was, it would help."

"Wrong, Lauren, it would only drag you deeper into this mess. Forget it, and forget about sneaking a look at the evidence. I shouldn't have asked. You're in enough hot water. As you pointed out, this could cost you your job."

"I've already lost my job," she said evenly. "It's just a matter of time. If you don't reappear at the courthouse, and soon, Jason's going to have to fire me."

"I can't give myself up."

"I expected you'd feel that way." Lauren spoke without any bitterness at all. If she were in David's shoes, she didn't know if she'd walk into a murder charge.

"You'd better get out of here before someone comes along to check." David sounded terribly tired. "I promised Dr. Smith I'd help him with some things at the clinic. Lauren, if you should need me, you can leave word with Alan."

Touched by the concern in David's voice, Lauren smiled. "You seem to have a full plate, David. I hope I don't fall prey to the Sheriff of Nottingham."

"The trouble with this rendition of the legend is, I'm not certain who the sheriff is," David said.

"It's a quandary, but..." Lauren heard the crack of a gun just as the front window of her car exploded. Tiny sparkles of glass rained against her face and hands, stinging but not cutting her skin.

Before she could speak or move, David opened the car door and dragged her down onto the ground beside him. "Lauren?" He rolled her over and brushed the glass from her face. "Are you hit?"

She shook her head. "What . . . ?"

"It's someone on the bridge." David held her down to the ground, covering her with his own body. "Wait here."

"David, don't go!"

"Lauren, he can sit out there all night on the bridge and if we even try to leave, he'll kill us. I'd say we have about fifteen minutes before someone reports the gunshot and the sheriff's department is here. Do you want to be caught here, pinned down with me?"

"I don't want you to get killed."

"That's a relief."

His breath touched the sensitive skin by her ear, and her stomach knotted suddenly. Thrown off balance, and frightened by the teasing note in his voice, she tried to wiggle out from under him. "Get off me," she said. "You like danger. You enjoy putting your life on the line. Well that's juvenile and disgusting." Her heart was pounding.

"That's true," he said, completely unmoved by her struggles or her words. "That's why I spend so much of my time with you."

"David—" she panted twice "—let me up or..."

"Or what, my pretty?" His imitation of the Wicked Witch of the West was passable. "I'll have those ruby slippers, and your little dog Toto, too."

Lauren groaned. Somewhere—not very far away—a sniper was watching them. And David was replaying favorite movies on the grassy bank of the river.

"You've stopped wiggling. And just when I was beginning to find it enjoyable."

"You've been sent from hell to torment me to death," Lauren said softly. "I don't know what I did to deserve such a curse."

"You moved to Natchez," David answered.

His breath was once again at her ear, and Lauren couldn't help her reaction to his whisper. What would it be like to welcome his caresses? She held herself very still.

"Now if you agree to stay here, I'll get off you and see about our friend on the bridge."

"Okay." Lauren took a deep breath as his weight shifted. "Let's see if we can't crawl away from here, David. It isn't that far to the road. Maybe we can hitch a ride." She rolled slightly so she could look at him. He was only six inches away, his profile clear and rugged in the moonlight.

"Maybe the sniper will pick us up. We could get a drink at Riverbend, maybe talk about why he's trying to kill you."

"Me?" His sarcastic accusation drove all romantic thoughts from her head. "Don't be ridiculous. He's trying to kill you. Why would he kill me?"

"This guy may be blind as a bat, but I think he can see the car he's shooting at. I'm fairly certain, in the moonlight, he could see me outside the car. With your hair down around your shoulders, and it is a lovely sight, you're obviously a girl. Think about it, Lauren."

She didn't want to. She only wanted to get out of there—with David.

"What are you going to do?"

"The obvious answer would be to climb up on the bridge and see if I can't disarm the guy."

"Still playing Robin Hood?" Lauren flared. "Don't you realize he could kill you?"

"You are a feisty wench," David answered drolly. "Perhaps you'd like to audition for the role of Marion?"

"Dream on," she snapped.

"Nicole does seem to relish that role." David's drawl was more pronounced than necessary.

"Go on," Lauren answered, shoving him with her foot. "Do whatever you want, because you're going to, anyway."

"In that case..."

David's lips were warm as he brought them against her own. He was gentle, yet hungry. His hand slipped up beneath her hair and steadied her head as his fingers wound in her thick hair. After a long kiss, he drew back.

"If I really had my way, I'd stay here and do a lot more than kiss you."

"Be careful," she said, all angry remarks dissolved. The man had a way of keeping her constantly off balance. His kiss had been gentle, yet exploring. Her stomach was still knotted from her reaction.

"Give me ten minutes. If I don't call out to you, get in the car and drive away."

"I won't do that!"

"You will, because I might be in danger. If you start to leave, you might distract the sniper."

"You're lying, just to get me to leave." Lauren wanted to reach out, to touch him in the moonlight.

"I'm not lying, Lauren. It could save my life."

"And I should leave you here, alone with a man who has a gun?"

His finger traced the line of her jaw. "Your concern touches me. And your willingness to share the danger. But you really have to promise me, or otherwise I'll be so worried about you, I might get hurt."

"Ten minutes." She swallowed her arguments. "And you'll call me?"

"When I get home safely."

Before she could protest, he was gone. Lauren watched the hands on her watch and the black outline of the bridge. She wondered about the sniper. Who was it? And if David's assumption was right, why was he after her?

Because she'd seen him at Bedford Tanner's? Or he thought she'd seen him. Her head throbbed with the dizzying possibilities and worry for the man who even now was climbing beneath the underbelly of the bridge.

Five minutes elapsed and she strained her eyes for sight of him in the dark. For a second she thought she saw a dark shadow moving along the base of the bridge, but before she could be certain, the image disappeared.

Three minutes later, she pulled her keys from her pocket. She'd given her word. Torn as she was between her desire to stay and her promise to go, she slipped into the driver's seat of her car.

The windshield was a pinwheel of glass fragments. There was a hole the size of a golf ball in the center, and she looked through it as she watched the bridge. Another minute and she'd have to leave.

The shot that rang through the night made her hands clench the steering wheel. She heard a shout of dismay, and then a loud splash as a body hit the water that fed into the fast currents of the Mississippi.

Chapter Eight

David's cry of dismay sent Lauren thrashing through the undergrowth to the edge of the water. The sound of the body striking the water spurred her fear to gigantic proportions. Without considering the danger of the currents, she waded into the eddies. Although the backwater appeared still and quiet, the currents tugged at her legs, pulling her away from shore.

Afraid to call David's name, Lauren swam. She made her way under the bridge, hoping to find him clinging to one of the supports. Night and water merged into a black nightmare that gave no sign of life. Fighting the current, she made her way back to shore and waded along the edge. At points the bank dropped sharply and she fell into the water. Once she regained her footing, she continued on until she was at the Mississippi.

The wide river stretched into the distance. "David," Lauren called softly. At least half an hour had elapsed. If the sniper was still on the bridge, she had to risk calling for David. He might be wounded on the bank, thinking she'd abandoned him.

"David!" Her voice rose to full volume. As she struggled through the weeds and brambles at the edge of the water, she called his name again and again.

There wasn't a trace of him. A submerged root snagged her foot, dragging her beneath the waters. She struggled free and clutched at the bank. Only the thought that she had to act kept hysteria at bay. Forcing her body up, she stumbled to her car and drove away from the river.

She had to get help. The Mississippi was deceptive. Though it looked wide, muddy and sluggish, eddies and currents were treacherous. A swift current could have pulled David far downriver by now. Hands clenched on the steering wheel, she drove straight to the Natchez Police Department and alerted authorities. With mingled hope and horror, she listened as a dispatcher sent out the call for emergency vehicles. The station house sprang to life.

A cop pressed a cup of coffee into her hand and wrapped a blanket around her shivering shoulders as he helped her to a chair.

"We're going to have to talk with you, but it can wait a few minutes," he said with a degree of kindness.

"Thanks." Lauren didn't even look up at his face. She kept replaying the sound of the gun going off in the night and the splash of the body as it hit the water. Was David wounded and floating helplessly in the river? Was he hanging on to some tree or limb, his blood ebbing away with the current? She felt the tears threaten as she sipped the hot, bitter coffee.

In the distance, sirens echoed, and she was aware that emergency units and paramedics had taken over the search for David. Lauren felt completely numb. The possibility that David was actually dead hovered at the fringes of her mind, but she refused to acknowledge it. She made her mind think of the rescue workers pulling him from the water—injured but alive.

"Lauren, are you okay?"

Jason's voice stirred her to look up. She pushed her glasses up on her nose and tried for a smile.

"When I told you to bring David Malachi in dead or alive, I didn't mean it literally." Jason grinned. "You get an A-plus for effort."

"I wasn't..."

Jason's finger on her lips silenced her. "We'll talk about it later. There will be a lot of questions. For now, don't say anything." Jason sighed. "Not to anyone."

She heard the warning in his voice and nodded her head. She was in deep trouble now. But it didn't matter. Nothing mattered until she found out that David was alive.

"I'm going to talk with the chief," Jason said. "The sheriff's here, too, so I'll find out what's going on. If there's any news, I'll let you know."

"Thanks," she whispered. Her throat felt like sandpaper, irritated and angry.

She checked her watch and shook it. Surely it had to be later than eleven o'clock. A lifetime had passed since David had started toward the bridge. She was shaken out of her reverie when a police captain took the chair next to her.

"Are you certain the person who hit the water was David Malachi?" he asked.

"Yes."

"You saw him?"

"I spoke with him just before it happened."

"And was he armed?"

"No!" Lauren looked up, the coffee sloshing out of the cup she held. "He was not armed. There was someone shooting at me, and he went to find out who. I couldn't leave because the gunman—" Jason's warning came back to her too late. "I'm sorry, I don't feel like talking," she whispered.

"We'll need to take a statement." The policeman rose. "You know Malachi is wanted for murder?"

There was an accusation in his words, and Lauren felt her temper rise to the occasion. "I am an officer of the court, just like you," she said coldly, placing her coffee cup on the chair beside her. "It isn't your place to question my behavior, or my decisions. That's up to my superior."

"And I'll bet Jason Amberly's going to have quite a few questions," the policeman said as he walked away.

Lauren buried her face in her hands. More than anything, she wanted to be away from the police department, but she knew she couldn't leave.

"I just talked with the head of the search team. They haven't found anything." Wyatt Reed took the chair the police officer just vacated. "Is there a chance Malachi escaped without injury?"

Lauren didn't answer for a moment. "I heard the shot, and then there was the sound of a body hitting the water. David didn't have a gun, so I'm sure he didn't fire the weapon." She couldn't stop the scene from playing again and again in her mind. David climbing; the orange flame of the gun in the dark; David falling. She shuddered.

"If he's alive, will he contact you?" Wyatt asked.

"No," she answered. "There's no reason."

"You were trying to talk him into giving himself up, weren't you?"

Lauren looked up and met Wyatt's sympathetic look. "If he had done that, he would be alive now," she said. "He wouldn't listen to reason." She didn't have the heart to lie to save herself, but on the off chance that David was hurt and that he might try to call her for help, she didn't want Wyatt—no matter how well-intentioned—hanging around her.

"Burton's gone over to the river. He's working with the search party in one of the boats. I think I'm going, too."

"How did you find out about this?" Lauren was suddenly curious. She'd never known Burt or Wyatt—or Jason—to show up at the police department during an accident or emergency. How had they learned about this so quickly?

"The chief called Jason, and he called us. This is personal with him, Lauren, you know that. His butt is on the line because of you, and he's got that thing with Malachi anyway. David's like salt in Jason's wounds." Wyatt shrugged. "I also thought you might need a friendly face."

"I did, and do," she answered, ashamed that she'd lied to him again, but knowing she had no choice. "Thanks, and thank Burton for me. If you find anything. Anything at all..."

"We'll let you know," he assured her. He stood and went to the door. As he started to leave, he gave her a thumbs-up signal, and she forced a smile.

As Wyatt disappeared, Lauren was left to consider how seriously Jason viewed the situation if he'd called his two best prosecutors down to the police station for a midnight search of the Mississippi River.

Her life was chaos. In less than a week's time, she'd been shot with an arrow, shot at with a gun, nearly drowned in the biggest river in the United States and was on the verge of losing her job in a manner that would end her career. She'd also fallen under the spell of a crazy man who might be dead. She just couldn't sit in the police department and wait.

Looking in both directions, Lauren found that no one was paying much attention to her. She had no plan—except to escape and wait for David to contact her. Of all the places in the world he would call her, the police station would be the last. She was out the door before anyone noticed she'd moved. Since her car was evidence in the shooting, she didn't bother with it. The night air felt invigorating, and even though her clothes were still damp, she knew she could jog home. There might be a message on her machine already, letting her know that David wasn't injured, that he was safe. That he was alive. She set out at a steady, block-gobbling run.

Panting slightly from the distance, Lauren flew into her house, almost tripping over the cat as she rushed to the answering machine. The little red light blinked happily and there was one message. She felt such a sense of relief, she almost didn't want to play the message back. But she hit the playback button and froze.

"It's all over town that David is dead. Call me," Nicole's voice commanded her. The mechanical voice of the machine came on, announcing that the call had been made at 11:25 p.m.

"In a toad's eye," Lauren muttered under her breath. If Nicole Sterling wanted information, she could get on her broomstick and fly to the police department.

She went to her bathroom and found the giant, industrial-size bottle of aspirin and poured three into her hand. The pounding in her head was going to deafen her, if not drive her completely insane. She swallowed the painkillers and drank a large glass of water, then changed into a dry sweat suit. Pulling Gumbo into her lap, she settled down on the sofa with the telephone at her side. David would call. He would. He'd promised. And he had to be alive. She leaned her head back and closed her eyes.

A frantic knocking at the door made Lauren leap from the sofa. Gumbo gave an angry hiss, arched her back and turned to stare at the front door.

"Who is it?" Lauren demanded.

"Where's David?" Nicole's equally angry voice penetrated through the wooden door. "This is another one of his tricks."

"Get off my property," Lauren said, her back arching almost as much as Gumbo's. Beneath the anger, a small flame of hope burned hotter. There wasn't an iota of grief in Nicole's voice. She sounded so positive David was alive.

Nicole's body thudded against the door. "Let me in or I'm going to make such a scene the neighbors will call the police." To prove her point she threw herself against the door again and let out the beginning of a scream.

Lauren jerked the door open and glared at the petite brunette. "Please remove yourself from my property."

"Do you ever comb your hair, or is the matted look some new fashion from the Kansas wheat fields?" Nicole slinked into the room. "Where are you hiding him? I know David, and this is bound to be one of his brilliant ploys."

"David isn't here and I don't know where he is."

Nicole looked her up and down, taking in the old and faded black sweat suit, her red-rimmed eyes. "He isn't dead, is he?"

"I don't know. But he isn't here."

"No, I believe he isn't here. He wouldn't stay. Not even *his* stomach could take such a sight."

"What do you want?" Lauren was too tired to argue. Nicole's surprise visit had reawakened her hope, and she simply wanted to be left alone to wait for him to call.

"David will call here, won't he?"

"Nicole, how can I guess what David will do. But if he wants to talk with you, he'll call *your* home. You've chased him so hard now whenever your name is mentioned he tries to bolt." Lauren could see the fiery anger that sprang into Nicole's eyes. A direct hit!

"He'll tire of your milksop ways—"

Lauren cut her off. "This isn't some game in which he's a toy that you and I fight over. Go home, Nicole. If he needs help, he might call you."

"René asked me to tell you something. We both believe David's alive and René had a message for you." She turned around and started walking toward the door. "Maybe tonight I don't feel like playing René's messenger boy, though."

Lauren saw the glint in Nicole's eyes that warned of some trickery. "Tell me or not, that's between you and René."

Nicole whirled around, her smile suddenly too sweet. "Since it's past midnight, the event will be tonight. At nine. We're all going to meet at David's aunt's home. If he's able, David'll try to get there. René wants you to be there, too."

"What makes you think David would go to his aunt's? *If* he's alive and able to get there."

"It was prearranged," Nicole answered. "René and David have been playing these little games since grade school. They've both fought to have me."

"And no doubt both have won, along with many others," Lauren noted pointedly. "So why me? Why am I invited to this...gala?"

"That's exactly what I asked René. He wouldn't say." Nicole's smile was cruel. "Perhaps he, too, has a taste for Milquetoast." Nicole walked to the front door. "If you care about David, I'd advise you to be there."

"Or what?" Lauren could smell the trap a mile away.

"Or I might turn David in to the police when he shows."

"Hell hath no fury like a woman scorned," Lauren said dryly. "I've heard that all my life. Now I know what it means."

Nicole laughed. "You only think you know."

THE WHITE LACE curtains moved gently back and forth in the window as Lauren sat at the kitchen table in David's Aunt Em's house. She remembered the kitchen well. Her pulse quickened at the memory of David's gentle hands dressing the arrow wound on her arm. She'd been terrified of him then. And now? She was terrified for him. And for herself.

The kitchen clock showed nine o'clock. There was no sign of René, Nicole, or David. She'd come early to check out the house and make sure she wasn't walking into a trap. Nicole was no friend of hers, and she wasn't sure of René. Either way, it paid to use caution.

The only thing she'd discovered was that David obviously lived in this house—or had lived here. It was a beautiful place. Large rooms, wraparound porch, hardwood floors and Oriental carpets with family heirloom furnishings. David's bedroom held a masculine four-poster covered with a beautiful quilt. The oak dresser had been recently dusted, as if someone came in to care for his possessions, even though he might never come back.

She choked on that thought and forced it away. David was alive. He hadn't drowned in the river. Search parties had turned up absolutely nothing, and now the riverbanks were being searched by helicopter. The bodies of drowned people sometimes stayed submerged, and then later floated to the top to snag in a tree on the side of the river. She shuddered at that gruesome picture. Working in the legal system, she'd heard a lot about death. Too much.

She turned the kitchen light on, wondering if she should or shouldn't. Was David waiting for some signal? Would the light scare him off? She checked the clock again to find that only five minutes had passed.

The day at work had been the worst in her life. The skin on her forehead felt bruised from the assault of Jason's questions. Why? How? Why? What were your intentions? She could hear the battering questions again and again. She knew that he was toughening her for the inevitable grilling by police, but he'd acted so aggressive and angry at her. No doubt he was. Every time he turned his back, she was in some kind of trouble again, usually public.

Her own heart was troubling her more than Jason, though. She'd done as David requested and gone to the evidence room to find out what they had in the Bedford Tanner murder. It was bad. The arrow that killed Tanner was hand-crafted and perfectly matched the ones that were in David's quiver when he was charged with the robberies. The robbery was also in the "Robin Hood" mode.

Who had killed Tanner? That was the question Lauren had avoided. It was also the one she had to answer. She could not believe David was capable of such an act. Robbery? Yes, absolutely. Because it was more than simply stealing, it as an act of justice—in his eyes. But Murder? Even in the name of justice? It wasn't possible. But how to prove that? She had to make contact with David, and they had to find the killer. Otherwise the evidence against David was overwhelming.

David had been on the scene. That couldn't be denied. But so had she. And though she had no proof that anyone else was there, she knew it was true. A third party had been at the Tanner home on the night of the murder. The crucial question, in her opinion, was who knew David would be there? Who would want to set him up?

Was it someone he considered a friend? She snorted. If Nicole was an example of his friends, he didn't need any enemies. A pure shot of jealousy hit her nervous system full strength. That was another thing that troubled her. If David's fling with Nicole had happened fifteen years before, why wouldn't the woman throw in the towel? Fifteen years was a long time to carry a burning torch.

Unless Nicole was in this mess up to her eyeballs. Unless she was using her past with David to shake Lauren's confidence in him.

"Rationalization can be an interesting process," she said aloud. "And not profitable at all."

She got up and started through the house, turning on every light she could find. If David was waiting on a signal, she'd give him one. "Only just let him be alive," she whispered.

When the house was ablaze, she made a cup of tea in the kitchen and took it into the living room. She settled in a plush wing chair with her cup and a family portrait album to while away the time until someone showed.

She went through an album of David and his cousins, she assumed, and Aunt Em. There was a lot of love in the photos, happy smiles and hands on shoulders. She laughed at the image of David, so young and terribly thin, with a big head and enormous gray eyes. Written beneath the picture was the nickname "Punkin'head Malachi." She grinned to herself at the obvious family joke. David's head was big, but he had definitely grown into it as a man. In another photo, a beach snapshot, she had a vivid view of how David's body had matured. It was a fascinating process to watch via the family pictures.

Another album contained people she didn't know. More Malachi relatives, she assumed as she thumbed through it. The third album was very old. The photos were sepia-toned and cracked around the edges. The men wore long black coats with tight collars. Hair was either long with a beard, or short, slicked back and parted in the center with a clean-shaven face. She guessed the style had more to do with profession than wealth. All of the Malachis had been financially secure, if she could believe what she read in the newspaper.

And the women! They were a stern-faced lot, except when they held a baby in a photo. Someone had scrawled carefully beneath some of the photos the dates and names. Lauren stopped when she got to Dr. James Malachi. He was almost the spitting image of David! It seemed as a doctor he straddled the line of occupations and sported slicked-back hair and a mustache. He looked more like a barber than a physician, and Lauren recalled with a shudder that often, back in the 1800s there wasn't much difference between the two professions.

She flipped the page and stopped with a sharp intake of breath. Her gaze was riveted to a gruesome picture of several men standing on a gallows, one with a rope around his neck and an unrepentant look in his eye. It was a tableau that was macabre, yet very much a part of the times.

The same careful script identified the four men in the photo. Dr. Malachi stood on the left, beside the condemned man, who was identified as Joshua Denton, leader of the Trace Outlaw Gang. Beside Denton was Sheriff Reb Tatum and the executioner, who wasn't named. The four men stood and stared into the lens of the camera.

Lauren's eye went back to Denton. If he was certain of his death, he didn't show it. If anything, he defied death. He was a handsome man, for his time. Dark of hair and eye, there was a power that radiated from him that not even time or the gallows could destroy. She went back to the doctor. His expression was one of forced calm. He seemed more disturbed than the condemned man, almost as if he would twitch out of the picture, but was holding himself steady by an act of supreme will. Once again, Lauren was struck by the likeness to David. Was Dr. Malachi, too, obsessed with his own version of justice?

Dreading the thought, but unable to stop herself from looking, Lauren flipped the page. To her relief, there was no documentation of the actual hanging. Carefully posed shots of the family continued. There was the new baby, by all counts, David's great-grandfather. A wedding photo of a Malachi man and his new bride, and on and on. She gently closed the album. In a moment she clutched it to her chest and hugged it.

Her arms were still locked around the album when the impact struck her. She didn't have time to register what was happening—only the blurred sensation of something slamming into her chest. The force of the projectile knocked her back into the chair. Survival instinct took over, and she flipped the chair backward and herself in it. Only the solid frame of the chair saved her when the second arrow struck.

There was a gleeful laugh. "The deer of Sherwood Forest are not as fleet nor cunning as one fair maid. Another time, my love." There was the sound of another arrow striking the chair, and then silence.

Lauren heard nothing except the sound of her heartbeat in her ears, as she hunkered behind the chair. She was afraid to make a sound as she waited for her heart to slow its frightening beat.

When ten minutes had passed and there was no sound from anyone else, Lauren crawled to the lamp and turned it off. Very carefully, she made a circuit of the room, snapping off all lights. When she felt more secure in the cover of darkness, she went back to the chair.

The photo album was pierced by a single arrow, the handcrafted shaft and white feathers too familiar to her. Of the two arrows stuck in the chair, one bore a note.

Suspicion is a crooked finger. It works best when curved. Thursday at 11:00 p.m. You have served me well.

The hand that held the paper trembled. The first arrow had been meant to kill her. She had no doubt of that. Had she not lifted the album at exactly the moment she did, the arrow would have pierced her heart as surely as the one that had found Bedford Tanner's. The chair had saved her from the second and third arrows.

The tremor from her fingers found its way up her arm and into the rest of her body. She was tucking the note away in her pocket when the front door burst open.

"Put your hands in the air!"

The command that came at her made her knees almost buckle. She held herself erect and did nothing.

"Put your hands in the air and walk toward the door."

Her mind registered the bullhorn and the voice of authority. Her hands went up and her legs moved her forward one small step at a time.

Light flooded the doorway and the porch as she stepped out of the house.

"Well I'll be damned!"

She heard Jason Amberly's angry voice.

"Lauren, get over to the car right now," he ordered. "For God's sake, don't kill her. She works for me."

Lauren stood perfectly still on the front porch. She didn't know what to do. She wasn't even certain what had happened. Her mind refused to think about it.

"Lauren!" Jason snapped. "Put your hands down and get over here. Is Malachi in the house?"

"No." Her voice was only a whisper. "No!" She finally yelled. "There's no one in there, or at least I don't think there is."

"What are you doing here?" Jason advanced toward her and the grip on her arm was filled with frustration and anger. "Every time I turn my back, you wind up in trouble. Lauren, I've had it with you. You're suspended!"

Lauren let him push her into the front seat of his car. He stormed around and got in behind the wheel. "What on God's green earth were you doing in that house? How did you find out about the setup?"

"What setup?"

"I'm going to break Burton's— And Wyatt's, too. Which one told you? Or did both of them dash to tell?"

"No one," Lauren said. "I mean, neither. They didn't tell me."

"Then what were you doing in that house?"

"Looking for some answers," she said.

"And did you find any?" Jason's voice was so sarcastic it almost hurt.

Lauren caught the sob in her throat and held it. "I think so." She could barely whisper the words.

"And what answers did you find?" Jason put his arm across the seat of the car. His profile was a knot of fury. He seemed to watch the activity in the old house where policemen circled and prepared to enter, guns drawn at the ready.

"Someone tried to kill me, Jason. They shot three arrows at me."

"What?" All anger disappeared, replaced by shock, then doubt, and finally worry. "Why didn't you say something sooner? Is he in there?" He was halfway out of the car.

"Wait." Lauren grabbed his sleeve and tugged him back inside the car. "He's gone. He knows he didn't kill me, though. He was laughing about it."

"Who was it?"

All of the air seemed to leave the car. Lauren felt the return of her dizziness, and for a moment the lights of the police cruiser circled red and blue across her entire mind.

"Lauren, do you know who it was?"

She nodded. "I'm afraid it was Robin Hood."

"Then he isn't dead?" Jason was triumphant. "I knew it. I knew it was all a trick to throw us off guard. He planned that entire fall from the bridge and he used you to make it convincing. He's a sly one, but I'll have Malachi behind bars before the week is over."

Lauren drew a steadying breath. "I didn't say it was David Malachi. I said it was Robin Hood."

"They're one in the same!" Jason insisted.

"Maybe at first, but I'm not so certain anymore." Lauren rubbed her forehead as the headache started with a dull throb. "The only thing I'm certain about now is that someone *is* trying to kill me."

Chapter Nine

Lauren took the pen Jason offered and signed her name at the bottom of the typed page. How many lies would she tell before the night was over?

The statement she'd just signed said that she had gone to Emma Malachi Schlagel's estate on her own with the idea of looking for clues to David's whereabouts. There was no mention of René or Nicole. Even more damning was the fact that the note tucked in her pocket was not mentioned at all.

Jason had used his authority as D.A. to put a rush on the crime lab, and the arrows had been determined by the crime experts as exact matches to the ones found at Bedford Tanner's and the ones already held in evidence against David Malachi. Lauren had not embellished on her statement to Jason that someone had tried to kill her.

In light of the turn of events, Jason had relented, a bit, on her suspension. She was still suspended, but with pay. He'd also spoken with the law enforcement agencies to make sure that someone would guard, protect, and watch over her twenty-four hours a day. As Lauren gathered her purse, she watched a stout, middle-aged policeman rise to accompany her. She was too tired to even argue the point. Whether he was called guardian or watchdog didn't matter. She knew she couldn't buck Jason on this issue.

The patrolman, Tim Prentiss, chatted in an easy way as he drove her home. He'd stay in the kitchen with a pot of coffee, if she didn't mind, until his relief came. She nodded at everything he said. She didn't care if he stood on his head and whistled "Dixie." All she wanted was some time alone, in a hot bath, to sort through the events.

Had David tried to kill her?

Her mind shied away from the idea and her body felt a physical cramp. It wasn't possible, was it?

You've served me well. She didn't have to bring the note out of her pocket to read it. That part was branded into her mind. *You've served me well.* It made her want to crawl under a rock and hide. It shamed her, and embarrassed her, and degraded her.

"You okay?" Tim Prentiss asked, concern on his face. "Want me to pull over?"

"No." She sat up straight. "I'm fine. Just tired."

He drove on, his gaze shifting back to her every few minutes. When they pulled in the driveway, Lauren got out her keys and opened the door. Gumbo greeted her with a cry, completely ignoring the patrolman.

"Help yourself to anything you want," Lauren told him as she scooped the cat into her arms. She held the purring Gumbo. "I'm going to bathe and then sleep."

"Thanks, ma'am," Prentiss said as he went to the kitchen. "If you need anything, holler. And remember that I'm out here, so don't worry. If someone's trying to hurt you or frighten you, we'll find them."

Lauren hurried down the hall and into the privacy of her own room before she even let her thoughts turn to who might be trying to "hurt or frighten" her.

An hour later, her skin scrubbed and soaked to a new height of cleanliness, she had a list of suspects. A very short list. Nicole was at the top, followed by René. David's name was third.

Her mind flinched away from looking at the note, but she knew she had to explore what it might mean. She pulled it from the pocket of her jeans and carefully unfolded it. The hole where the arrow had pierced it made her hands tremble. It was typewritten, just like the one that had been stuck to her desk the first day she met David.

The wording was enigmatic, odd, but not exactly the same. The first note had had a lyrical quality. Perhaps the author hadn't had time to mull this one over.

It was obviously a riddle, a puzzle that spoke of a meeting. At eleven o'clock. She checked her watch and discovered that it was nearly two in the morning. She had twenty-one hours to make up her mind whether she wanted to attend or not—if she could figure out the location.

She forced her mind back to the arrow incident the night before. The voice that had called out to her was nasty, mean, condescending—very like the voice that belonged to the man who'd chased her through the woods at Bedford Tanner's and shot her with an arrow.

The question—the most important question she'd ever answer—was whether that person was David Malachi. It should have been a purely clinical question, but it wasn't. It was weighted with a million emotions. Was it possible that Malachi had a split personality? Was he David, the robber bandit with a passion for justice in his own mind, and David, the man capable of murder and manipulation to attain what he thought was justice? Was he both men in the same body? A schizophrenic? A split personality? For Lauren, who knew the ramifications of such a mental disease, it was an anguishing question. She'd discounted the possibility once before—because she'd begun to care for this man. Care deeply. But caring couldn't fix what might be wrong with him.

She went over what she knew about him, his background, his life, his decisions. He'd never married, a strange fact for a man his age, and with his good looks. He'd given up a lucrative legal profession to run a company with a lot of manual labor. That wasn't necessarily a wrong move, but it wasn't exactly ordinary. He also had a strong belief in what he called justice, a belief outside the accepted system.

Lauren stretched out on her bed and pulled Gumbo up beside her for comfort. The cat snuggled into the crook of her arm and prepared to sleep. Wide awake, Lauren stroked the cat while her thoughts spun. She didn't like the way she was answering her own questions. She didn't like it at all.

She examined the note again. " 'You have served me well.' " It made her sound like a dupe and a moron. She read the rest of it. " 'Suspicion is a crooked finger. It works best when curved.' "

This was much harder than the first riddle she'd solved. And that one had led her into a chain of events that began with Bedford Tanner's murder. Whatever she decided, she had to remember that Tanner's murderer was still on the loose. Whether it was David, or someone else, that person was capable of killing again, and whoever it was had something to do with David Malachi's life.

Fingering the note, she tried to compare it to the paper of the first message. This paper was heavier, more expensive. Elegant. René Devereau's face leapt to her mind. René was an archer. Hadn't he competed with David during their adolescence? She was certain of it. And for that matter, she wouldn't put it past Nicole to be able to hit a bull's-eye at a hundred yards. There was something deadly about that woman, and it wasn't just her tongue. And Nicole had a taste for the expensive. She could have written the note.

The crime lab would be able to identify the type of paper and where it had been milled and maybe purchased. But the option of drawing on that expertise wasn't open to her. She was suspended. If she asked for any help, she'd bring a mountain of questions and suspicions down on her head. This was something she was going to have to figure out without technological assistance. It was a matter of reasoning.

Nicole, and possibly René, had set her up once—at Aunt Em's house. She had gone like a lamb to the slaughter. To see David. Just as she'd gone to Tanner's house. Anger began to boil under her skin. That was the trouble. She'd been maneuvered and manipulated from the get-go.

Lauren decided she would trust no one. Not a single person she knew in Natchez. The only person she could rely on and trust completely was herself.

"Suspicion is a crooked finger. It works best when curved!" She spoke the words aloud, knowing immediately what they meant. "Suspicion is a crooked finger," she said again. "It works best when it is curved." Yes! Exactly! When suspicion is self-directed at the owner it could be a perfect blind. The Robin Hood Robber, or someone impersonating him, was going to rob the Malachi home! But which one? Aunt Em's or the "ancestral home" set on about two hundred acres?

At the thought that David was going to rob himself to throw suspicions off his trail, Lauren felt a thrill of appreciation. He was very clever. Untangling her arm from Gumbo, she got up and began to pace the room. The plan was brilliant . . .

Except that David had already covered his tracks with a fall from a bridge into a dangerous river. *She* believed he wasn't dead, but everyone else had been looking for his body. Except Nicole. Until now. Until the incident at his aunt's home. This self-robbery would be overkill. It was a great assumption, but it didn't pan out. It would only serve to make David look guiltier than ever, and give notice that he was still alive.

Deflated, she sat on the bed. David wouldn't stage a disappearance only to reappear the next night to shoot at her and rob himself. Unless he was really mentally ill. Unless in his own mind, the "good" Robin Hood was drowned in the river. The complication of all of it made her fall backward, almost crushing Gumbo, who gave an unhappy sputter.

"What should I do?" Lauren asked the cat. Gumbo disdained the question and curled into a calico ball.

The shrill of the telephone almost made Lauren scream. She bolted off of the bed and picked up the receiver.

"Sorry to call so late, or so early, but I had to talk with you."

She was shocked and surprised to hear Jason Amberly's voice. "Jason, where are you?"

"At the office. I couldn't sleep, so I've been waiting for some of the reports to come in. Lauren, I've been doing a lot of thinking, and maybe I haven't been fair about Malachi."

Suspicion made Lauren's pulse race. What was Jason up to now? He was too smart, and far too ambitious for early morning confessional calls. "What do you want?"

"I want to help you."

"Jason, I understand why you had to suspend me. There's really nothing you can do until this mess is cleared up. I've been in the wrong place at the wrong time too often in the past few days."

"I had begun to wonder if it was part of your character, like clumsiness or foot-in-mouth disease," Jason said, and his voice was a bit more lighthearted.

"No, I swear it. I've never had a bit of trouble with anything like this until I came to Natchez. It must be something in the water." She tried to match his humor, even though she was wary. He was up to something.

"I get the feeling that you're not telling me the complete truth." He waited, but Lauren didn't respond. "Maybe you're protecting David because you truly think he's innocent?"

"I don't know what I think," Lauren said with complete honesty. "If I knew what I believed, it would be a lot simpler."

Jason heard the note of honesty in her voice. "Did something else happen at the old Schlagel house?"

"No." Lauren shook her head as she held the telephone.

"Was David at the house? Did you see him?"

"No." She wanted to say more, but she couldn't.

"Lauren, I know David is alive."

"How?" she blurted. "Did you find something?"

"He's alive, suffice it to say that I know that much for a fact. There's something here that I don't understand. This is a very interesting case."

There was speculation in Jason's voice, and Lauren clamped her lips shut. She was torn between loyalty to her job and loyalty to David Malachi, strange man that he was. But if he were mentally ill, and capable of killing, what were her duties then? If another person died, it would be her fault.

"Lauren, how well do you know Nicole Sterling?"

The sudden change in direction made Lauren even more wary of Jason. "She's a bit... I don't know her that well," she answered.

Jason's chuckle was easy. "She is a tigress. She called me earlier this evening. She said you were involved with David up to your ears."

"Nicole Sterling has a healthy imagination and a vicious tongue."

"This comes under the heading of a friendly warning, Lauren. David Malachi has been paying the bills on Nicole's estate for the past two years. He may not be the culprit I think he is, but he is definitely involved with that woman, so watch yourself."

"I have no reason to watch myself." Lauren made her voice completely emotionless. "David Malachi is free to spend his money any way he chooses."

"I thought it might interest you to know that Nicole's mortgage was paid yesterday evening. By cash. The teller at the bank couldn't identify the man who left the money at the drive-up window. He was wearing a hat and sunglasses. When I spoke with Nicole, she admitted that David has been taking care of that little matter for her."

"It must be nice," Lauren said.

"Don't protect him, Lauren. He isn't worth the loss of your career or your future. If he's innocent, then justice will be done. Now, if there's anything you need to tell me, call anytime. Otherwise, don't leave your house without a police officer. That's an order. We've had our differences in the past, but I like you. I may not be able to keep you on the payroll, but I don't want to see you dead."

"Thanks, Jason," Lauren said before she replaced the telephone receiver. She crawled beneath the sheets before her body had a chance to really wake up to the shock and hurt of what she'd just learned. David had blown his cover to pay Nicole's mortgage. Then perhaps he had been at his aunt's home, shooting arrows. This was not the work of a sane mind.

She turned off the bedside light and shut her eyes, pulling Gumbo into her arm. She'd sleep. She had to rest; she was so tired her eyes burned. Tomorrow she'd deal with things. Tomorrow. Just like Scarlett O'Hara and that damn book that had just about wrecked her life.

LAUREN PUT HER FORK and knife on top of her plate. Across the table, Tim Prentiss smiled at her.

"That was some fine cookin', Ms. Sanders. I'd never know you were from Kansas by the way you can cook."

"People in Kansas have taste buds," Lauren said easily. She liked the older police officer who had taken off during the day and recently returned to keep her company for the night again. She had a shooting pang of guilt at what she was about to do to the poor man.

Sometime during the hours of the morning, a plan had come to her. To put it into motion, she had to escape her watchdog. She meant Tim Prentiss no harm. In fact, she liked him greatly. He reminded her of her Uncle Harry. She watched in satisfaction as he took another sip of the only glass of wine he'd allowed himself. The tranquilizer she'd ground up had dissolved in the ruby red liquid, just like on television. Tim wouldn't be hurt. He'd snooze for a few hours, and by the time he awoke, she'd be safely back and tucked in her own bed.

"There are some books in the den if you'd like to spend a while reading," she suggested. "I know I slept most of the morning, but I'm exhausted. I think I'll read for a while and then sleep."

"It's the best thing for you," Tim answered, his smile simple and concerned. "It's hard, being suspended and all. But sleep is a healing process in a situation like this. Otherwise, the stress will get you. You go on and rest and I'll wash up these dishes and maybe turn on the tube."

"Thanks, Tim," she said, another pang of guilt making her stand up immediately. He was a *lot* like Uncle Harry.

In her bedroom she locked the door and listened for several moments. She could hear Tim rattling around in the kitchen, the water running. He started whistling and Lauren crept to the telephone.

She'd done her homework. Nicole Sterling's phone number was memorized. It took three rings for Nicole to answer.

"Listen up and listen good. I've got a watchdog on me and I can't escape. David is hurt and he needs help. Meet him at the Malachi mansion at eleven. He needs clothes and several things I don't know where to find—his passport and traveler's checks."

"Where's he going?" Nicole asked, her rich voice breathless. "He can't run out now."

"Settle that between the two of you. I can't help him. I've got a police escort watching every move I make. It's up to you, Nicole." Lauren set down the receiver.

When the telephone rang again immediately, she waited for Tim to answer. She stepped into the hallway and listened.

"Officer Prentiss here."

There was a pause, and then the policeman replaced the phone. Lauren hugged herself and hurried back into her room. Nicole had taken the bait. She'd called to see if Lauren was lying about the policeman.

So far, so good. Now came the more difficult part. She dragged out a pair of scruffy jeans, not as dark colored as she might wish, but tough and durable. She found a dark shirt and her winter gloves. If she was going to commit a crime, she didn't want to leave her fingerprints around.

Checking once more to make sure her bedroom door was locked, she switched on the radio beside the bed and eased out the window. She had two hours to kill before it was time to meet Robin Hood. But there were some things she had to do first, and the mode of transportation she'd chosen wasn't going to make it easy. As she crept down her street, she could only thank heaven that Natchez was a small town with small-town trust. Little Joey Anderson's bicycle was propped against the magnolia tree in the front yard where he left it every night.

She took the old balloon-tire Schwinn and started peddling.

Nicole's house was on the way, so she paused there for a few moments. The house was ablaze with lights. Hiding the bike under a tree, she crept across the yard. Nicole was too mean to keep a dog. No self-respecting hound would stay around, Lauren thought with a glint of satisfaction.

She stopped short at the driveway and dove into a shrub. There was the sound of footsteps crunching in the white oyster-shell drive. No doubt Nicole had had the entire driveway imported from the coast. At the thought, Lauren couldn't help but wonder if David had paid for it.

She had no time to debate her answer. René Devereau stopped only inches from where she hid.

"I told you not to antagonize her," René chided. "She's smarter than you think. She's on to us."

"She doesn't know a thing."

"Nicole, she didn't say if David had called her or not. This could be very dangerous. It's suspicious. If we're caught on his property, it will look as if we're trying to rob him."

"We won't be caught," Nicole said. "Lauren suspects us. If she had any other avenue, she'd never have called me, don't you see?"

"Unless she's setting you up."

"She might be smart, but her hormones are all worked up over David. No woman thinks straight when her pulse is jumping." Nicole laughed and stepped close to René. "David has that effect, you know."

"Anything in pants has that effect on you," René replied coldly.

"Even you, darling," Nicole responded.

"Are you going to meet David?"

"Do I have a choice?" There was anger in Nicole's tone. "I hardly think Lauren Sanders has planned this, but she's put the onus back on me. If David is hurt—and we both know he's alive—I have to help him.''

''Otherwise we'll never find . . .''

''Shut up.'' Nicole's voice was harsh. ''I'd better get going. I want to be there first, to make sure it isn't a trap.''

''Be careful, Nicole.''

Lauren heard the wistfulness in René's voice. If he truly cared for Nicole Sterling, then he was certainly living in hell.

''Don't worry about me, Robin,'' Nicole said confidently. ''Just improve your aim. If you get another chance, I want you to be able to hit the target.''

''You were always the better hunter, Nicole. You have that killer instinct.''

Nicole laughed as she got into her car. ''See you at River Bluff,'' she called as she drove away.

For a long time René stood watching the empty drive. It was too dark for Lauren to see the expression on his face. Hunkered down in the shrub, she tried to keep perfectly still. René was, literally, only three feet away. What she wouldn't give to know what thing he and Nicole were searching for. Another time, though. At the moment she could only pray that he'd get in his car and leave immediately. If she was going to bicycle out to the Malachi mansion and make it by eleven, she was going to have to get pumping.

As if he'd read her thoughts, René turned away from the empty drive. He got in his car and left. Lauren waited as long as she dared before she crawled out of her hiding place and hurried back to the hidden bicycle.

River Bluff, the Malachi estate, was about five miles north of town. It was on the banks of the Mississippi, set on a high bluff, with a long, private road leading in to it. Lauren had never visited the estate, but she'd gleaned all of her information when researching the newspapers. It had been a showplace of the South for years, and part of the tour of historical homes until David had taken it off four years before. The lands surrounding it, a fertile two hundred acres, were still farmed, but she wasn't certain what crop was grown. Lauren went over everything she knew as she furiously pedaled the bicycle toward her destination.

No one lived at the house now, or at least none of the Malachi family. David had moved his residence to Three Dog Trace, his Aunt Em's house, for reasons that she could only guess at. She wasn't certain if there was a live-in caretaker on the property, but she was guessing no. David would send his landscaping crew over to tend to the grounds. But if there was a housekeeper, sending Nicole over had been a stroke of genius. As much as she knew about everyone's business, she'd know exactly how to avoid any trouble.

Now all Lauren had to do was get to the estate and find Nicole. Then wait for whoever was destined to show up. Nicole would be there. And René. And the person who'd arranged the meeting. And David? Maybe he was one and the same. Maybe not. This night she'd know for sure, though. If she was being used by David Malachi, she intended to find out and put a stop to it.

Panting, her breath whistling in her lungs, Lauren finally made it to the top fo the hill where she could see the driveway to River Bluff. It was another three-quarters of a mile to the house, and somewhere along the way she had to hide her bicycle. She didn't relish the ride back home, but she wasn't going to worry about that now.

The road to River Bluff had been dark. The streetlights had ended at the edge of town and for the past four miles she had ridden on blind faith that the road would continue around the next curve. As she walked the bicycle down the driveway, she felt the darkness close in on her.

The estate was secluded. Very secluded. Trees canopied overhead, and she felt a glimmer of claustrophobia as she took several deep breaths. It didn't help that the setting reminded her of the deceased Mr. Tanner's property. Why did all of these wealthy Southerners have driveways that evoked all of the fears she'd felt as a child.

The wheels of the bike scrunched along in the gravel as she walked. When she came to a thick clump of bushes, she decided to leave the bicycle. She pushed it into the heavy undergrowth, only to find that the branches had been stacked on top of Nicole's car.

A small chuckle escaped Lauren as she put her bicycle across the road and hastily rearranged Nicole's camouflage job. So, she was taking this seriously enough to hide her car. For a brief moment Lauren was tempted to let the air out of the tires. It would be ultimate revenge to think of Nicole having to hoof it five miles back to town. Only the shortage of time forced her to hurry toward the house. She didn't want to miss a second of what was going to happen, and she had to pick out her vantage point.

When the first glimpse of the lawn came into sight, Lauren ducked off the driveway and hid in the fringes of the woods while she examined the place. The manicured lawns swept up to the old antebellum house. Wide steps invited a visitor up onto the front porch, which ran the length of the house and was duplicated on the second floor by a balcony. The house seemed all windows and doors. Vines and big magnolias shaded the porch at every point. There was a gazebo to the right, and a fountain to the left, and rose gardens in between. It was an impressive sight.

As Lauren studied the grounds, she was trying to decide where it would be best to hide. The gazebo looked promising. It was shaded, and she could hide easily there and still have a good view of the lawn. She had to figure out where Nicole was before she made any move though.

She scanned the grounds again as she looked for a sign of another woman. A movement caught her eye, and she saw Nicole's slender figure, dressed in black, dash from the shadows of a magnolia to a deeper shadow by the front steps. She was almost in the house.

Lauren grinned. As soon as Nicole moved to climb the steps, she'd make a dash to the first tree beside the gazebo. It was a game of cat and cat. The nice thing was that Nicole didn't realize she was being watched. Not yet.

It was only a few seconds before Nicole made her move. Lauren tensed, ready to run to the safety of the tree she'd selected when she felt the pressure on her shoulder.

"Don't try it," a voice softly warned her.

The pressure on her shoulder increased as she felt fingers dig painfully into her still healing muscle.

Chapter Ten

In the second that Lauren hesitated, she lost the chance to struggle. Strong arms circled her and a large, calloused hand covered her mouth.

"Guess who? It is Robin or the sheriff?" a familiar voice asked.

Lauren felt all of her false hopes tatter and fall apart. She recognized David Malachi's voice. He was there. At his estate. So he had sent the note to her. Pain and shame combined at the memory of his words. "You have served me well." She struggled with every shred of energy to evade his grasp, but he held firm.

"Why is it that every time I see you, I have to physically subdue you? Not that I'm complaining. The contact is, well, stimulating."

David's warm voice in her ear brought reality and fantasy to a shattering collision for Lauren. Disappointment made her go limp in his grip. She wouldn't give him the satisfaction.

"Will you be quiet if I release you?" David asked. There was the suggestion of playfulness in his voice, in the gentle brush of his fingers on her mouth.

She nodded. More than anything, she wanted to bite his hand, but she knew it was pointless. It was all so pointless. She'd misplaced her trust, and her affections. Her career was ruined. The carefully planned life she'd imagined in the beautiful river city was all gone.

Although his hand traced the contour of her face, he could feel the passive resistance in her body. His finger outlined the edge of her bottom lip and then fell away. "Are you okay?" he whispered into her ear.

Lauren felt a shiver of delight at his words and her heart twisted even more painfully. Even now, knowing him to be capable of such cruelty, she couldn't kill her feelings for him. "I'm fine," she answered as she tried to step away from him. He held her close, his body warm against hers. She fought for control of her emotions and her voice. "I'm glad to see you finally dried out," she managed. "Nice of you to let me know you didn't drown."

"I thought the ploy of drowning in the Mississippi would gain me some time, but it didn't work." He drew her closer to him and brushed her cheek with his own. "I tried to see you, but there was always a cop around. I was beginning to wonder if you'd rented space to the police department."

The sharp prickle of his unshaved beard made Lauren want to press back against him, but her anger saved her. "I was worried sick."

"I was sorry to do that to you, Lauren," David continued. "I asked Dr. Smith to give you a call. Didn't he?"

"No, not that I know of. My guard usually answers the phone." The concern in his voice was confusing her. He sounded—and acted—as if he cared about her feelings. Her mind struggled to concentrate on why she had come to River Bluff. What was David up to? "I have to find Nicole. She's running around here."

"Nicole?" David was shocked.

"Yes, I told her you wanted to meet her here, and just like me, she was willing to risk everything for you." She could hold back the bitterness no longer.

"Nicole never risks it all," David said slowly as he allowed his arms to fall down to Lauren's shoulders. He turned her to face him. "Lauren, why are you at River Bluff?"

"To do your bidding," she answered. She could feel his gaze searching her face, but she knew he'd find little of her true emotions revealed. The woods were dark, and she could see his features, but not clearly. He was dressed in the long tunic and dark jeans. His quiver was strapped to his back. "I guess you found another way I could 'serve you well.'"

David's hands reached up to her face. "I could think of a way, but I wouldn't have picked River Bluff for a rendezvous."

"Stop it!" Lauren's voice was a restrained hiss. "Stop pretending, David. This isn't some book or movie or TV show. What is it you want from me?"

David's gaze searched the contours of her face. "Maybe you'd better explain what you're doing here."

"You deny nearly shooting me with an arrow—again? You've conveniently forgotten the little note attached to it?"

"I deny shooting you the first time, or again. What note?"

If he was acting, he was good. If he wasn't, then he might really be insane. Lauren felt her body prepare to bolt. If she valued her life, and her sanity, she had to get away from him.

"Lauren." His hands clamped around her waist. "Don't run away from me. Tell me what you're doing here."

"You tell me why *you're* here."

"I followed you. Every mile, up hill and down. You have a very nice posterior, and excellent pedaling form."

For a moment, Lauren didn't know what to say. "Why?"

"I was headed for Nicole's house when I saw you slink from the bushes and mount that bicycle. My curiosity overrode my desire to strangle Nicole, and I followed you instead." He held her with one hand and brushed a strand of her honey-blond hair from her face. "When I realized you were headed for River Bluff, I thought perhaps you'd been tricked, or baited into coming here."

"You sent me a note." The accusation was laced with hurt. "Another riddle that led me here."

"*Someone* sent you a note, but it wasn't me. What did it say?"

Lauren repeated it word for word. When she came to the part about serving well, she could see the trace of a smile on David's face. "It isn't amusing. At least not to me," she concluded.

"I can see where that would gall you. The wording is pretty high-handed, and sure to draw you here if nothing else would. Whoever sent it is very clever."

"You didn't send it, of course." She knew David would deny sending it. Didn't liars always lie? But he sounded so sincere. And even more importantly, he sounded sane. If only the light was better so she could see his eyes.

"No, Lauren, I didn't send it. Furthermore, I wasn't near Aunt Em's house last night. I was..."

"Where?"

"I had a meeting with someone. I'll explain it all later. And I can prove it," he added before she could interrupt. "Besides, it doesn't make sense that I'd show up at Aunt Em's when I almost killed myself setting up a fake death."

"Then who?"

"The same person who shot you and killed Bedford Tanner, that's who. It's clear someone wanted to set up evidence that I wasn't dead. I had hoped to give myself a little time to do more hunting, but whoever is behind this knew they could draw me out by using you as bait."

"David...I don't know if I believe you or not." She felt her hope stir slightly, and she wanted to squelch it. She couldn't afford to be manipulated again. On the other hand, if he was telling the truth, then they'd both been maneuvered. Someone else had a reason for wanting them at River Bluff. Together. At this particular time of night. "If you're in any danger because of me, I'm sorry."

David pulled her against him. "Don't be, Lauren. I don't regret that you're my point of vulnerability. My only regret, about any of this, is that I've involved you. It isn't fair that you've gotten caught up in this."

She knew she should resist, but her body refused to obey her command to push away from him. She allowed herself the luxury of resting her head against his chest. Held close in his arms, she wanted to forget the past few days.

She could care for this man. Care deeply, in a way that swept aside all obstacles. She sensed the power of the emotions she felt for him, and it frightened her. She needed time to know him. If only they could slip away somewhere for two weeks. Someplace where they could talk.

But reality wouldn't fade away. She couldn't ignore the fact that they were hiding in the woods, waiting for another incident to unfold. She couldn't forget that David Malachi was a criminal wanted for murder.

"What are we going to do?" she said.

"Watch for Nicole." David's hands moved gently over her back. "She and René are up to something. I suspect he was the archer of yester eve. He's a good shot."

"But he lacks the killer instinct Nicole has."

David chuckled softly. "How true. But Nicole lacks the force to power the bow. That's why they're such an effective team. She can goad him into doing the dirty work she thinks up."

"What are you looking for, David? All of you. There's something here that I'm not getting."

David's lips brushed the top of her head. "You're a smart woman, Lauren. But there are some things you shouldn't know. For your own protection."

"I've been shot, chased, harassed and fired. Now I'm being told I don't need to know something or I might suffer dire consequences? Please!"

"Let's get out of here first. Then I'll tell you," David said. "I was going to at Bedford Tanner's but I thought you wouldn't believe me. I thought if I could find it, then I'd show you and you'd have to believe."

"It? What it?"

"Hush," David whispered.

Lauren felt his body tense even before he spoke. Her gaze went immediately to the beautiful old house. A shadowy figure crept across the lawn. In the distance she couldn't be certain who it was, but the figure was tall, slim.

"Nicole?" she breathed.

"The hips aren't right. It's a man," David answered, his gaze never wavering from the dark figure that moved from shadow to shadow on the lawn.

His observation stung Lauren, but she said nothing. She, too, watched the man move across the garden. "What are we going to do?" she finally asked.

"Nothing."

The lack of emotion in David's voice was chilling to Lauren. "David, Nicole is in that house. We can't let someone sneak in there and harm her," she muttered the last of her sentence under her breath, "even though she deserves it."

"Did it ever occur to you that perhaps this person is meeting Nicole? Maybe it was Nicole who sent you here. The wording of that note has her touch."

"I've thought of that." Lauren shifted slightly and brought her body more fully into contact with his. She could feel his sudden response. It occurred to her that she should let the goblins take Nicole. She and David could escape simply by walking away. She'd been tricked into going to River Bluff, and David had innocently followed her. They should leave while the leaving was good.

"Who else do you think might have sent the note?" David asked.

She hesitated. "Possibly René."

"Possibly. Those two are like Tit and Tat. Where one goes, the other follows. But I wouldn't put it past Nicole to walk off and leave René if she found what she wanted."

"She doesn't strike me as the loyal kind."

She felt David's hand caress her rib cage as he chuckled. "And I was hoping you and Nicole could become good friends."

Lauren applied her heel to the arch of his foot with just enough pressure to let him know that she could hurt him, if she chose to do so.

David's grip tightened around her. "No need to get violent. Let's save that for our friends."

The tableau on the front lawn had changed slightly. There was movement on the porch as the unknown man made his way to the front door.

"Shouldn't we try to trap him?" Lauren asked. She was amazed at David's lack of initiative. It was almost as if he were letting some scene play out before he decided to intervene. He definitely knew something.

"I want to see how deep Nicole is in this."

His answer was a woman's shrill voice screaming through the night.

David didn't wait to explain. He leapt around Lauren and headed straight across the lawn toward the house. Lauren recovered her footing and started after him. Her stride was no match for his, and he was leading by thirty yards when she saw someone else in the shadows of the trees not forty yards to her left. She dove to the ground instinctively, and she felt the whistle of the arrow as it passed over her head.

"David!" she called out. "Get down!"

David had almost gained the porch when he heard her cry. He turned to see her sprawled on the grass. He headed back toward her, running.

"Get down!" she called at him, signaling with a free arm. She rolled twice so that she didn't remain an easy target. An arrow slithered into the grass only inches from where she stopped.

Looking up, Lauren saw that David was a perfect target. He was moving across the lawn, without a bush or shrub for protection, heading straight for her. Yet the archer aimed at her and another arrow struck the earth only inches from her shoulder.

She rolled again, grunting with the effort. A cry of terror escaped from her throat as she scrabbled to her feet and then lunged forward, deliberately falling flat on her stomach. She had to keep moving and she had to develop an erratic path. Someone was trying to kill her. Not David. Not Robin Hood. Her! Lauren Sanders, who never had an enemy in the world until she'd moved to Natchez, Mississippi.

"Lauren!" David's voice was commanding. "Roll!"

She did, throwing herself in a crazy ball that moved ever constantly toward David and the house. In a moment she felt his strong fingers around her arm and he pulled her to her feet. Using his body as a shield, he half carried her as they ran toward the porch.

It seemed to take forever, but they finally gained the safety of the high steps. David pushed her behind the steps and then put his body in front of hers.

"He...wanted...to kill...me," Lauren panted. "Why?"

"I don't know." David's jaw was clenched, making his words harsh. "But I'm going to find out."

"David." She hated her weakness, but she grabbed his arm. "Don't leave me. Please. He could come back."

His answer was to wrap his arms around her. "I thought he'd kill you before I could get there. I could see the arrows burrowing into the dirt only inches from you. I thought I would be too late." His arms held her tighter.

"We have to see about Nicole," Lauren said. The scream still seemed to hang in the air.

David searched the line of trees where the archer had hidden. There was no movement, but he hated to give up the relative safety of his niche. To gain the porch, they would both be exposed targets, at least for a few seconds.

"I'm going to lift you onto the porch. Throw yourself in the door, roll, and dodge to the right. Okay?"

"Yes." Lauren didn't think her body could take one more tumble, but she also knew she didn't have a choice. There were only two alternatives. She could stay where she was, or she could walk in the door like a prime target to get shot. Actually, there wasn't a choice.

David's hands clenched around her waist and he easily lifted her onto the high porch. Lauren rolled toward the door, kicked it open and did as David had instructed her. The house was eerily empty. The only sound was her own scuffling on the beautiful polished oak floors. David followed right behind her, almost tumbling on top of her as he rolled into a formal drawing room that could have been a setting for a nineteenth century documentary.

"Glad to see someone keeps the floors clean," Lauren remarked in a dry whisper as she gained her feet.

"We don't make it a habit of inviting people who scoot about on all fours." David kissed her cheek as he drew her against the safety of a wall and whispered in her ear, "My mother wouldn't approve of you, I'm afraid."

"Nor mine you," Lauren answered. "She'd be a little uneasy of a man who ran around in the garb of a fictional outlaw."

Another nerve-shattering scream made Lauren flatten her body against the wall. Shrill, high and demanding, Nicole's voice seemed to echo off every wall in the room. There was something wrong, but Lauren couldn't put her finger on it.

David took her hand and pulled her out of the drawing room into the foyer. He stopped abruptly, once again shielding Lauren behind him. He held himself perfectly still as he looked up the graceful curve of stairs.

Unable to see why he had stopped, Lauren looked around him. Nicole was standing on the stairs, one hand resting casually on the banister.

"You took your sweet time," she said. "Someone could have cut my throat by now."

David didn't have time to respond. The front door crashed open and a shot rang in the night. A vase beside David shattered.

David threw Lauren to the floor and sprawled on top of her.

"On your feet, Malachi."

Beneath David's very solid weight, Lauren recognized the voice of Burton Brecktel.

"Move slowly, and don't make any funny attempts." Burton's voice was steely, greased with success. "I can't believe we finally have you back. Jason's going to be a very happy man tonight." He started reading his rights as David got slowly to his feet.

Lauren felt herself being lifted, and she turned to look directly into the bore of Burt's gun. He motioned toward her. "Get away from him, Lauren. Do it now and do it slowly."

"Burt, how did you...?"

"A lucky guess, I suppose you'd say." He waved the gun at her. "Now get away from him. He's a dangerous man and he's used you enough."

"Go ahead, Lauren." David gently pushed her aside. He turned to look over his shoulder at Nicole, who stood on the staircase completely unruffled by the turn of events.

"Why were you screaming, Nicole?" he asked, acting as if Burt wasn't there with a gun. There was a dangerous edge to his voice.

"I had to do something to get you into the foyer." She shrugged. "It's for your own good, David. You'll be safer behind bars. If you keep on the way you've been going—diving off bridges and crashing through doors—you're eventually going to get hurt."

"Thanks for your concern." David's reply was bitter.

"Think nothing of it." Her smile was dismissive. "You were becoming dangerous to yourself, David. Someone had to step in and see that you didn't hurt yourself, or anyone else."

"Are you implying..."

"When you told me you killed Bedford Tanner, I didn't believe you. The David I knew in grade school couldn't do such a thing. I should have called the police then, but I thought you were hallucinating. I never believed you could murder a man, not even Bedford Tanner."

"Stop it, Nicole." David's order was angry. "This has gone far enough." He locked his gaze on her.

She took two steps down toward him, then stopped. Her fingers trailed on the banister. "It's for your own good, David. You won't be able to hurt anyone else, or yourself." Nicole's voice was filled with sympathy. She looked over David at Burton. "He's basically a good man. He's just become deluded with the Robin Hood business. Look at him."

"Did he confess to you that he killed Bedford Tanner?" Burton kept the gun trained on David as he spoke to Nicole.

"Oh, absolutely. The very night it happened. But I didn't believe him. Everyone hated old man Tanner. Probably everyone in town has fantasized about killing him at one time or another." Her elegant right shoulder lifted in a half-shrug. "I tried to explain that to Ms. Sanders, here. She simply wasn't capable of understanding."

Lauren felt as if her muscles had turned to stone. Events were happening, and she knew she should act, but she couldn't seem to make her legs respond. Nicole was crucifying David.

"You're very sly, Nicole, and more desperate than I ever thought." David clenched his hands at his side. "You'd do anything to get me out of the way, wouldn't you? Anything. Even frame me for a murder you know I didn't commit."

"Isn't that a symptom of mental disorders?" Nicole directed her question to Lauren. "I mean, I've read that a person with a split personality can commit an act with one personality and the other personality would have no awareness of what occurred."

"David isn't schizophrenic." Lauren found her voice, and the desire to fly up the stairs and strangle Nicole with her bare hands.

"I hope David doesn't trust his mental future to you," Nicole drawled. "I doubt you could house train a dog."

"I'd be glad to try—with you," Lauren answered. She felt David's restraining hand on her arm and she shook it off angrily. She turned on him. "How can you let that…rabid, lying, manipulative, greedy…" She turned back to Nicole. "I'm going to show you the first step in training a mongrel." Out of the corner of her eye, Lauren could see that Burton was edging into the room. His gaze shifted from Lauren to David, and he was clearly torn about what to do. She took three rapid steps toward Nicole.

"Stop her," Nicole said as she backed up the stairs. "Stop her, Brecktel," she commanded.

"Lauren!" Burton shifted the gun away from David and toward Lauren. "Don't do anything foolish."

"Oh, I'm not." Lauren advanced toward Nicole with a slow step. "This should have been done long ago. I'm going to snatch her bald-headed. How's that for a turn of Southern phrase, Ms. Sterling? As you noted, 'some folks just need killin'.' And there are those who need other things." She was at the foot of the steps, and she took the first one. "It looks to me like you need a new hairstyle."

"Stop it, Lauren. Get against the wall." Burton's voice was strained. "You're behaving like a fool."

"Shoot her!" Nicole directed. "Shoot her, you dolt!"

Lauren advanced steadily up the stairs. She glanced back once to see the grin on David's face. The drama of the moment would give him his only chance. "Gotcha!" she yelled as she lunged up the stairs at Nicole, caught her by an ankle, and jerked her legs out from under her. Nicole fell on the steps with a heavy grunt.

Before anyone could stop her, Lauren grabbed both of Nicole's legs and started down the stairs with her, bumping her bottom harshly on each step.

"Lauren! Stop!" Burton moved toward her and was caught by David's shoulder in his midriff. The two men tumbled to the floor with David on top. The gun swirled across the parquet.

"Terribly sorry," David said as he slugged Burton one time on the jaw hard enough to leave him momentarily senseless. David stood up and walked toward Nicole and Lauren.

"I hate you," Nicole sputtered as she struggled to free her feet from Lauren's grasp. She was half sprawled on the bottom step.

"What should we do with her?" Lauren asked.

"She's much too tough to cook and eat. There's an old abandoned well behind the house. A few days in the well might teach her the value of telling the truth and good manners. She was awfully rude to you, wasn't she, Lauren?"

"Terribly." For the first time in days, Lauren was enjoying herself. Nicole's face was gratifyingly afraid. "And if we get too busy, we may forget to bring any food or water."

"Oh, God, don't do that. David, you know I'm terrified of the dark." Nicole turned her big eyes on him. "Please, David. Remember what we shared. Please don't do this."

"Begging won't do a bit of good, Nicole. Remember, I'm a cold-blooded murderer."

"I'm sorry. René told me to say that. He said you'd get out of it but it would keep you in jail and out of the way. He staged this whole thing so we could get you arrested."

"So, it's René, is it? You didn't have a thing to do with it?"

"David, I swear it. René thought it all up, and he forced me to help him. He blackmailed me."

"René is such a naughty, naughty boy." David leaned down to put his face level with Nicole's. "I don't believe a word you're saying, Nicole. You're a compulsive liar and you'd accuse your mother to save your own hide."

"Believe it, David. He said he'd kill me. He said I had to help him. René's close to bankruptcy. I swear it." She looked at Lauren for help. "Check his finances. You can do that. Subpoena his bank records and see if I'm not telling the truth. He's the one who set all of this up."

A low moan from Burton on the floor made everyone look at him.

"I suppose René called Mr. Brecktel?" David asked.

"I don't know." Nicole shook free of Lauren and stood up. "René said he'd have the authorities here. He didn't say who."

Lauren held up a hand for silence. There was the thin sound of sirens in the distance. She knew without a doubt they were headed for River Bluff.

Nicole's smile held a thread of victory. "Too late, Robin," she said. "Better scamper off to Sherwood Forest before the evil deputies get here." She nodded to Burton, who was coming around. "This is going to look very, very bad."

"I'm already accused of murder. I doubt a clout on the chin will finish off my case." David was amused.

"Not for you. For Ms. Sanders. It isn't considered the best of business etiquette to go around with someone who knocks your associates unconscious. But then, what would someone from Kansas know about manners?"

"A point well made," David said. The amusement was gone from his face. He strode to the window and cut a length of cord from the curtains. He returned to Nicole, and this time his face bore a look of anticipation. Before she could protest, he caught her hands behind her back and lashed them together.

"You sorry—"

"Save it for later," David said sweetly as he pulled a handkerchief from his pocket and quickly gagged her. In another moment he had her kicking feet tied.

"Now it's your turn," he said to Lauren.

"What?" For a moment she thought she'd misunderstood. But when he cut another length of cord, she knew he was planning to tie her, also.

"Lauren, if I don't, they'll accuse you of being an accomplice. You can lie and say that I forced you here. That you tried to stop me when I hit Brecktel."

"Fat chance Nicole will go along with that." Lauren could see the black-haired beauty had no intention of complying with such a scene. Nicole shot her a look that would have melted stainless steel.

"Nicole has no choice. Besides, it's your word against hers."

There was a muffled protest from Nicole.

"Hurry," David urged as he pushed her down beside Nicole.

The sound of the sirens was growing much louder. There was only a matter of minutes before they arrived. "Tell them that you were forced. Tell them that Nicole was here, robbing my home."

At that suggestion, Nicole quit struggling.

"I want her behind bars, at least for the rest of the night. And if René is so determined to have her help, he can pay her bond in the morning."

Nicole thumped her feet so furiously on the floor that David released her gag. "Would you like to say something?" he asked.

"René knows where the key is. If you don't let me out of this, he's going to find everything and we'll never see any of it."

"And if I let you go, the two of you will give me a call, correct? I don't think they allow condemned murderers to have telephones in their cells." David's anger showed clearly in his words. "Forget it, Nicole. I'll handle René on my own." He replaced the gag.

Turning to Lauren, he bent close to her face. "Before I go," he whispered, and his lips touched hers. "Now scream, Lauren. Scream for all you're worth."

He was laughing as he disappeared. Lauren heard a door slam just before the screeching tires of the patrol cars pulled up at the front steps.

She began screaming as loud as she could. "Help! Help! We're in here! Help!"

Chapter Eleven

Lauren strolled into the questioning room, closing the door carefully behind her. The guard outside the two-way mirror could see them, but he couldn't hear. There was only a table, two chairs and Nicole. Lauren's satisfaction was hard to subdue, but she tried to control her glee as she approached the table where Nicole sat.

"How's life in the county jail?" Lauren asked.

"David will spend the rest of his life in prison, and you will be run out of town on a rail. I will personally see to it." Nicole's eyes were alive with anger.

"What? René didn't come to rescue you?" Lauren took the chair across the table from her. "That's too bad. I thought he would show more manners than to leave his partner to while away the long hours in the women's holding cell. Meet any interesting businesswomen? Maybe you picked up some clients for your decorating business?"

Nicole's dark eyes blazed across the table as she glared at Lauren. "You told the police that I was attempting to rob the place. That is an outright lie."

"Tell me what David is looking for and I'll change my story."

Nicole's eyes widened. "You don't know?"

"Not exactly." Lauren hated to admit it, especially to Nicole.

"David doesn't trust you enough to tell you." Nicole's confidence rose, and she straightened her back. "I wouldn't tell you the time of day," she said.

"Your preliminary hearing is coming up. Since I'm somewhat underemployed, I have plenty of time to spend on the witness stand. I think Judge Clinton, who's taken a personal interest in the Robin Hood robbery cases, will be very intrigued by what I have to say to the court about you. There's the business of aiding and abetting Mr. Malachi when he originally escaped from jail."

She smiled at Nicole's angry expression. "You did tell me that, Nicole, remember? Then there's robbery, blackmail, and verbal assault. That should up the ante on your bond considerably."

"You filthy carpetbagger!" Nicole half rose, and only the quick movement of the guard made her sit back down.

Lauren grinned. "It isn't considered good manners in the courthouse to physically threaten a member of the D.A.'s office."

"You don't work for Jason anymore. You've been fired!"

"Suspended. With pay." Lauren leaned her elbows on the table. "Listen, Nicole. My advice is to come clean. I still have a lot of influence with Jason. I could explain the situation in a light more favorable to you."

"If David wanted you to know what he was hunting, he would have told you." Nicole tossed her hair. "Can't you understand that you're an outsider? This doesn't involve you, and you have no part in it."

"Thanks to you, David and I haven't had a chance to discuss anything. Every time he tries to tell me, someone tries to kill one of us. Now what is it he's looking for?"

"Forget it." Nicole stood and went to the door. She knocked sharply three times. When the guard opened it, she turned back to look at Lauren. "You'll never really belong here. No matter how hard you try, you'll never be a part of David's life. We have a history together. We share common friends and family. Our past goes back to the time when the Natchez Indians controlled this territory. If you want to know what David's all about, you'll find it in the past." She turned and walked back toward jail.

Lauren's smug satisfaction had turned quickly to disappointment, and a small, grudging admiration for Nicole Sterling's considerable grit. The woman might not be a rocket scientist, but she was hard as nails. And mean to boot. David had never spoken truer words when he'd said she was too tough to cook and eat.

"Ms. Sanders?" The guard looked at her questioningly, then glanced at his watch. "Are you done?"

"Thanks, Charles. I know you risked yourself by letting me in here like this. And when you see Officer Tim Prentiss, please tell him I apologize sincerely for putting that little sleeping potion in his wine."

"That wasn't a nice thing to do, Ms. Sanders. Poor ole Tim got a dressing down for that."

"I am sorry." Lauren frowned. "I just had to get away."

"Well, Robby's out there waiting on you, and he's not as nice as Tim. That's too bad for you, and for Tim."

As she left the questioning room, Lauren caught sight of the big, burly cop who waited for her. His uniform was flawless, and his hat perfectly in place. Everything about him gleamed and squeaked. She knew without any doubts that slipping away from Robby would be a very different ball game than easy-going Tim.

She was stuck. And just when she'd thought of a plan.

WHEN SHE'D FINALLY convinced her new guard to wait outside her office, Lauren picked up the phone. She soon found, to her delight, that both René's home and River Bluff were opened for the annual Natchez Historical Society's Spring tour. She phoned the NHS to volunteer to work at River Bluff during the tours. With a great deal of delight, she agreed to replace Nicole Sterling, who was unfortunately detained for several days in the county jail. Amid gasps of horror and titillation, Lauren quickly explained Nicole's unfortunate position—and was rewarded with a role in opening River Bluff. Since Lauren didn't know any of the history of the homes, she agreed to work with the cleaning crews to supervise and make certain that flowers were in place before the flood of tourists arrived.

That was the easy part.

René Devereau was the challenging chore next on her list. As she picked up the phone to call him, she felt her nerves bunch into a painful knot that almost paralyzed her. Now was not the time for turning chicken, she reminded herself. In the books she'd read, the women in the South were strong, determined, tenacious when it came to protecting their men, families and homes. Even Nicole, who could hardly be considered the stuff of books, had that unfailing courage. She held her head high in the time of danger.

Lauren dialed René's number. She expected a servant to answer and was surprised to hear René's clipped voice.

"It's Lauren Sanders," she said clearly. "We have to meet, and I've got a guard dog on me that's tighter than a tick, to borrow one of your Southern phrases."

"Lower middle-class Southern phrases," René said coolly. "I've never personally experienced a tick."

Lauren couldn't help but smile at the well-aimed reply. "How can we meet?"

"That is assuming I want to meet with you, Ms. Sanders. I don't know what angle you're playing in this game, but it's too dangerous. Last night, someone tried very hard to kill you. Not David. Not Nicole, but you. I'm not certain your company is healthy."

He was right. The arrows had been relentlessly directed at her. And David had been a clear target not twenty feet away. He'd even come back for her and used his own body for a shield. The arrows had stopped. Almost as if they were afraid of hitting him.

"Lauren?"

"Yes," she muttered, pulling her mind back from her thoughts. "How did you know that?"

"I was at River Bluff. In the house the entire time. I was hoping David would discover..." He drifted into silence.

A million questions popped into her head. Why didn't he rescue Nicole? Who was the shadowy figure that had slipped into the house? All of her questions had to wait, though. She finally asked, "Can you meet me?"

"Can you shake your guard?"

"Tell me one thing, first. Do you know who killed Bedford Tanner?"

"Where are you, Lauren?"

"In my office."

"Let's discuss this in person." René's voice had developed a nervous edge. "The police have been all over my house. The phone could be tapped."

"Do you know?"

"There are things I know that I wish I didn't."

"Meet me at River Bluff. At noon. I'm on the committee to make sure the property meets all the high standards of tour time. David said there was a trail behind the house that led to the bluffs. Meet me there at noon. I may be delayed a bit—" she had to get rid of Robby "—but I'll be there as soon as I can."

"What do you have for me?"

"The location of the key," she answered, and hung up the phone.

She smiled. She'd done it. She'd brazened her way into the meeting. René wouldn't fail to show. From there, she'd have to play it by ear. Now, what key would René be interested in? Surely not a house key. Something else. Apparently something very valuable. That's what they were all hunting for. She'd heard David mention it but hadn't let it register until she was sitting in the empty questioning room. A key to money, or a fortune of some kind. René was bankrupt, according to Nicole. Maybe to a safe-deposit box. She didn't know, but as long as she could convince René she knew where it was, that's all that mattered, at least for the moment.

She worked at her desk, or at least pretended to, for another thirty minutes. Her one effort to get Robby to go down to the cafeteria for coffee failed miserably. He only smiled and said he would be glad to accompany her.

"Damn," she said as she went back to her desk. She didn't want coffee, she wanted freedom. She had to think of a way to escape. Another burning question had entered her mind. Where was David, and what was he up to?

At the sound of a light rap on her door, she looked up to find Burton Brecktel waiting to enter.

"Come in," she said, and she could feel the guilty flush creep up her face. "I'm glad to see you weren't injured."

"Nor you," he said slowly. He eased into the room and closed the door. "I thought at first that you really were with Malachi. It looked as if you were." He waited for her to answer.

"Burt, there's a lot about this I don't understand."

"I have the time to listen."

Lauren dropped her gaze to the papers on her desk. "Why were you at River Bluff last night? I mean, who told you to be there?"

"I don't have to tell you this."

"I know." She looked up again. "I was tricked into going there. That's the truth. And I'm not certain who did it. I was as surprised as anyone to see David Malachi there. If I knew who sent you, I might be able to determine, for positive, who tricked me."

"And why?" Burton relaxed a little as he settled into the chair.

"I think the why is obvious. I've been a scapegoat in several unseemly situations. But last night, someone tried to kill me."

"This wasn't in your report." Burton's face did not change in the slightest.

Lauren noted his lack of concern, and a flicker of uneasiness tingled along her skin. He had every right to be angry at her, but was this anger or something else? "That's true. And I know that I should have included it, but I have my reasons for not doing so. Now will you tell me who sent you to River Bluff?"

"It was an anonymous call." He smiled.

Lauren didn't say a word, but she knew her face had registered a split second of disbelief. It was too pat, too cozy.

Burton's voice was almost lazy as he continued. "I know that sounds like a crock, but it isn't. Some guy called me at my home. He said to go to River Bluff if I wanted to take the Robin Hood Robber. He said not to tell anyone else, that a lot of cops would ruin the whole setup. He said to go there at eleven-thirty, and to take a gun."

"Did you see anyone else in the house or on the grounds?"

Burton shook his head. "Should I have?"

The thought occurred to Lauren that he wouldn't have seen anyone else, if that someone was himself. She decided to try for a reaction. "Someone was in the trees on the north side of the front lawn. Someone with a bow and arrow."

"Like David Malachi?"

"No. David was with me." Lauren stopped. She wasn't getting a thing from Burton. He was too cool—or still too angry. She was only giving away information that might best be kept to herself. "That's all I can tell you now. It wasn't David, and whoever it was tried to kill me."

Burton leaned forward in his chair. "Be careful, Lauren. You're dealing with people in this town whose families go back for generations. They do things that seem crazy to normal people. It's like the Hatfields and McCoys, and I'm not exaggerating. Grudges are held for generations. And some of the families who've descended with money..." He rolled his eyes. "Let's just say that great wealth is not necessarily a contributing factor for mental stability and common sense."

Lauren smiled. For just a moment Burton had sounded as if he cared what happened to her. "I couldn't agree more." She stood up and walked around the desk. Stopping in front of Burton, she put her hand on his shoulder. "I will be careful, and thanks for the information."

"Some help. An anonymous caller. It could have been anyone."

"A male caller. That does narrow it down. I had thought perhaps our latest guest of the county, Ms. Sterling, might have done it."

"And now who do you suspect?" Burton's eyes flickered with alertness.

"No one. And everyone."

"A healthy attitude, but beware, Lauren. Don't forget that you can trust me, and Jason and Wyatt."

"I won't. And thanks."

"ROBBY, WOULD YOU check the drive to see if the Mini Maids have arrived. This place is supposed to be spit-shined. Mrs. Falstaff assured me the maid service would be here this morning." Lauren fluffed the bright, lacy curtains that adorned the kitchen window at River Bluff. The room was big enough for a staff of chefs, and there was also a kitchen table. Out of the corner of her eye she looked hopefully to see if the burly policeman would go around the house and check the front for her.

"I'll be glad to accompany you while you look," Robby Prescott said without cracking a smile.

"What do you think, that I'm going to fly away? You have the car keys and there's nowhere I can go on foot. For goodness' sake, the driveway's half a mile long!" She was exasperated and sick to death of being watched. She couldn't even go to the bathroom without Robby dogging her footsteps to the door.

"You might, and you might not. I don't want to suffer the consequences if you do." He leaned against the kitchen doorway and said nothing else.

Without checking the time, Lauren knew she had only a half hour at best to shake Robby and get to the bluffs. The cleaning crew was scheduled to arrive any minute. Maybe she could divert Robby then.

As if she'd summoned them mentally, she heard the front doorbell. When she hurried to open it, a vanload of five women and one man poured into the house with buckets of cleaners and long poles, mops, brooms and dust cloths. One woman began giving orders, and the troupe of cleaners dispersed throughout the house.

Lauren attached herself to the two workers who headed up the beautiful staircase. She chatted easily with them as she volunteered to show them the house. To her chagrin, she saw Robby head up the stairs after her.

"Excuse me, sir," the grand marshal of the cleaners grabbed Robby's muscular arm, "could you help me with the rug cleaner in the back of the van?"

Lauren couldn't believe her luck. She slowed on the stairs to see if Robby would comply with the woman's request.

"Certainly," he said somewhat reluctantly.

Lauren knew she had only moments. She left the cleaners, who were already busy with their work, and hurried to one of the back bedrooms. A balcony stretched around the house, and she knew from an earlier surveillance that room also contained a vine with a beautiful coral, bell-shaped flower. She had no idea what it was, could only pray that it wasn't poisonous and that it was strong enough to support her weight. Afraid that if she looked at the ground she'd lose her nerve, Lauren climbed over the balcony railing and laced her fingers in the sturdy vine as her feet struggled to find a foothold. She was on the ground sooner than she expected. Hugging the house, she used it for cover as long as she could before striking out to the north where David had said the trail to the bluff could be found by a small family cemetery.

She passed the wrought-iron enclosure of the cemetery but didn't linger. A marble angel guarded the plot with a fierce gaze. Lauren was already ten minutes late. René was not the most patient of men. She could only hope that the bait she'd offered would tempt him to wait.

Once she left the lawn of River Bluff behind, the woods were thick with trees and foliage. The air seemed even more dense. She found the trail with no difficulty and jogged along as fast as she could. The smell of the river came to her before she could see it. Still, she wasn't prepared when she halted on a high red bluff that gave her a view of the swirling currents the Indians had named The Father of Waters.

"Inspirational, isn't it?" René stepped from behind a curtain of kudzu.

"It is." She had to proceed carefully. "René, what is going on between you and David and Nicole, other than the obvious fact you've known each other all your lives?"

"It wasn't very nice of you to lie about Nicole trying to rob River Bluff." There was only amusement, no censure in René's words. He smiled to prove it.

"So? After all the dirty tricks she's played on me."

"You have to accept Nicole for what she is, Lauren."

"You and David might have to do that, but I don't."

"Well spoken. Now where is the key?"

"Tell me, why is this key so important?"

René stepped closer. "You haven't any idea, do you? Not really. That's amazing. I was positive David had told you in the beginning. I thought that was why you clung so tenaciously to his innocence."

"Nicole says you're bankrupt. Is it true?"

"Close enough." He smiled. "Mama warned me not to play the stock market. She said to keep the family money in land and products. I should have listened." He shrugged.

"Is David in distress, too?"

René's laugh echoed on the water. "David has no idea how much money he has or hasn't. The noble Mr. Malachi doesn't spend his family money. It's tainted."

"What does the key belong to, then?"

"The past, Lauren. It unlocks the past for David. An innocent man died. And David can't let it go. There's some vow in the Malachi family that he believes he has to honor. That's David. Can't you see that—his obsession with Robin Hood, with doing good deeds, with righting wrongs. He's a very sick man."

"But he isn't a murderer."

"No, I don't believe David killed Bedford Tanner."

"Then go to the cops and tell them who did." Lauren touched René's arm. "Please, René. If this continues, someone else is going to get hurt. The police view David as a dangerous man. They could easily kill him while trying to apprehend him. They think he's a murderer."

"I can't tell them who killed Tanner."

"Why not?" She frowned, unable to understand.

"Where's the key, Lauren? How does it work?"

"Not until you tell me who killed Bedford Tanner."

"I don't think you really want to know." He smiled slowly. "All of us thought Tanner had the key. It's been passed from one old Natchez family to another. David may give the proceeds of his robberies to the poor, but it's the key he's looking for when he robs the homes of his... social contemporaries. We searched River Bluff, my home, and Nicole's house. It wasn't there. So it had to be with some of the other older families. Where did David find it?"

"He didn't." Lauren felt the finger of fear lightly touch her spine. She'd bluffed her way this far. Now she was cornered. "At least, not that I know of."

"What are you saying?"

"I don't have any key. I don't even know what it unlocks." As she watched René's eyes darken, she suddenly wished that Robby Prescott would bird-dog her to ground right now.

"You little fool, it doesn't unlock anything. It's the key to a map." He gripped her shoulders with both his hands. "I should have known you were up to something, but I didn't believe you had it in you to be so deceptive. Nicole warned me. She said you were capable of anything, no matter how corn-fed and wholesome you looked."

The facade of manners slipped from René's face, and Lauren confronted his cold rage. She hadn't bargained for the fear that made her legs weak and quivery. René Devereau was a desperate man, and she'd forgotten that desperation could force a man to acts he might otherwise find unspeakable. Who had killed Bedford Tanner? René had said she'd rather not know, and at this particular moment in time, she knew he was right.

"Hurting me won't help you any," she said as calmly as she could manage.

"You're a complication I don't need, Ms. Sanders." He pushed her roughly toward the bluff. "I have to find that key. Now that you know what it is, you'll be looking everywhere, won't you? I've gotten rid of David. I can't let you interfere with my search."

"I'm not interested in maps or treasure. I only want David's name cleared," Lauren said. She backed up two steps as René approached her. Behind her, she knew the bank of the bluff dropped away sharply. It wasn't a long fall to the waters below, but she had no idea how deep the river was, or how dangerous the current. There were places where a suction could catch hold of a log, or a body, and pull it to the bottom for a long embrace.

"You should have gone back to Kansas when you had the chance. Jason should have fired you. He thought he could keep you out of trouble."

"Jason?" Lauren thought she had misunderstood.

"You don't think ambitious district attorneys run political campaigns on slogans and convictions, do you?" René grinned. "Natchez is an old town, with a long history of how things work. You should have learned that by now, Lauren. You've been told often enough." He stepped closer.

Lauren took the last step backward she could afford. She had only inches of bluff left before she'd step off into thin air—and the Mississippi River. She met René's black gaze. To her astonishment, his head snapped forward and a blank look entered his eyes before he sagged to his knees. A large stone fell beside him.

Uncertain what had happened, Lauren knelt over him. He was unconscious. She turned his head and drew in a sharp breath. Blood oozed from a gash in the back of his head. A large ugly gash. The rock beside him was coated with blood.

Chapter Twelve

A hush settled over the thick blanket of kudzu that covered the woods. Lauren caught a slight movement to the left of a white oak and held her breath. Who had followed her? How much had they heard?

The forest green of the kudzu shifted and fluttered, and the figure of a tall man stepped into clear sight. Sunlight touched his brown hair, sparking highlights of gold in the midday sun.

"And what is a fair maid like yourself doing gamboling among yon woods with the likes of this rogue?"

Lauren's heart pounded painfully in her chest, first from fear, now from relief, and a surge of another, powerful emotion she didn't care to examine. David Malachi, a crooked grin on his face, walked toward her, bow in hand.

"Why the rock, Goliath?" she asked. "Why not an arrow?" Her voice was firm and revealed none of her turmoil.

"I only wanted to knock him out. I didn't want to kill him. Contrary to what you might have heard, I'm not in the habit of shooting arrows into people."

"Well, rock or arrow, thanks for the help. I get the feeling I was going for a swim."

David's grin was nonchalant. "It's obligatory for Robin to show up in the nick of time to rescue the fair maiden, isn't it?" He knelt beside René and checked his pulse quickly. "Let's get out of here before he wakes up. He's going to have a nasty headache, and René wasn't in the best of moods to begin with."

Lauren felt his strong hand circle her wrist, and she let him pull her to her feet. "Where to now? Back to Sherwood Forest?"

"Your guard sounded the alarm. He was storming around the house in a vile mood. There are probably about four squad cars at River Bluff now, preparing for a manhunt. Or womanhunt."

"I don't want to go back," Lauren said. "I want to stay with you, David. And I want the truth from you."

She stopped him as he almost stepped back into the thick green of the kudzu vines. "It's time you told me everything. I know about the key and the map."

"I see." A shadow passed over his face. "I wish you didn't. The more you know, the more danger you're in."

"You were going to tell me at Bedford Tanner's," she reminded him.

"I was, until Tanner was murdered. That increased the risks and I decided that as long as you were truly ignorant of all the facts, no one would hurt you."

"René was going to. The archer last night..."

David shook his head. "I can't believe that he would have done anything to injure you. He wanted you to think he was going to hurt you. If you knew anything, then you'd tell him. René isn't a killer, but someone is."

"Who?"

"If I knew that, Lauren, I'd do something about it." He turned back toward River Bluff, listening. There was some activity in the distance. "They're coming."

"Can't I go with you?" She knew he was going to tell her nothing else. Nothing at all. If she was going to help him, she'd have to do it on her own. But she wanted some time to be with him. She'd crossed the line, long ago if the truth were known. She believed him—and believed in him. Now she knew there was no turning back.

"The best thing you can do for me is keep yourself safe, and away from any of this."

"Tell me about the map and the key," she said, and she knew she was begging.

David shook his head. "It's a family matter, Lauren. I'm not certain where it leads, but it's my own personal quest."

"René said that an innocent man died, and that you were determined to uncover the truth." She started to blurt out what she knew about Darcy Woodson and the Sarah Malachi-Lee murder, but David might think she'd been prying into his past. And she wanted him to tell her of his own free will. "Won't you let me help you?"

A blue jay called a sharp warning in the top of the white oak. David tensed. "They're on the trail now. I have to go. Tell them René fell and hit his head. He won't deny that story." David started to leave, but turned back and pulled Lauren into his arms. "One kiss?" he asked, but he didn't wait for her consent.

Lauren felt the sunlight on her closed eyelids, a warmth that matched the honeyed feeling of David's lips on hers. For the first time in her life she understood the meaning of total surrender—a moment when all is given and everything is returned. Whatever David Malachi was, or would become, she knew her feelings for him wouldn't change. Slowly she ended the kiss. "Go, David," she whispered. The sound of men thrashing through the thick foliage could be clearly heard. "Go now."

"It would almost be worth getting caught to stay here with you. For one more kiss."

"Go now, and the kiss will be waiting for you. But be warned, I don't intend to sit back and do nothing. I'm going to help you."

"I'll be in touch."

The green of the woods swallowed him as if he'd never been there. Only the lingering warmth of his lips remained.

"Lauren!"

Jason's voice snapped her out of her reverie. She turned to confront her glowering boss.

"Arrest her." Jason's order whiplashed down the sunny path.

"On what charge?" The officer at his side looked dubious.

"I don't gave a damn. Think of a charge and arrest her."

Lauren had never seen Jason so furious, and his temper was legendary. She wasn't even tempted to try an explanation. Not yet, at least.

"Shall I handcuff her?" the police officer asked Jason. It was clear that he didn't like the idea, but he was too much in awe of Jason's fury not to obey.

"Cuff her. Gag her. Chain her to her desk. I don't give a damn what you have to do to keep her contained, but do it! I won't have her traipsing all over Adams County interfering—" He shut himself off abruptly. His gaze bored into Lauren.

She took a half step backward. The force of his stare was almost physical. It was as if he'd said too much.

"Don't bother with cuffs. Just escort her back to one of the cars and put her in the back seat. Leave her there and I want a word with Officer Prescott."

"I tricked Robby," Lauren said clearly.

"You seem to be making a habit of tricking law officers. Emulating your friend, Mr. Malachi?" Jason's voice was ugly. "Well, it's time you learned that there's a price for your shenanigans. And this time Robby will have to pay it. Just like Tim Prentiss did. When it finally dawns on our finest that you're slick and not the delicate little thing you appear to be, maybe they'll take their job seriously. I want you guarded."

Lauren knew that arguing in Robby's defense would only make it worse for him. "There's an injured man up the trail," she said. "It might be more appropriate if you worried about that." She walked to the officer. "I surrender." She held out her wrists.

"What man?" Hope sprang in Jason's voice. "Is it Malachi?"

"No, it's Devereau." Lauren had intended her words to shock, but she was completely unprepared for the look that crossed Jason's face.

"How badly is he hurt?"

"I'd say he's going to have a whopping headache. He threatened me and I pushed him down. He hit his head on a rock."

Jason's expression turned from distraught to sly. "That's my charge. Take her to the station and book her on assault with intent."

"I was defending myself." Lauren felt her own temper rise. "He was going to hurt me and I only defended myself."

"That remains to be seen," Jason said. "And make sure she shares the cell with our captive damsel of Natchez society."

"Not Nicole." Lauren spoke the words as if they were a sentence of death.

"Exactly," Jason said with a grin. "I think the two of you have more in common than you'd ever want to acknowledge."

"WHAT'S THE OLD saying? Politics make strange bedfellows? Apparently so does crime." Nicole swung her legs from the top bunk and jumped to the floor. "So nice to see you here, Ms. Sanders."

Lauren took in the cell with distaste. There were two bunks with dingy sheets and coarse blankets, a toilet in the corner and a smug Nicole. "Why don't you call your office and have some prints delivered? Maybe a few plants and some colorful bedspreads." Even as she spoke, Lauren knew she didn't have the heart to fence with Nicole.

"I would if I could use the phone." Nicole leaned against the wall, her own attitude showing a moment of defeat. "I can't believe René left me here," she added.

"I wouldn't blame him too much. He's been a tad on the busy side." Lauren hadn't meant to tell Nicole anything, but what would it hurt? She knew what it felt like to think someone who cared for you had betrayed you. She could spare Nicole that. "He may stop by later. He's on his way to the hospital now, I'd say."

"Hospital?" Nicole pushed off the wall. "Why?"

"His head and a hard rock met in a harsh collision. The rock won."

"Is he hurt?"

Lauren couldn't tell if there was genuine concern or simply inconvenience in Nicole's question. "Not permanently, but I'm betting that his head aches."

"He couldn't get brain damage. There's nothing in there." The smile she gave Lauren was tentative.

Lauren responded, despite her caution. Nicole was a slippery thing. It wouldn't do to trust her, or to listen to her.

"Why don't we pool our resources?" Nicole suggested. She walked to the bottom bunk and sat down. She patted the seat next to her.

"Not on your life." Lauren kept her voice agreeable.

"You think I'm a snake, don't you?"

Lauren nodded. "I haven't determined whether you're poisonous or not, but you're definitely a snake."

"I've always had to scratch and hustle for everything I've ever gotten." Nicole's face was emotionless, but her hands were clenched at her sides. "That kind of life makes a person hard." She glared at Lauren. "Don't think I'm apologizing, 'cause I'm not. I've done what I had to do. The trouble with this town is when a man does it, he's clever. When a woman does the same thing, she's a hussy or a whore. I married money, an old man with money. I never loved him, but I liked his bank account. Do you think I'm the only person in Natchez who's ever done that?"

Once again Lauren was aware of Nicole's strength. There was a cockeyed dignity about the woman that touched her. "I doubt you're the first, or the last," she answered. "That doesn't make it right."

"Or wrong! I made Leonard Sterling a happy man while he lived."

"Then it doesn't sound like you owe anyone an explanation. Least of all me." Nicole was making her uncomfortable. She couldn't tell if this "confession" was sincere, or an attempt to gain sympathy.

"David doesn't think you'd marry for money."

Lauren had been staring at the gray cement cell floor. She looked up into Nicole's eyes. "Why should he?"

"David's rich. Wealthier than even he knows. He would have married me, except he thought it was his money I wanted. But it wasn't. Never his money." Nicole stood up and smoothed her hands down her lean thighs. "Isn't that a kick? When I really didn't care about the money, I couldn't make him believe me."

The one thing Lauren did not want to hear was Nicole's declaration of love for David Malachi. "Look, we're stuck here together, let's call a truce. Let's not talk about your past or each other."

"It makes you uncomfortable to think about David and another woman, doesn't it?" One lean hip cocked to the right, Nicole stared at Lauren. "You're a strange one."

"Not so strange..." Lauren started to protest.

"Maybe even a touch of nobility." Nicole continued her unblinking evaluation of her cell mate. "I'll bet you'd back away from him if you thought another woman could make him happier. I never really believed that kind of woman existed—except in books. The noble heroine type."

"Stop it!" Lauren had reached her limit. She eased slowly from the cot. "Stop it now, Nicole. My feelings for David are none of your business."

Nicole paced the room again. "I told René you were more clever than anyone believed. He couldn't believe your motivation. He said you had to be after the money. No matter how hard I argued, I could never make him believe you'd risk everything because you loved David."

"I..."

Nicole waved her protests away. "Deny it if you want, but it's all over your face." She stopped pacing and reached into the collar of her shirt. Drawing out a gold locket, she held it in her hand a moment before unfastening it from around her neck. "This was David's Aunt Em's. He values this necklace a great deal. I want you to give it back to him for me. He'll understand what it means." Nicole dropped the necklace into her hand and turned abruptly away facing the bars. Her shoulders moved slightly, then calmed.

Lauren held the beautiful locket in her hand. It was a masterful work of art, beautifully created. Judging by the feel of it, Lauren knew that it probably had a secret compartment for a photo or lock of hair. The heart was scrolled with leaves and violets no bigger than pinheads but exquisitely wrought. It was one of the most magnificent pieces of jewelry she'd ever seen.

Nicole's shoulders straightened and she turned back to Lauren. The smile on her face was cool, detached, and her emotions were once again under rigid control. "David will understand what I'm telling him if you give him back his aunt's locket." She drew a deep breath. "I never really had him anyway. Now, let's cut through the games and pretenses and be honest. Where is David?"

"I don't know. He was at River Bluff at noon. Where he went is anyone's guess." Lauren went to the lower bunk and sat down. She patted the spot beside her with genuine sympathy. If she understood Nicole's gesture correctly, Nicole was yielding all claim to David's affections. She was, essentially, telling him that the past was over.

"Even if you knew, you wouldn't tell me." Nicole shook her head. "I don't know why I thought I could establish some basic link with you. You wouldn't even tell me the correct time if I asked you."

"Nicole, you want to be honest, let's give it a try. I truly don't want David's money. And I don't think he cares about it, either. I do want him freed. It would help if I knew what he was looking for. The key to the map—what does the map show?"

For a long moment Nicole stared at Lauren as if she didn't believe her. "You really don't know." The amazement in her tone wasn't pretend. "What does it matter if I tell or not?" she asked rhetorically. "You'll find out soon enough. It all goes back to David's family."

"To Darcy Woodson and Sarah Malachi, right?" Lauren shifted her weight to make more room for Nicole on the cot.

"Darcy was innocent. He loved his cousin, and he spent his entire life trying to protect her." Nicole sighed. "From the little I know, it was a tragedy. You know Darcy was David's Aunt Em's uncle. She loved him a lot, and when he hung himself in prison, it hurt her in a way that she never completely got over."

"I can certainly see that. But if Darcy was innocent...surely she knew that. Why didn't someone do something?"

"It's the map. Darcy and Sarah were supposed to have acquired a great deal of money."

"How?" Lauren interrupted her.

"The Malachis always had money. Some folks thought it was family inheritance, maybe Sarah's dowry. Some say she blackmailed her folks and got the money. Some say that they found it buried on the old estate. River Bluff is vast. There's lots of places to hide things. Then there's always the rumor that it was a pay-off, that one of the Malachi family was a Union sympathizer and that it was money paid for his services."

Lauren cut back an expletive. "Does everything in this town eventually turn back to that war?"

"Some believe so." Nicole grinned, and there was an impish spark in her green eyes and the first glimmer of a real camaraderie. "Of course for someone like me, with no breeding or background, the war is just a history lesson."

Lauren laughed. "Touché. Now go on. I didn't mean to interrupt."

"Anyway, the story I've always heard is that Darcy and Sarah found the money and hid it. They felt that it was tainted money. That anyone who spent the money would be corrupted by it. To prove that they weren't spending any of it, they began to live in near poverty. But that wasn't good enough. Some of the old families in town wanted a cut. Those two old codgers refused, and the result was that Sarah was murdered and Darcy framed. Then he was murdered in his jail cell and it was made to look like a suicide.''

''And the money was never found?''

''That's right. Time passed and it became part of the local folklore, like haunted houses and such. Up until last year. Then René found the map.''

''Where?''

''At Timbermain. He'd hired me to re-wallpaper one of the upstairs bedrooms. I had a crew steaming the wallpaper off, and I just happened to be there when they found this old piece of paper wedged between the felt and the wooden wall. It was the map.''

''But none of you can read it.''

''True enough. We've all been looking for the key. Even David.''

''Why, if he doesn't need the money? Why should he care?''

''Family. He believes that wherever he finds the key, he'll know who was responsible for killing Sarah and hanging Darcy. See, it was our understanding as children that Sarah and Darcy had devised the method of using the map and key to hide the money so that if someone found one, it would be useless without the other. It was double protection. On the night that Sarah was murdered, David believes someone found the key—the same someone who murdered Sarah and Darcy. That key disappeared with the murderer.''

''And how did the map get to Timbermain?'' Lauren wasn't so certain that René's forefathers weren't involved in the treachery.

''When René showed David the map, we figured that Sarah put it there. See, she helped in some of the decorating at Timbermain. It would have been easy for her to slip the map in the wall when the felt was going up.''

''What better place to hide something than in the midst of the very people who wanted it,'' Lauren mused.

''And believe me, the Devereaus wanted it. René's family has been up and down in the market since before the Civil War. They've hung on to Timbermain through thick and thin, but there were times when it was on the tax roles to be sold. There was talk that René's great-grandfather shot a carpetbagger and buried him in the rose garden when he showed up at Timbermain after the war with enough hard cash to pay the taxes owing on the estate.''

"He was never prosecuted?''

Nicole grinned. "Like I said, some folks just need killin'. There wasn't a lot of sympathy during those times for carpetbaggers.''

"Nor these times, either,'' Lauren added.

Nicole laughed. "True or not, it makes a good story, and it accurately sums up the financial history of Timbermain. If there was a great deal of money buried, René's family would have been in hot pursuit. I have to confess, the idea of good money moldering away in some damp hole keeps me awake at night.'' She shivered dramatically. "Wouldn't you like a cut?''

Lauren didn't answer immediately. Of all of her fantasies, finding buried treasure had never been one. No, her dreams ran more to moonlight and magic, love and embraces, Spanish moss draped oaks and verandas complete with a tall, handsome man.

Nicole shook her arm. "Hey! I asked you if you wouldn't like a cut? The money may very well be gold, which means we'll all be rich. There's enough to share.''

"I think the question is whose money is it?''

"You sound like David. That's how he and René got at opposite ends with each other. David insisted that the money be spent for a hospital or a school or something like that. René needed it for Timbermain and refused. He said if we found it, then he'd take his cut and use it for what he wanted.''

"And you?'' Lauren was curious.

"You can never be too rich or too thin.'' Nicole gave her characteristic shrug. "I wanted it for myself.''

"So David began robbing all of the wealthy houses in Natchez, hoping to find the key hidden in some of the items he took.''

Nicole shook her head. "Yes and no. He stole to make a point. He searched those houses thoroughly, and then picked out a few expensive things to take. He wanted to serve notice to the old families in town that justice was on the way. You know, Robin Hood and all. I think he was hoping someone would turn over the key to him—to prevent having their home desecrated."

Nicole's ideas made a lot of sense to Lauren, but there were still so many answers missing. "I suppose David gave up his law practice about the same time René found the map."

"No, actually it was a year or so before. David was defending a man charged with robbery. I remember the details, because I thought David was taking the entire case too personally. The man had robbed one of the branch banks in town and was caught. The teller identified him and the bank's cameras had clear photos. David's defense was that the man was taking the money because his daughter needed a kidney transplant. David seemed to think that the motive made a difference. He argued that his client had committed a crime, but that there were mitigating circumstances."

"And the jury didn't buy that defense?"

"The man was sentenced to twenty years in prison and just after he was transferred to Parchman, his daughter died. David had tried to help the girl, but they couldn't find a donor or a match." Nicole shook her head. "It really tore him up. He felt personally responsible, like he could have done more."

"So he gave up law and went into landscaping." Lauren was getting a clearer and clearer picture of the man for whom she'd risked everything. He was rash and difficult and unreasonable—and willing to live out his convictions.

"I think he tried to hide by working twenty hours a day. There were some days when I'd stop by to see him when he'd be so tired he would fall asleep over a glass of wine. That's about the time he moved out of River Bluff and into his Aunt Em's house."

"So who killed Bedford Tanner?" Lauren leaned against the metal post of the bed so that she had a clear look at Nicole.

"You were there, who did you see?" Nicole countered.

"No one but David, but I know he didn't kill Tanner."

"Why were you there?"

"I'm not sure. David wanted me there. I think he expected to find the key."

"Tanner was his last option. Except for René, of course, and since the map was found at René's we never considered that the key might be hidden at Timbermain, too. David had burgled every other family that might have been involved. He did expect to find the key at High Knoll."

"Do you think it might still be there?"

Nicole shook her head. "David went back to hunt. Unless the key is hidden in the structure of the house, it isn't there. If that's the case, it could be in any of the old homes. It would be hopeless to keep looking for it."

"But you don't believe that, do you?" Lauren was beginning to see the entire picture. Instead of feeling defeated, René and Nicole had begun to believe the key was within their grasp.

"It's somewhere right in front of our eyes." Nicole slapped her leg with her palm. "That's what's so frustrating. It has to be someplace so simple that we've all looked at it a million times, and none of us has seen it."

"That's why you and René wanted to trick me into going to River Bluff. You knew David would follow me, and you wanted him arrested so he wouldn't find the key before you did."

"We knew David wasn't guilty of murdering Tanner. As soon as we had the money, we'd help him clear his name."

"That's a mighty dangerous game to play, Nicole. What if you couldn't clear his name? He might have gone to prison for the rest of his life, especially with Jason prosecuting him."

"Jason does hate David." Nicole's voice took on a musing tone. "Haven't you ever wondered why?"

"That one seems fairly clear to me. David represents everything Jason hates. Jason even put it in words. David's had every advantage, and Jason feels like he's thrown it all away. It enrages him."

"You're the psychologist, but isn't that a little too pat?" Nicole's features held an expectant look.

"What now? You're going to tell me that both men have vied for your affections."

"Oh, no. Well, I mean, yes, but it doesn't enter into the picture. There's no love lost between Jason and me. It's just that I've never completely bought that line from Jason about his noble suffering. Jason is an ambitious man. Extremely ambitious. He's got his eye on the attorney general's seat, and then the governor's. From there, I'd say the U.S. senate. David could have helped him out with those ambitions."

"As in campaign contributions?"

"That, and other means of influence."

"And David refused."

"More than once."

"So?"

"If Jason prosecuted David Malachi successfully, it would make headlines for months. He could broker that case to a very nice position in the next election."

"Jason's ambitious, but he isn't unethical."

"He wants David to be guilty. And he wants it bad. Maybe even bad enough to kill." There was no hint of teasing in Nicole's face or voice. She was deadly earnest.

Lauren felt a ripple of genuine shock. "Are you saying that Jason killed Bedford Tanner just to frame David?"

"All I'm saying is for you to watch your step. If the Tanner case isn't airtight against Malachi, the man who killed Tanner is capable of taking other action. If you suddenly turned up conveniently dead, say shot with an arrow, David Malachi would fry."

"My sweet . . ."

"And Jason would be swept into the attorney general's office on a wave of public acclaim," Nicole finished. "Just watch your back, Lauren."

Chapter Thirteen

"Okay, Sanders, the charges against you have been dropped. Sterling, you, too. Get your things and get out." The guard indicated that they were to scurry out the cell door he held open.

"Remember what I said," Nicole whispered as she passed Lauren.

"Thanks," Lauren called after her halfheartedly. Her fingers found the locket that dangled beneath her shirt. She still wasn't sure if she believed Nicole's accusations. Something about the woman defied complete trust. Nicole was a gamesman. Was there ever a time when she wasn't playing an angle? Even when she sounded so sincere.

Outside the lock-up, Lauren paused. Where was she supposed to go? She no longer had a job, and she didn't want to go home. Nicole had vanished. She'd taken off like a scalded dog. Lauren smiled at her own turn of phrase. She was getting better and better at this Southern stuff.

Since she was already downtown, she'd take a look in her office to see if anything had been changed. It was late afternoon, and the halls seemed abnormally empty. She hurried up the steps to her third-floor cubbyhole. Strangely enough, she'd been let out of jail and there was no police officer to guard her. Had Jason forgotten? Or was this a trick?

Slipping into her office, she closed the door softly and turned the lock. It didn't take long for her to discover that someone had been through every one of her files. If she hadn't been looking for it, she might not have noticed the slight disarrangement of her papers, a few items in her desk drawers tumbled about. Whoever had searched had done so thoroughly, and carefully.

She left her office feeling like a felon and headed down to the evidence room. With a bit of luck, the officer on duty wouldn't know that she'd been suspended. Nicole's accusations had created one or two possibilities in Lauren's mind, and the evidence room was the best place to begin.

The officer on duty checked her identification and unquestioningly brought out the quiver of arrows. Lauren stopped him before he could go back to the ledgers he was pursuing.

"There were fifteen arrows in this quiver when it was brought down. There are only six now. Where are the others?"

He gave her a puzzled look. "I was on duty the day those came down. I booked them in personally. There were only six."

"I'm positive there were fifteen. They came from my office and I saw them." Lauren couldn't believe it. No one would be stupid enough to steal from the evidence room.

"I'll check the book to make certain. I always check everything before I sign an item in," the officer said with a slight frown of aggravation. "I'm positive it was six arrows. An even half dozen."

Lauren could barely prevent herself from drumming her fingers on the counter as she waited. The officer drew out another ledger and carefully went down neatly printed items.

"Here it is. March 1. One genuine leather quiver and six hunting arrows, white feathers, oak shaft, appears handmade. It's listed as the property of David Malachi and is to be held until trial." He slapped the ledger with a show of satisfaction. "I told you so."

Lauren knew the chill that made her head ache was from her thoughts. Everyone in the D.A.'s office had access to the quiver and arrows. Everyone. But Jason Amberly had the easiest access, and he had assured her that the quiver and all fifteen arrows had gone into the evidence room. He'd *personally* seen to it. And she'd believed him.

He'd also had complete access to her office, and to her files. When Burt and Wyatt had shown up unexpectedly at Timbermain, again at the police station and yet again at River Bluff, Jason had sent them.

"Anything else I can do for you?" the officer asked pointedly.

"No thanks." Lauren tried for a smile that felt brittle even to her. She hurried from the room and out into the sunshine. There was only one thing to do—get a look at the map. She could kick herself for not dragging the information where René kept the map from Nicole. After their last scene at the bluffs of the river, René was never going to voluntarily help her out. He'd view her as just one more cog in his already cogged-up plan.

Her car, windshield still cracked like a malevolent spider web, was behind the police station. She took a path that would eventually lead her around the building without detection—she hoped. It was odd that Jason had given up the idea of bird-dogging her, but there wasn't a tail in sight. Of course, her experiences with finding a tail were a bit limited. Back in Kansas, she'd never dreamed that she'd ever have need of such a skill.

When she finally slid behind the wheel, she felt certain that no one followed her. To be on the safe side, she drove straight home, her thoughts on her plan. Jason had returned Joey's bicycle the night before. She glanced at it to be certain it was, once again, parked beneath the tree. A smile eased over her face and crinkled her eyes. Only in a small town where trust came easily would a bike that had once been stolen be returned, unprotected, right back into the front lawn from which it had been taken. This time when she borrowed it, she'd leave Joey a little cash for his trouble. The way things were going, she was becoming an expert cyclist. If anyone followed her, she'd give them a run for their money.

The only person to greet her in the house was a hungry, slightly put-out Gumbo. The cat sharpened her nails on Lauren's shoes at the front door, then haughtily turned and walked away, tail in the air.

"I haven't exactly been on vacation," Lauren said dryly as she searched through the cabinets for Gumbo's favorite tuna in sauce can of food. "Remember the kennel? Well, I've been in the human equivalent, so don't grump with me."

The whir of the can opener restored the cat's sense of humor, and Gumbo tucked into the food with a healthy feline appetite. Lauren took a long shower and changed into shorts and a blouse. It was easier to pedal in short pants.

Getting to Timbermain was going to be the easy part. Once she got there, what was she going to do? She'd have to wait and see if René was at home before she made any decisions. He had the map, and she was determined to get it.

"AN EMISSARY OF DAVID's, no doubt." René didn't offer any hint of hospitality as he folded his arms and stared at Lauren. "So you want to see the map. I think not. David's seen it once, and that's one time too many."

"I don't care about any buried treasure—if it even exists, which I doubt. I want to clear David's name." Lauren felt calmer than she expected. She was a bit winded from the bicycle ride, but she was also exhilarated. No one had followed her, she was certain of that. To increase her chances even more, René had opened the door himself, sans servant. He was obviously distraught and maybe willing to listen to her plan. If she could talk him into letting her see that map, she'd have some idea where to begin looking for the key. Nicole was so insistent that she, Lauren, was the outsider, that Lauren had come to the conclusion that such a fact might be the biggest plus in her favor. Nicole had said they'd all looked for the key and failed to find it. As an outsider, Lauren might have sharper eyes—the terrain was unfamiliar.

"I fail to see how examining the map could help or hinder David's case." René rubbed the back of his head. A large knot the size of an egg gave him a slightly disfigured look.

"I intend to use the map as bait. To draw out whoever is trying to frame David." Lauren stated her plan without unnecessary words.

"Don't be a twit. Even if you did manage that, Bedford Tanner's killer would kill you. Only some extraordinary luck has kept you alive this long. I don't think you have any idea how charmed you really are. Some saint must be protecting you." René relaxed his arms.

"David insisted you wouldn't have hurt me." Lauren crossed her arms. "He insisted that you're an honorable man, even though I didn't think so. You see, David has some allegiance to his friends. I'm finding that in Natchez, loyalty is too often a one-way street." She gave a snort of derision. "I guess in Kansas, friendship is a lot more important and meaningful."

"You don't know enough about the circumstances to judge." René's eyes sparked anger. "This is a very complicated..."

"Oh, so circumstances dictate friendship. Like maybe if a good friend gets a disease, well, then, they aren't such a good friend." She let her lips curl up in what she hoped was a sneer. "I'm sorry I bothered you. I thought I could come here and plead with you, on David's behalf. He led me to believe that his welfare would matter to you. I can see what a fool I was to listen to him." She took the two steps back to the front door and twisted the knob with enough force to nearly wrench her arm.

"It isn't that I don't want to help David." René put his hand on the door and held it closed as Lauren tugged at it.

"I know. It simply isn't convenient." She gave the last word a venomous twist and jerked at the handle simultaneously. "Let me out of here. When I first saw this house I looked on Timbermain as a place of elegance and beauty, a place where the qualities of gallantry and courtesy and integrity lived. It was right out of a book. I know that's romantic drivel now. Just because a person lives in such a place, that doesn't make him a gentleman." She looked boldly at René. "And just because you live here doesn't mean you deserve to."

His jaw clenched, and for a second Lauren wondered if she'd pushed too hard. He wanted to slap her, she could almost see him draw back his hand, but he didn't.

"You play with words very effectively, Ms. Sanders. Your training has given you an advantage. You see people's weaknesses, and you bore into them."

"Have I struck a nerve?"

"How can I trust you? You said you knew where the key might be once before. You lied. Why should I bother with you now?"

Lauren's breath was coming in short gasps. Her struggles with the door, and her temper, had left her breathless. She dropped her hands to her sides and leaned against the wood. "I lied about that. I had to, to get you to meet me. I didn't know what you were looking for, and I had to find out. Now that I know about the map and key, I can help. I swear that if I find anything, I'll tell you. My motives haven't changed at all."

René's smile was steeped in cynicism. "I'm supposed to believe that because you say so. And you wouldn't lie."

Lauren matched his stare. "You can believe it because David is more important to me than any amount of money. And I don't think the money is important to him. He wants to clear Darcy Woodson's name and find out who really killed Sarah Malachi-Lee and Darcy. Don't you think it's time this town put all of the ghosts to rest?"

"You make it sound so simple." René was more amused than angry. "You think you can breeze into town and clean up generations of secrets and double-dealing and corruption. Just because you find that you're fond of a man." He shook his head. "David has indeed found the perfect Maid Marion. The two of you are a real trip."

Lauren held onto her temper. She did feel foolish. She'd felt that way ever since David Malachi had walked into her office and pulled the wool over her eyes. Even so, she couldn't back down from what she believed. He was an innocent man—and she intended to prove it.

"I'm not asking you to believe in me or to like me. I am an outsider. But David is your friend. You've known him since he was a child, and you must know that he has a code of honor. I swear to you, on David's name, that I have no interest in the treasure. I make no claim on it, nor will I try to steal it." A lump formed in her throat, and she fought against the strong tide of emotion that threatened to wash away her fragile self-control.

René watched her face. "You're just as crazy as David," he said, his voice slightly hushed. "For some reason, I do believe the money doesn't mean anything to you. Maybe you think you're going to get David's family money. Maybe you really don't care about it. Whatever the reason is, it doesn't matter." He signaled for her to follow. "Nicole will have me skinned alive for this, but we've searched everywhere we know to look. We can't find a damn thing, so you might as well give it a shot."

Lauren quickly caught up with René as he walked into the drawing room of Timbermain and on through to the library. The beauty of the old house struck her anew. It would be a shame to see Timbermain change hands. René might not be a good money manager, but it was obvious he loved his family home and took great pride in its care.

As she watched, René pulled out a large leather-bound book. For some reason it reminded her of an ancient tome of alchemy and not for the first time she wondered if perhaps she had read one too many novels. René's dedication to his home was almost the stuff of heroic behavior. Almost. But the sliding panel of books that moved beneath his hand was definitely the fabric of some sinister work of fiction.

For a brief instant Lauren was transported back to her childhood and heard her mother's disapproving voice.

"Lauren, put that horror book away and find something else to read. That stuff is going to warp you. You'll have nightmares about something evil under the bed."

Reality reasserted itself and Lauren held her breath as the entire bookcase swung open to reveal a safe.

"I thought the wall safe was behind the family portrait," she said.

"Too obvious for the Devereau family." René said with a laugh. "As if no one would think of a moving bookcase." He turned and smiled at her.

Lauren answered with a wry smile of her own. For all of his faults, and they were too numerous to count, René had a certain charm and sense of humor. She watched with interest as he twisted the dial of the safe and opened the door. After a moment of shuffling among some papers, he brought out a carefully rolled-up piece of paper and another folded sheet.

"This is the original." He shook the roll at her and then put it back in the safe. "We'll work from the copy, if it's all the same to you. If nothing else, I believe the map is a valuable heirloom of David's. Once all of this is over, I'd like to return it to him."

The map, if it could actually be called that by any sane person, was a montage of colored figures and alphabet letters that made no sense. There were trees colored in, and some areas that might have once held significance. Lauren reminded herself that Natchez had changed tremendously in the sixty years that had passed since Darcy's death.

"René, where did Sarah and Darcy get all of this supposed money?"

René unfolded the copy and motioned Lauren to join him at a library table in front of an unlighted fireplace. Outside the window, the backyard of Timbermain was aflame with the pink, coral and orange of blooming azaleas. In one brief flash, Lauren realized that spring had touched the South. Sometime while she was running around in the dark of night or in jail, the magic of dogwoods and bridal wreath had swept through the town like the brush of a fairy godmother's wand.

"The Malachis always had plenty of money. Plenty. I'll bet David has no idea what he's worth."

"Then why were Sarah and Darcy living in near poverty?"

René anchored three corners of the map down with a crystal weight, a silver letter opener and a Rolodex. "Of course I never knew them, but even to this day they're legendary. They actually had goats living indoors with them."

"That doesn't sound too sanitary."

"Life had gotten far beyond sanitary for those two. No one knows why they didn't marry. It was obvious they were deeply in love, even when they became so eccentric that they hardly ever came into town."

"Were they living at River Bluff?" Lauren's eyes searched the map, but at first glance she couldn't make head nor tail of it.

"Oh, no, not in the house itself. Sarah determined that it was haunted. She lived there as a teenager and well into her middle years, but then she moved out to the cabins behind the house. That's another little bit of the story that never seemed to fit. About two weeks before she was murdered, the slave quarters caught fire and mysteriously burned. A large portion of the structure they lived in was destroyed."

"And Sarah?"

"She got out without a scratch. Darcy smelled the fire before the smoke could overpower her. He got her out."

René's attention was on the map. His fingers quested over it as if he could draw the meaning from the lines and blocks of color by sheer determination.

Lauren started to speak, then paused, cleared her throat and went on with her question. "Don't you find it strange that Darcy was so conveniently around at the time of the fire?"

"You're not the first to ask that question. Of course the prosecution used that same way of thinking to send old Darcy to prison for the rest of his natural life. They presented the fire as a failed murder attempt. They said Darcy tried to burn her to death, chickened out at the last minute, and saved her. His second attempt with a shotgun was more successful.'' René looked up at her for the first time since they'd stretched the map across the table. ''Of course, the other reading of that situation is that Darcy actually saved her from the first murder attempt. So the murderer came back—with a gun.''

''True.'' Lauren was undecided on how she felt about Sarah's murder. Did it really matter what she felt? Was this the family battle that David was so compelled to win? It had all happened so long ago and there was no changing any of it. ''Why did Sarah renounce her family money in the first place?'' she asked.

''No one can figure that out for certain. She was the apple of her father's eye and found no shame in wearing the best of Paris fashions or throwing lavish parties. She was the center of Natchez society for forty years. Then about three years after her folks drowned on a voyage to Paris, all of a sudden she said the Malachi money was tainted by blood and she wanted no part of it.''

''And Darcy?''

''He was living at River Bluff, too, in the back wing where the smallest of the guest rooms were. When Sarah moved out to the slave quarters, he did, too. He said he loved and respected her, and that if she felt the Malachi money was evil, he'd denounce it, too.''

''Sounds awfully pat to me.''

''I wouldn't let David hear that kind of talk. He's more than a little sensitive about his family.''

''On the contrary. I wouldn't say that I'm overly sensitive.''

Both Lauren and René whirled around to face the library window. David sat in it, feet dangling into the room like a small boy's. He was dressed in jeans and a cotton knit shirt.

''René failed to tell you that my Aunt Em nearly died of grief and shame when Darcy was convicted. She was a teenager, and that incident colored her entire life. Until the day she died, she had nightmares about it. The idea that anyone would think Darcy would hurt the woman he loved was appalling to her.''

David's rigid posture belied his softly spoken words. Lauren took a step toward him. His presence made her heart drum, and a trace of flush heated her cheeks.

"Can you read the map without a key?'' she asked. The coded letters and colors made no sense at all to her. "Have you tried some of the more common cryptograms?''

"No, Lauren, we got out a box of crayons and decided—''

"That's enough sarcasm, René.'' David slipped to his feet. "I believe we've tried everything we know to figure out the map. Of course, René has refused to allow me to see it. He lifted an eyebrow at René.'' But that has apparently changed.

"Nicole and I have hit a brick wall.'' René motioned David and Lauren back to the map. "Without the key, we'll never have any idea how to find the money. The map is meaningless.''

David smoothed the creases out of the paper as he bent to study the unintelligible collection of letters and colors and symbols. "I suspect a lot of the stuff is simply for the sake of confusion. From what I understand, Great-Uncle Darcy had a real sense of humor. He fancied himself a poet, an inventor and a number of other gentlemanly occupations.''

"He certainly wasn't a mapmaker,'' René said sourly.

"Did it ever occur to you that the only other person that mattered to Darcy, also knew where the money was,'' David said with mild reproof. "Sarah knew and Darcy knew. The map was something they concocted together probably more to amuse themselves than to actually tell anyone about the money.''

"Well, if we ever do find it, my share is going into my bank account,'' René said, an edge of challenge in his voice.

"The money will go toward the public good," David answered. "We both know that our families amassed great wealth from the Natchez land, sometimes using very unethical means. It's time we gave some of it back."

René's lips thinned dangerously. "You have more money than you'll ever spend. River Bluff is cared for by an escrow account. You'd feel differently if you thought it would be sold out from under you."

David looked at Lauren for a second before he spoke. "You've had more than one chance to protect your assets, René. The state of Timbermain is the result of some bad decisions, your decisions. Don't act as if it were my fault."

"And will you ride to my rescue and pay my mortgage like you do for Nicole?" René's face drew into an angry sneer.

"Nicole never had the opportunities you had. She's done well with what she's acquired."

"And she's more your type in bed." René walked abruptly away from the table. "Get out. Both of you."

David casually picked up the copy of the map and folded it into a neat square. "I know this isn't the original. You have other copies, and I need this."

"Take it, just get out of my house. You spent part of your childhood here, David. You were always welcome. I can't believe that you'd want to see Timbermain put on the auction block."

"I don't. But we've had plenty of chances, René. Our time has passed. For generations your family and mine took from the land and the people around us. We inherited a fortune, not because we worked hard for it or because we deserved it, but because of a freak of birth."

"Deny yourself if you want. Turn River Bluff into an orphanage or a free clinic or a hospital. Do whatever the hell you want with your property, but don't tell me what to do with mine!" René took a deep breath. "Now get out before I say something that neither of us will ever forgive."

David nodded to Lauren and they walked out of the library. René made no effort to walk with them, so they let themselves out of the house.

"David..." Lauren was hesitant to say anything after the emotional exchange between the two men. "How much money is involved, do you suppose?"

"Several hundred thousand, maybe more, if it's jewels. What René refuses to consider is that it also might be worthless, or even nonexistent."

"You think this treasure is real?"

"I do. Some of it was money Sarah and Darcy had collected. They'd begun to sell valuable items from River Bluff. Trinkets and collectibles. I think they had it in mind to sell the entire estate, piece by piece." He sighed and shook his head. "And I wish they had."

"Why, David? River Bluff is a beautiful home. I'd hate to see it change. There are people who would divide up the property and build subdivisions. I can..." She hesitated again, then pushed on. "I can see why René wants to keep Timbermain. He loves that house. And I don't think I blame him for fighting to save it."

David reached his arm around her to draw her close as he moved them both down the broad sweep of steps that led to the lawn. "I don't, either, Lauren, but you have to realize that much of that little scene staged today was for your benefit, not mine."

"Staged? Timbermain isn't in jeopardy?"

"Indeed it is. René may well lose it. But that's the case whether René finds the money or not. You see, René's habits are expensive, and his business sense is nil. That's a bad combination. The loss of Timbermain is more a matter of René's behavior than anything I could ever do."

"It's easy to judge other people's flaws." Lauren put her hand on David's arm and stopped him. "If he loses that estate, he'll hate you for the rest of his life."

David smiled, but it was not the expression that made his eyes dance. It left only bitterness in his face. "He already does, Lauren, and don't let his act fool you for a minute. René is capable of doing almost anything to save Timbermain—this time."

Chapter Fourteen

David picked up the bicycle Lauren had ridden and rolled it out of view behind the house. "You're going to have to buy that kid a new bike," he commented. "You're wearing this one out."

"I left a twenty dollar bill in an envelope in the fork of that old magnolia tree where he parks it." Lauren looked over her shoulder. She had the uneasy feeling that someone was watching them. The windows of Timbermain were empty, but that fact did not calm her sense of foreboding. How far would René go to eliminate David? David's implications had really unsettled her. What did he actually believe? At one moment he'd defended René, saying he wasn't capable of murder. Now he was saying René would do whatever was necessary to save Timbermain.

"You've got bad news written all over your face." David's hands touched her cheeks and his thumbs brushed over her eyebrows, easing the frown away. "What is it?"

"David, there are only six arrows in the evidence room. Someone stole at least nine."

"So, the ones that killed Bedford Tanner and almost killed you were actually my own handiwork." David's hands dropped from her face. "I couldn't understand how someone had copied my style so perfectly. Now I know. It wasn't a copy."

"The evidence clerk lists only six arrows. There's no record of the ones that are missing. For all official purposes, they never existed."

"Care to guess who took them?" The worry in Lauren's eyes was easy to read. David couldn't help but feel responsible for the light smudges beneath them. She'd been so perfectly in control of herself and her life when he'd first met her. Now all of that was changed. Even her straight honey-colored hair was whipped and unruly by her ride on the bike. He'd done nothing but wreak havoc in her life.

Lauren was unaware of his silent scrutiny as she verbalized her thoughts. "Anyone in the D.A.'s office could have done it. Then I guess the patrolman who delivered the stuff down to evidence could have taken them. Or even the officer at evidence, but I think that's unlikely. He was positive about the quiver and arrows. Very serious about his job."

David brushed her hair from her forehead and turned her face up to his. She was tired, and she was fighting so hard for him. He wanted to kiss her, to hold her safe. It was impossible, though. Whenever she was with him, she was only in more danger. He sighed and asked, "Who would you put your money on?"

"Jason." She felt a twist of disloyalty as she spoke. Jason was her boss, a man who deserved her allegiance. A man who'd kept her out of trouble, or so he wanted her to believe. His only flaw was his ambition, and yet of all the people who might have done David harm, or who might want to, Jason was the most promising candidate. Every time the wind changed, Jason was appearing and reappearing, hot on the scene. It was as if he had no other thoughts in mind but capturing David and making him "pay his debt to society."

She watched the subtle shift of expressions on David's face. It was impossible to tell if he agreed with her choice or not. He seemed deep in thought. "Am I correct?" she prodded.

"Jason had plenty of time to take the arrows. He also hates everything I stand for." David shrugged. "When I was practicing law, he'd come in the courtroom where I was trying a case and watch. Since I defended a good many of the less-than-wealthy clients that his office was prosecuting, we were on opposite ends of the scale. It was only natural that he would check up on me, but there seemed to be something more to it than that."

"His political ambitions?"

"Not even that. Jason knew I didn't support him, but I was never any threat to him. I didn't support anyone else, either."

"What then?"

"I've never been certain, Lauren. It was just a feeling that he watched me, hoping that one day I would . . . make a serious mistake, or grow horns, or something personally devastating. I get the idea that he wants to see me suffer, he wants to shame or humiliate me."

"Jason can be vindictive. But to go to such an extreme . . ."

"There was something with Nicole, too. I've never asked what the relationship was, and I'm sure the fact that you've defended me hasn't made him care for me any more."

"That doesn't sound like grounds to frame a guy for murder."

"True enough, but just remember that the person who would kill an old man by shooting him with an arrow through the heart isn't thinking rationally. He might not need a real reason to frame me."

"Who would you put your money on?" Lauren asked.

"Could René or Nicole have gotten to the arrows before they went down to the evidence room?"

"Only in my office." Lauren couldn't follow his thinking. "I've never seen either of them in the courthouse."

"I just asked because the person who killed Tanner used those arrows in such a deliberate way. I'd be inclined to believe whoever killed him hated him as much as I did. Or else it was a coldly professional job." David's eyes opened wide. "We haven't considered the possibility of a hired killer. Someone who dressed like me and was paid to murder Bedford Tanner in that brutal fashion. Up until now, we've always assumed that it was the map and key the murderer was after.''

"If it was Jason, then it's personal revenge. Against you."

"Unless he knows about the money." David gave a crooked smile. "There's always been talk about this buried treasure, but no one took it seriously until René found the map. We were supposed to keep it to ourselves. Just René, Nicole and me, but who knows who Nicole might have told in a moment of wanting to prove that she's important.''

"David, if it's Jason, your life could be in danger." She put her hand on his chest, testing the steady rhythm of his heart. The vivid scenes she'd played over and over again in her imagination of David being injured during a capture sprang unbidden to her mind.

He covered her hand with his. "We have to find the key."

"How?" Lauren felt the hopelessness sink in. One look at Darcy's map had shown her the futility of trying to decipher any portion of it.

"I believe the key must still be at Bedford Tanner's home. It has to be there!" David's brows drew together and he shifted his gaze from Lauren's face to the driveway. "Listen."

At first Lauren didn't hear anything, but then there was the sound of a car approaching in the still day. It was coming very slowly, tires easing over the scrunchy gravel. "Company?"

"René could easily have called the cops. He wants me out of the way."

"So I've gathered. You'd better go." She couldn't help reaching up to touch his face. It seemed that every time they had a few moments together, danger pushed them apart. Her feelings for him surfaced strong and charged. "David, I..."

"No time," he said as he kissed her. "No time for talk, but I swear to you, as soon as this is over, we'll talk. Until we know everything about each other." He kissed her again, a long kiss that contained much of what Lauren wanted to hear.

"How will we find the key?" she asked, almost dizzy when he stepped back from her. "I want to end this."

"It's going to be dangerous, but meet me tonight..."

"Wait a minute. Every time I hear those words from you, something terrible happens."

David's smile was quick and self-deprecating. "I haven't planned it that way. Now that you mention it, though, what I have in mind will be dangerous." His fingers moved to lightly brush the smooth skin of her throat. "Maybe you shouldn't come. I'd rather go to prison for murder than have anything happen to you."

"You know wild horses couldn't keep me away." She placed her hands on his shoulders and squeezed with a surge of strength. "I'm going to be there. Tell me where."

"Midnight. Bedford Tanner's. Bring two flashlights and wear gloves. I'll have everything else we need. Listen!" David turned his head back to the drive. "The car we heard. It's stopped."

He started to step around the house for a view of the drive, but Lauren's hand stopped him. "Allow me," she said. "If it's someone looking for you, why give them such a lucky break."

He nodded, all of his attention set on listening for someone approaching.

Using the thick azaleas that surrounded the base of the house in a show of spring color, Lauren ducked around the corner. An unmarked patrol car lurked down the drive, barely visible through a screen of blossoming dogwoods, azaleas and the massive oaks that made René's yard so exquisite. She couldn't be certain who was in the car. Two men, it appeared. A driver and a man who shared a common silhouette with Jason Amberly. As she watched, the man ran his hand through his hair in a characteristic Jason gesture.

She slipped back to David and motioned him toward the back of the property. "Go," she whispered. "It's an unmarked car and I'm pretty sure Jason's in it. René must have called him and told him you were here. They're waiting."

"Not very unobtrusively," David said, a worried look on his face.

"Go!" Lauren urged him. "There could be others moving in on us."

He picked up her hand and kissed the palm. "Be careful, Lauren. Promise me?"

She nodded. "Go!" She could feel the net drawing tighter around them. David had to escape. There was something odd about that single patrol car parked down the drive. It was too obvious, too easy to spot.

Like all of the old homes Lauren had visited, Timbermain had an impressive garden. David disappeared among the neatly trimmed shrubs and borders as if he'd never been there.

"You be careful," she said under her breath as she pushed the bicycle out of the safety of the house. The sense of someone watching sent a shiver along her spine, and she looked up. René Devereau stared down at her from a second-floor window. Her hand went to her throat, and she felt the locket Nicole had given her. She'd forgotten to return it to David.

Beside René the curtain ruffled, and Nicole's face appeared. The smile that touched her face made Lauren's heart triple beat. It was the coldest expression she'd ever seen.

Lauren stepped down hard on the right pedal and the bicycle sped down the drive. The patrol car had disappeared. Why hadn't the police made some effort to apprehend David, or at least question her? If René had called them, surely they knew he was nearby. Why had they parked in the drive without making a move?

Lauren pedaled furiously toward home, her thoughts in a tangle of unanswered questions. Where could the key to Darcy's map be? David had seemed to believe it was still at High Knoll. Why there?

Instead of going home, she headed west toward the downtown area. Maybe a little deeper probing into the files of the *Natchez Democrat* would yield some answers. No one had ever bothered to explain the relationship between David and the families he'd robbed. If all of this involved the past, then she wanted to know everything. A clue to the secret of the map could be hidden anywhere.

She parked the bicycle at the front of the newspaper office and left it with a renewed feeling of bemusement. Few people in Natchez felt the need to lock bicycles, or even cars. She hurried inside and was soon seated at a desk with several spools of microfiche to go through.

Her right arm cranking the handle of the machine, she whirred back through the years to 1932 when Darcy Woodson's face appeared on the front page of the paper. He was a haggard man with a look of sadness in his eyes.

She flipped back screens of the paper until she came to the first mention of the murder—a bold 72-point Bodoni type splashed across a banner headline: Natchez Heiress Found Murdered in Home.

In lurid detail, the newspaper described the discovery of the body and the search at the crime scene conducted by Sheriff Sammy Tanner.

It took a moment for Lauren to register the significance of the name. She made a hasty note on a scrap of paper from her purse. The county birth and death records should be easy enough to trace Sammy Tanner to Bedford Tanner if there was a direct link. Or she could probably ask the first stranger she met on the streets. Folks in Natchez knew who was related to whom way before Civil War days.

Apparently Sarah Malachi-Lee had been an artist of some merit, a fact Lauren hadn't gleaned from her other brief exploration of the murder. As she read the details in the newspaper, she stopped to wonder about the destruction of Sarah's paintings. Whoever had committed the murder had slashed through each and every one of her canvases, shredding them from the frames. Other personal family items had been trashed, also, including all of the family pictures.

When Darcy had been arrested for the murder after the body had been recovered from a well on the property, he'd stopped in the main drawing room of the house and picked up a portrait of Sarah that had once been in a silver frame. The frame, glass smashed out of it, was still lying on the floor. He'd taken only the picture of Sarah and refused to part with it during his trial and imprisonment.

Lauren blinked back the threatening tears as she read. From her vantage point in history, it seemed so clear that the old man wanted a keepsake of his beloved Sarah. Others had interpreted his actions as that of a murderer wanting a memento of his kill.

Ignoring the dull throbbing behind her eyes from straining at the microfiche, Lauren kept reading. She went through the long stories about the investigation, and finally the arrest of Darcy. She felt tears threaten again as the newspaper stories recounted how Darcy had requested the picture of Sarah in his jail cell. Only the interference of a local minister in his behalf got his simple wish granted.

There were angry accounts of how the townsfolk stood outside the courthouse, calling for a public hanging of the "fiend" who would shoot an innocent woman with a shotgun and then dump her body down a well. Through it all, Darcy never said a word in his own defense. He stood in the courtroom, gaunt-eyed and frightened in his dirty, bloodstained clothes. In his cell, he simply held the picture of Sarah and stared at it. He would not talk to anyone.

For a long minute, Lauren closed her eyes. There was a striking similarity between Darcy and the David Malachi who'd first appeared in her office. Both refused to say anything in their own defense. Both seemed to dare the system to do its worst. And it did for Darcy Woodson. He was convicted of a murder he did not commit.

The similarities ended there, though. Darcy was a man caught in circumstances over which he'd had no control. David had deliberately constructed his own circumstances. Had anyone else recognized the parallels? Was it deliberate or unconscious on David's part?

Rubbing her eyes, she went back to her research. She was almost to the tragic conclusion of Darcy's life, and even though she knew the ending, she couldn't control the building compassion she felt for the old man she'd never met.

The trial was given extensive coverage, even down to naming the jurors who'd been picked from "a membership of his peers." She read the prosecutor's opening statements, far more verbose and flamboyant than the style used by modern-day D.A.s.

Caught in the rhetoric, she read how each juror, according to the prosecutor, had been carefully picked. All were educated men. All businessmen. All contemporaries. It was not to be a jury of the have-nots judging the haves.

Lauren laughed aloud at that thought. Based on what she knew of Darcy and Sarah, they'd renounced the Malachi fortune and were living in the slave quarters in virtual penury.

That, indeed, was the spine of the prosecution's case— that Darcy was sick of living in poverty and since Sarah held the purse strings, he'd killed her, knowing that he would inherit the bulk of her estate.

The defense, led by an able-witted man called Jerritt Brill, built a dramatic case labeling Darcy as much a victim of the crime as Sarah. It was pointed out that the two were life-long companions, and that Darcy had not spoken a word in his own defense, so grief-stricken was he.

Lauren felt a stab of sympathy for Brill. How could he possibly defend a man who refused to give his own account of what had transpired? Brill was doing an admirable job in his opening statement of weaving possible motives out of thin air.

She skimmed through the names of the jurors and went on to the next issue of the paper, which showed a family shotgun—that belonged to Darcy—identified as the murder weapon.

Lauren's fingers clutched on the handle of the crank. Her arm reeled the microfiche backward in a jerky motion and she searched the previous page with an avid eye. The gasp she gave as she re-read the list of jurors brought the newspaper morgue librarian out from behind her desk with a questioning look.

"I'm fine," Lauren said apologetically. "I'm almost done."

"Too much of looking at that stuff will ruin your eyes," the librarian noted as she returned to her seat, and her filing.

Lauren read the list of jurors again. Arwin Davis, Jeb Games, Calvin Peoples, Adam Hamner, James Keel, John Welford, Quint Rutledge, Cotton Winters, Pascal Howard, Buford Linton, Jameson Radney, Lemeul Yawn, and alternate, Perot Benefaux. And the sheriff had been Sammy Tanner.

With a shaking hand, Lauren picked up her pen and began to write. Davis, Games, Hamner, Winters, Howard and Yawn. Six men whose names should have meant nothing to her. Six men who had long ago died, taking their ghosts and guilts to the grave. Except it was the same six men—seven counting the sheriff—whose ancestor's homes had been burgled by the Robin Hood Robber.

They were also names still prominent in Natchez business and social circles. They were names of wealthy men— men who had judged an innocent man guilty and set him up to die. Had possibly even murdered him in his jail cell.

Lauren flipped off the machine and rewound the spool of film. Her hand was shaking and she tried to stop it, to no avail. Now she had the link she'd missed. She'd also unearthed another bit of evidence that locked David securely into the role of murderer. She had given Jason Amberly the motive he needed—if he ever found out about this information.

Holding the spool of history in her hand, Lauren was tempted for the first time in her life to steal. Not permanently, but for long enough to keep this from the D.A.'s office. She struggled with the idea for a long moment. Face flushed and heart beating, she slipped the spool into her purse. She would make sure that no harm came to the film. Before the librarian could stop her, Lauren fled the building. She jumped on the bicycle and pedaled away before anyone stepped out of the newspaper office to stop her.

MIDNIGHT WAS ONLY half an hour away, and Lauren drove a slow circle around the outskirts of Natchez in the rental car she'd leased for several days. At a four-way stop, she took a right down Old River Road one more time. Behind her, the road was clear of all headlights. No one followed her.

As she turned toward High Knoll, her hands clenched the steering wheel. David would meet her there. The whole, mind-boggling mess might be solved if David recovered the key to the map. But would it determine who killed Bedford Tanner?

Lauren almost applied the brake at that thought. A faint unease tingled through her. The killer might be waiting at High Knoll. Lauren knew that the irrational surge of fear was partly due to her past experience at the Tanner estate. She could too easily remember the beautiful gardens with the life-size statues gleaming eerily in the moonlight—the panic of being chased through the thick woods by someone who had no qualms about killing her.

Her mouth was dry and she swallowed. David would be there. He'd look out for her. But the closer she came to the old estate, the harder the fear locked in on her.

She turned her car down the long drive and continued almost to the house. With deliberate care to keep as silent as possible, she turned around in the narrow drive and headed the car out in an escape direction.

The house was completely dark. Lauren approached, dread multiplying with each slow step. It was a house for ghosts and haunts—vengeful spirits of murdered men. Whatever Bedford Tanner had been, he hadn't deserved to die the way he had.

The dark windows of the house were like sightless eyes as Lauren slipped from shrub to shrub. Not even the moon cooperated. It shone thinly on the horizon, a sliver of light that was more promise than reality.

Her breath coming in short gulps, Lauren made her way around the house, retracing the steps she'd taken on her previous visit. As she spied the pool and the gardens, she halted. Had something moved among the hedges and rose-bushes? She could have sworn so. The longer she stared, the quieter the gardens looked. It was only her fear making her eyes play tricks.

Where was David? She'd expected him to meet her at the drive. Was he already inside, looking for the clue to the key that had eluded them all for so long? The flashlights, one tucked in the waistband of her jeans and the other in her left hand, gave her a small sense of safety. The heavy light could be used as a weapon if necessary. Using the side of the house as a shield, Lauren slipped toward the French doors.

Dread thicker than cold oatmeal choked her breath into short little gasps. There would be no body this time. The house was empty, except for David, and he was waiting for her to bring the flashlights and to help him.

She fought back her fear, but her hand shook as she twisted the knob of the French doors. They opened without a complaint. Lauren stepped into the library of the Bedford Tanner home for the second time. She made her way unerringly across the room toward the door where Tanner's body had almost tripped her. She moved quickly in the darkness, eager to leave this particular room behind her. Where in the hell was David?

Her foot caught the edge of something and she went down with a sharp pain in her right knee. Mumbling a curse, she used the doorjamb into the hall to pull herself to her feet.

For one terrifying instant, the night of Tanner's death came back to her. She'd tripped on his corpse that night. The idea that somehow the body had been forgotten coiled out of the night to signal her brain to scream. She fought back the impulse, but she knew she'd have to find whatever she'd tripped over. Her imagination would never stop if she didn't. She had two choices. She could turn on her flashlight, or she could get down on her hands and knees and feel along the floor in the same fashion she'd used to discover Tanner's body.

The light might endanger David. She dropped to her knees. Hands seeking in front of her, she began to go back toward the outside door. At last her questing fingers found a place where the carpet had doubled over. Lauren's laugh was shaky as she stood up and hurried out of the library toward the hall. She'd never realized what a grisly imagination she had. She hoped she never had reason to exercise it again. She made a silent promise to herself—never again a horror book or a Southern romance. Never.

The hallways echoed with the sound of her rubber-soled shoes, and she paused, listening for some sound that David was somewhere in the house. She wanted to call his name, but caution prevented her. Where was he? She didn't have to glance at her watch to know that it was at least ten minutes past midnight. He should have been waiting for her, watching as he'd promised. When she found him, he was going to hear about this.

The only idea she had for finding the key was perhaps the antique furniture that Tanner had consulted Nicole about. With that in mind, Lauren made her way up the winding staircase to the second floor. It was a beautiful home. The stairs seemed to float in the air, a tribute to the style and grace of the architect and the builder. Heavily carpeted, the steps didn't make a sound as she ascended.

Nicole had been commissioned—or almost commissioned—to redecorate guest rooms with Ballard antiques. Lauren wasn't an authority, but she felt she could recognize the heavy mahogany furniture. Each piece contained a carved half egg somewhere in the design, the Ballard trademark. Lauren had hatched her own ideas about those eggs. Perhaps one was trick, an empty little nest where something valuable could be hidden.

Courthouse records had proven that Sammy was Bedford Tanner's father. If Sammy Tanner had been in on the scheme to set up Darcy Woodson, then it might have been Sammy Tanner who held possession of the key. In his role as sheriff, he could easily have searched Darcy's belongings and taken anything he wanted.

As she climbed the stairs with slow care, Lauren went over her ideas. Tanner and his cohorts must have found the key, but failed to find the map. By her best calculation, Sheriff Tanner and the jurors had planned Sarah's murder. The jury, of course, had been rigged. They'd hoped to break Darcy by charging him with the murder. When the conviction failed to make him tell where the map was, they killed him, fearing that if he ever talked, they'd all go to prison. So the gang of Natchez businessmen who'd murdered two eccentric elderly people had ended up with only half of the necessary elements to find the treasure. Sammy Tanner had passed the key on to his son, who'd hidden it somewhere in High Knoll. Or at least that must be what David was thinking.

That was why he'd returned to Bedford Tanner's house.

If he'd returned.

For the first time, Lauren felt her faith in David's ability to show up at High Knoll slip. The house was terrifyingly dark and silent. She was at the top of the stairs, and the hall stretched forever in both directions. All of the doors to the rooms were closed, and she had no burning desire to open any of them.

Before she'd become an avid fan of *Gone with the Wind*, she'd dabbled a bit in mysteries and horror. Now every creepy sensation about big old houses she'd ever read tickled the edges of her mind.

Was that a faint scratching at the door to her right?

The sound of little claws against wood?

Terror effectively held her feet to the floor. No power on earth could make her move a leg. She was paralyzed, a fly in the web of some malevolent spider. Her grip on reality was pulled taut, and she closed her eyes tight and forced her mind to reject the terrors that had suddenly taken over.

She shook off her panic and started forward. She'd come too far to turn back now. Too far. David was up here, somewhere, expecting her help. Or he'd be here soon. If he were delayed, he'd have a damn good reason. Maybe he had another clue. She bolstered her shaky spirits with that thought and stepped to the right down the dark hallway that disappeared in blackness.

She distinctly heard scratching. Her overactive imagination was not in charge of her hearing. The sound of frantic, ominous clawing was coming from one of the bedroom doors.

Who, or what, was in the house with her?

The noise came again, just at the base of the door. About a foot and a half from the floor. Tiny scrabbling noises of wood scraped by nail. Or claw.

Maybe a raccoon or small dog had been accidentally shut up in the house. She clutched desperately at some rational explanation.

She listened for a bark or snarl that might give away the nature of the creature. Her hand inched toward the door, and she silently cursed each movie where the innocent victim feels compelled to explore a strange noise. No good ever came of that decision. Hiding behind the door, scratching in the darkness of the night was always something that would be better left alone.

Her fingers touched the cold brass of the knob. There was a soft bumping that gently shook the door and made her heartbeat accelerate another ten percent. Stiff fingers clutched the doorknob and her jaw clenched. She held the flashlight at the ready.

She turned the knob and pushed in. The door opened three inches and then held fast. A low moan escaped from inside the room, a pure sound of dread and helplessness. Lauren put her weight behind her shoulder and hit the door with all of her might. It inched forward, as if a great weight held it. The crack was wide enough to allow her to poke her head in, along with the flashlight. Clicking the beam on, she halted as the circle of light stopped on a body crumpled against the door. For one heart-stopping second, she thought Bedford Tanner's body had returned, this time in an upstairs bedroom. But something about the long legs and lean back made her realize that the figure on the floor was not that of Tanner.

"David?"

She couldn't believe it, but the truth slowly registered. The body on the floor, moaning slightly, was David Malachi.

"David!" She pushed hard against the door, wedging it further open until she could slip into the room. She was at his side, her hand searching over his back and neck, moving to his head for some sign of injury. The tape across his mouth was the first warning she had that she'd stepped into a trap.

"David!" She edged her fingernail beneath one side and slowly began to pull it away. The expression of pain in David's eyes made her reconsider. She snatched the tape with one violent jerk.

"Get out of here!" David ordered her. "Now! Get out!" He tried to push her away from him, but the rope that bound his hands to his feet wouldn't allow much movement.

"What happened?" Lauren asked as she went to work on the knots that held him prisoner. "Be still!" she ordered.

"Get out, Lauren. Don't worry about me. Just get out of here before they come back."

Lauren bent over David where she could make an effort to see the knots. The rope had been tightly tied, and David's struggles had only served to tighten the knots. She put the flashlight on the floor, pointed at the first section of rope.

"Lauren, please, just get away from here. Go call Dr. Smith. He'll come back to help me, but I want you out of here. These people are capable of anything."

"What people? Who are they?" Lauren demanded. She had the first series of knots worked loose.

"Lauren, get out." David heard the desperation in his voice. "They're in the house, and they're dangerous. I don't know how they knew I was coming, but they had everything set up. I walked into their trap like a kid." Bitterness flavored each word.

"I've almost got this one." The sound of something rustling in the hallway outside the room stopped Lauren. Her fingers held the knot but froze. On the far side of the wall, her shadow hovered over the shadow of David's prone body like a vampire. Her shoulder-length hair concealed most of her face. She listened intently, but there was no other sound.

"I've almost got this," she whispered as her fingers tore at the knots.

She never heard the footsteps outside the door, or saw the nightstick that was lifted high and then brought down against the back of her head.

Chapter Fifteen

Lauren woke in darkness. The wool carpet beneath her face muffled the soft moan that escaped as she pushed herself into a sitting position. Something hard was pressing into her back, and she reached around and removed a flashlight from the waistband of her jeans. Memory returned in slow increments; the terror much faster.

Snapping on the light, she searched the floor for David. A reddish-brown stain was the only sign that he'd ever been there. Tentative fingers touched the blood. Already dried.

It took Lauren a moment to realize that she was alone in the Bedford Tanner house. Or at least she thought she was alone. Dizziness made her stagger as she stood, but she kept her feet beneath her and tilted toward the door. The knob refused to turn and she almost fell.

Tears of frustration threatened, but she forced them back. Angrily she twisted the knob. The lock held. Solid oak with brass fittings, the door held. She was no match for the stoutness of the old house.

Whoever had hurt David had taken him away. An inessential part of their plan, she'd been left on the floor, unconscious. It was frightening to realize that she was of no use to them because she knew nothing. She could only assume that they hadn't killed David, and her, because they needed something from him. She checked her watch but found that it had been smashed. Deliberately? There was no way to tell.

How had the assailant, or assailants since she figured it would take more than one person to subdue David, known that she and David would be at the Tanner house? She'd made certain she wasn't followed. Her research at the newspaper morgue had gone undetected. She'd made sure of that by snatching the microfiche. But someone had known David would be at the Tanner house at midnight. And they'd suspected he wouldn't be alone because they'd waited quietly to eliminate her. How had they known? David would never have told anyone.

Her strength was returning with each breath, and she assaulted the door again. The lock was impossible. She thought about turning on the lights but decided against it. There was a chance that whoever had slugged her and taken David prisoner might be close enough to see that she'd regained consciousness. The other problem was that High Knoll was a crime scene. She, better than most people, knew that the house was off limits. Although the main investigation was over, the house was still officially "sealed." If at all possible, she wanted to escape the property without getting caught—and jailed. At last she fully understood David's compulsion to remain free. If she were caught and jailed for trespassing, who would look for David?

One thing she knew was that whoever had him didn't intend to turn him over to the authorities. If they had, they wouldn't have belted her in the head and sneaked off with him. What they did plan to do with him was something she couldn't afford to consider at this time.

On the other side of the bed a large window looked to be the only avenue of escape. Lauren hated heights, but there was little choice. She raised the window easily enough and straddled the sill. A small platform, a miniature balcony, was enclosed with an ornate railing. It would give her the extra two feet necessary to reach the tree limb—if the dainty-looking structure would support her weight. The house was old, but it seemed to be in excellent repair. She had to try. Tucking the flashlight into her jeans, she crossed her fingers and eased out to the railing. Balanced precariously, one leg hooked in the rail, she pondered the next step.

Several branches were within reach. The problem was that once she caught onto the branch, she'd have to travel hand over hand for a long distance to the trunk of the tree, which was a black mass in the night. There was no way to tell if she'd be able to get any kind of toehold to climb down.

Below her, the front lawn might have been grass or pavement, she couldn't see well enough. She could make an awfully big splat if she fell on pavement. But it was the tree now, or later. She could wait until dawn, but she had no idea how much time had passed since she was knocked out. Dawn might be hours away. Or the kidnappers might be only just ahead of her. She didn't have time to wait around. She had to free herself and then think of some way to rescue David.

Trusting that she'd manage the tree, she leaned out and lunged for the limb. The bark was rough against her palms, and she sighed, dangling a good thirty feet above ground. So far, so good. Looking up for a grip, she realized there was another fork to the branch. If she could reach over to it, she'd be close enough to another bedroom window to attempt entry. Chances were good that if she could get into another room, she could easily escape without risking the tree—or a fall.

Using her body weight to build up momentum she swung toward the second branch and grabbed it with her right hand. Lucky for her she'd learned to traverse the gym bars in grade school. It was never a game she'd greatly enjoyed, but one that she now appreciated. With another swing, she hooked her leg onto the ornate railing. Funny that she'd never noticed the tiny balconies before, but they ran along all of the windows on the second story. For one terrible moment, she thought she wouldn't get her balance and would fall backward to the ground. But her leg held and she pulled herself up to the window.

The glass slid up without making a noise, and she eased into another bedroom. In a flash she was across the room.

As she'd suspected, the door opened with the first turn of the knob, and she found herself in the hallway.

The highly polished floor was covered with plush runners, and Lauren slipped the flashlight out of the waistband of her jeans and examined the floor. There were two faint marks that looked as if someone's feet had dragged. David! She followed the marks down the stairs and lost them in the foyer. There was no trace which way David had been taken.

Lauren hesitated. Should she attempt to look for David, or should she try to find the key to the map. If she found the key, she might have something to barter for David's safe return. As it stood now, she had no idea where he might have been taken. There were several suspects, but no absolutes.

Running back up the stairs, she began opening door after door. She was hunting for a specific bed, a structure of wood with a massive headboard and posters. She'd know the unique egg design when she saw it.

The house was frightening in the beam of the light. The first two rooms she checked were beautifully appointed, but the furnishings were not as heavy as Ballard antiques. They were obviously children's rooms, probably young girls. She moved on down the hall, always catching her breath as she opened a door.

The fifth bedroom she tried revealed a ladder, paint cans, drapes and tools scattered about the room. The bed was shrouded in an enormous cloth. Once again horror-novel images and scenes invaded her. Only the foolish victim in one of those movies or books would actually pull off the shroud and awaken the sleeping menace.

On the other hand, any Southern belle worth her salt would never hesitate, especially not if her man was at stake. Lauren grabbed the sheet and tugged. The most beautiful bed she'd ever seen was revealed in the beam of her light.

Magnolias were carved around the massive headboard that was centered with a rising sun motif. The headboard extended almost to the twelve-foot ceiling, with supports for a canopy and netting. On each of the four posts, Ballard eggs were perched in grand display.

Lauren went to work, her fingers tracing the pattern of the carved knobs. One of them had to twist and reveal... what? An empty socket or the key?

To reach the top of the post, she had to climb on the bed. She'd seen plenty of antiques that were actually tied together with strips of leather or cotton rope. That sling-type of support had held up corn-husk mattresses—before cotton became king. The bed she put her feet on, after stepping out of her shoes, was firm. Thank God for modern conveniences, she thought as she reached up and began to wiggle the egg on the bottom right post. The wood was smooth beneath her fingers, and it seemed all made of one part. She twisted one way, then another. She pressed and pushed the grapes and leaves that decorated the post and provided the "nest" for the egg. Nothing budged.

Moving to the next post, she tried again. The process was repeated at each post. Lauren even traced her fingers over every inch of the headboard. If there was a secret cache, she had no idea how to open it.

What if she was wrong? What if the key wasn't hidden at High Knoll? She was wasting valuable time in her efforts to track David. But deep in her heart, she knew she had no tracking skills. She couldn't call the law to help her find him. And without the map or the key, she had nothing to offer his captors.

Her fingers went automatically to the locket at her throat. She fingered the delicate filigree that enclosed the heart, wondering even in the dark how she'd expected to find a hiding place that had eluded David when she couldn't even open a simple locket. As she handled the jewelry, she felt a sharp prick on her forefinger. Moving to a corner of the bedroom, she snapped on her flashlight and held up the locket for a closer look. A tiny nub protruded at the base. Using her thumbnail, she pressed. The locket opened in her hand, revealing two sides where miniatures should have been placed.

Instead, a small, black metal disk was nestled in a bed of gauzelike material. Lauren had seen a few similar devices in her work with police departments. Micro bug. She'd been planted with a listening device. And just as Nicole had planned, she'd worn the locket from the moment it had been given to her.

Aunt Em's locket! Only the beauty of the piece kept Lauren from tearing it off her neck and flinging it across the room. That and a half-formed plan that leapt to her mind. She closed the locket as easily as she could and let it fall back beneath her shirt. There were many things to think about before she took any rash action.

She felt a surge of pure adrenaline as she began to realize how she'd turned the tables—if her listeners had not detected that she'd found the bug.

Feeling as if she were suddenly under surveillance, Lauren had to force herself to move around the bedroom normally. She went down the hall, checking each room as she'd done before. Whoever was listening would get plenty of heavy breathing as she climbed around furniture, twisting various parts of the two additional Ballard beds she found. As with the first, she could find nothing that moved or shifted or turned. So far, the idea of the hidden cache was a bust.

Lauren sighed sadly, and she hoped not dramatically. She was tempted to try a few tears, just to let her audience know how disappointed she was. The entire time she'd explored the beds, she'd remembered her conversation with Nicole. She felt the anger and humiliation creep up her neck again! All along she'd thought Nicole couldn't be trusted! All along. Yet she'd allowed that viper to hang a necklace around her throat—and bug her. It was easy to see how everyone knew she and David planned to be at High Knoll at midnight. They'd talked about it—and someone had listened.

But another thought had crossed Lauren's mind. A thought that might well solve the mystery of who was behind Bedford Tanner's murder. It was so obvious, too. She'd had the evidence right around her neck.

Lauren knew the system well enough to know that prisoners weren't allowed to wear jewelry into jail. All personal items were taken, marked, placed in an envelope and put in the jail safe. Nicole would never in a million years be allowed to keep such an expensive necklace. Unless Jason Amberly had arranged it. Jason had the power to bend a few rules. And Jason had access to electronic listening devices and a whole lot more. The bug also explained the patrol car hovering around René's drive. They'd come as close as they dared to get a real earful. And she and David had blabbed away about their plans.

Obviously, Nicole and Jason were working together. For whatever reasons—romantic, financial or simply two ambitious people who never bothered to worry about the means that got them their end. The question was how far René had bought into the plan? Or how far did he think his ticket took him? Nicole and Jason were capable of betraying him at any turn in the road. Did René know that? If he did, or even suspected, she might be able to turn him into an ally instead of an enemy. But if he was still in love with Nicole, he'd never believe anything bad about her. Love was blind. And very often deaf.

The more immediate problem that Lauren faced was what to do next. She had to talk with someone so that whoever was listening could hear her plans. The clinic! It came to her like a bolt of lightning. Dr. Smith would help her. He'd be more than glad to play along to help David. She couldn't stop to consider that she might involve the doctor in something that would prove dangerous. David's life was very likely on the line. She and Alan Smith would have to take their chances. She never doubted that David was worth the risk.

She used the flashlight to negotiate the old house. Hell, she wanted them to know where she was. Slipping out the front door, she started running across the lawn. David had not been seriously injured when she last saw him. There had been a cut on his forehead that bled on the carpet, and he'd been tied tighter than a hog on a November morning. Not even her improvement in colloquialisms could make her smile as she trotted across the lawn toward the rental car. She could only pray that her unknown assailants had left her car. After all, the keys had been dangling from the ignition.

The Taurus was parked exactly where she'd left it, and it cranked on the first try. Lauren was beginning to think that her path to freedom had been a little too easy. Whoever had David wanted her free—and searching. So far so good. It looked as if she was playing into their hands.

Her one trip to Alan Smith's clinic had been after an arrow wound with a man she thought was trying to kill her. She wasn't sure she could find the place again, but she managed. The old house, renovated but still retaining the original grace of the structure, was completely dark. Dr. Smith was in bed. Since her watch was broken, Lauren checked the radio. It was nearly 4:00 a.m. Almost time to start a new day.

Alan Smith answered her fourth press of the buzzer. His white hair stood on end, as if he'd jumped from his pillow and into his clothes.

"Lauren!" He didn't bother to hide his surprise. "What's wrong?"

"Funny how everyone who sees me lately asks that very same question," she said as she followed him into the house and down a long corridor to the kitchen. He snapped on a light and pointed to a coffeepot. Lauren nodded. Caffeine. A hearty jolt might help her survive.

"Where's David?" Alan talked over his shoulder as he prepared the pot and turned it on.

"He's been kidnapped." Lauren eased the locket from beneath her clothes. Picking up a pencil and a scratch pad by the phone, she wrote, "I'm bugged, play along as well as you can."

Alan nodded his understanding. "Who's got him?"

"I have no idea. We were going to explore the Tanner home for the key. They knocked us both out and took David." Lauren let her voice rise in panic. She was frightened for David, but she also wanted his captors to think she was more afraid than she really was. "What should I do, Dr. Smith? I'll do anything to make sure he isn't hurt."

"It would have been simpler to kill him on the spot, so they must want him alive for something. Any idea what?" Alan watched Lauren's face closely for his cues. He smiled as she nodded her satisfaction with his response.

"It must be the key. They're after that treasure."

"David hasn't been able to find it or he'd have it himself. Surely they can't think he knows and won't tell?"

"Maybe he does," Lauren said. Whatever she and Alan Smith said, they couldn't imply that David wasn't valuable to his kidnappers. Once they believed he was of no use to them, they might very well kill him.

"Yes, you're right about that." Alan had picked up on her signals. "David has always kept so much to himself. I've known him since he was a child. He never flinched—or talked for that matter—when he came in for his exams. Took his shots without complaint. There's every possibility that he's known about the treasure all along and never told, just waiting to see who it would draw out of the woodwork."

"So that means it's up to me to find it. And when I do, I'll trade it for David."

Alan wasn't playing along when he went to Lauren and put a hand on her shoulder. "I know you're not from Natchez, Lauren, but wherever you're from, I'm glad you're here now."

"In a very strange way, I am, too. My life in Kansas was never such a mess, but then David wasn't in it." She smiled up at the elderly physician and took the cup of coffee he offered. "Now all I have to do is solve the map that everyone's been puzzling over."

"Can you do it?"

"I can and I will. In fact, I have a few ideas that no one else has tried."

"Care to talk about them?" Alan asked her for better direction with a shrug.

"No," she smiled, and made a gesture of blowing him a kiss. "That coffee hit the spot. I'd rather keep my ideas to myself. I don't want to involve you any further."

"Lauren, I owe David my practice, my health . . . my life. Involve me."

"If it's necessary, I will." Lauren stood up. "You know, the one place that no one has bothered to look is David's Aunt Em's house. It's a long shot, but think about it. From what I know, Darcy and Em were fairly close, or closer than anyone else in that scattered family except Sarah. It is plausible that he entrusted her with the key. From what David says about his Aunt Em, she wasn't the type to go around digging for buried treasure. She was too busy raising her children, and David, and instilling some values in her brood."

Concern filtered over Alan's face. "You could be right, Lauren. Righter than you want to be," he cautioned.

"I know I am. Now all I have to do is get over there and find the key. You know, I told Nicole and René I could find the key because I'm an outsider. I only half believed it at the time, but now I think I know exactly where it is. All I have to do is find it, decipher the map, and the treasure will be mine."

"To trade for David," Alan gently reminded her.

"Exactly."

"And how do you intend to go about this?" Alan asked.

"Once I have my hands on the key to the map, I'll decide then. Now I'd better go. If my hunch is correct, I could be a very wealthy woman in the next twenty-four hours."

"Or a very dead one," Alan warned her.

LAUREN GRAVITATED to the kitchen in Three Dog Trace. Even under the worst of circumstances she'd recognized the warmth of the room. On a chill March night, when she knew she'd set herself up as a target, the white ruffled curtains and bright copper pots made her feel a little better.

Part of what she'd told Alan Smith was true. She did believe the key to the map might be at Aunt Em's. Where, she hadn't a clue. But since it hadn't been found in any of the other homes, including River Bluff, then it could easily be in David's other family home.

There was something nagging at the back of her mind, some part of the entire story that she'd learned about. It niggled at her as she looked around the house, but she couldn't put her finger on it. Like a sore tooth, it acted up on an irregular basis, throbbed a few moments and then went away.

The last time she'd been in this house someone had tried to ventilate her with an arrow. She'd avoided the living room just because of that. The trouble was, she'd gone over much of the house, still looking for a Ballard antique that might have a "nest egg." She'd found nothing, and her idea that the key was hidden at Em's old home now seemed less than brilliant.

What would she do if she couldn't draw out David's kidnappers? Why had she ever thought she could? But realistically, what else could she do? If Jason was behind it all, going to the police would accomplish nothing. She couldn't risk it, either. She could find herself right back in jail—and David without anyone who cared if he was ever found or not. At this moment he had a lot more in common with Darcy Woodson in his last days than she cared to acknowledge.

Forcing herself to enter the living room, she searched several tables that looked promising. There were Christmas cards from two years back, a few unidentified snapshots, blank notepads, pencils, a pair of scissors and nothing vaguely resembling a tool to decode a map.

She edged over to the chair where she'd been sitting when she'd been attacked. Beside the chair the photo albums were neatly stacked. Well, if she was going to be a sitting duck, she might as well get it over with. Slumping down in the chair, she picked up an album and started turning the pages. It was the older one, with pictures of the 1800s. The shots were fascinating, even when the majority of her attention was attuned to a step on the porch or a bullet tearing into her heart.

She'd never made it toward the end of the album before, so she flipped there. To her surprise, several pictures of Sarah Malachi-Lee were cornered in place. One was a wedding picture, the only symbol of her brief marriage to a New York industrialist.

"The marriage didn't last long. It was scandalously dissolved amidst rumors that Sarah's husband had a fondness for others of his gender."

Lauren's heart almost stopped at the words spoken so softly, almost in her ear. She held the book rigidly in her lap as she turned to confront René.

"Where's David?" she asked, her voice sounding rough and unused.

"The last time I saw him, you two were conspiring against the side of my house. He took off through the woods like one of the noted deer in Sherwood Forest."

"Yeah, the Sheriff of Nottingham was parked in the driveway."

"I saw the patrol car and thought I recognized Jason. He must have changed his mind about coming to Timbermain. He left without knocking on the door."

"How convenient that he should arrive, just as David did."

"That is interesting," René agreed. "But I'm far more interested in knowing what you're doing here."

"Looking for the key."

"An interesting and possibly astute guess. You might have been correct. As an outsider, you might see clearer than any of us who are so intimately involved."

"Thanks for the vote of confidence. Where's your mistress, the queen of the night? I've been meaning to ask, does Nicole have a reflection when she looks in a mirror?"

"The answer to both questions is, I don't know. To be honest, Nicole doesn't check in with me. She left the house right after you pedaled away. She seemed to have something on her mind."

"I'll bet. And you haven't seen her since."

"That's correct. Have you?"

"Only the manifestation of her greed."

"That's Nicole's aura, I'm afraid. It doesn't take a sharp eye to detect that." René put both of his hands on the back of Lauren's chair. "Now that we've dealt with the subject of Nicole, why don't you tell me what you've found here."

"That's easy. Not the first thing. And I was positive I'd find the key. I could have sworn it was here."

"Mind if I look around?"

"Not at all. I'm sure David's house is open to all his friends, even when he's being held hostage."

René turned around, anger mingling with amazement on his face. "He's been taken?"

"Why so shocked?"

"It wasn't supposed to happen tonight. It was—"

The whish of the arrow was the only warning. René looked down at the shaft that had sped through the open window and into his heart. His right hand clutched the wood, as if he meant to break it off, before he fell backward to the floor.

Chapter Sixteen

Instinct took over and Lauren dropped to the floor. The lights in the entire house went out. Moving as gently as she could in the dark, Lauren found René. She tore off the lightweight jacket she'd worn and attempted to staunch the flow of blood from his wound, but even in the darkness, she could feel the sticky wetness was seeping too fast.

René moaned and whispered, "David."

"Where is he?" Lauren had to bend close to hear René's faint voice. "Please, René, tell me."

"The clinic." René's voice was slurred, indistinct.

Lauren could tell with each beat of his heart he was weakening. "Where is David?" she tried again. There was nothing she could do for René, but she had to try to save David.

"The clinic," René repeated. He coughed, a low rattle.

Lauren choked back panic and tears. René was dying and there was nothing she could do to stop it. "Please, tell me where David is?"

"Bitter irony…" He coughed. "Bitter…" His last breath left him.

In the silence of the room, Lauren heard the ticking of an old grandfather clock. Her mind was as clear and blank as a white page. She was unable to think, to accept that René Devereau was dead. There was only the sound of the clock, steady and unrelenting. It struck her as odd, but she didn't know why. In the horror and finality of René's death, time ticked on. Then she understood. Someone had been coming into the house to wind the clock. It didn't run on electricity or batteries. A human hand turned the key that fed the clock. And she knew it wasn't David Malachi. Another spike of fear tingled over her.

Inching away from René's body, she began to crawl around the room toward the door. Her knee slammed into the photo album she'd dropped, and she moved it with her. She'd been staring at a photo of Sarah Malachi-Lee when René had intruded—and died. It was very similar to the photo that Darcy Woodson had taken to his jail cell with him and something about it made her want to take a closer look at it, somewhere away from Aunt Em's.

As she crawled through the living room to the main front hall, she tried not to think about René. It wasn't possible that he was dead. It hadn't happened. Any moment now, he'd sit up and come explain that it was all part of some sick joke, some charade destined to make her spill her guts about the treasure. She clung to that thought, yet at the same time she knew that René would never move or speak again. Emotionally, she simply couldn't think about it.

He'd been brutally murdered, and it didn't take Einstein to figure out that the arrow that had killed him was one of the ones stolen from David's quiver at the courthouse.

He'd been framed yet again! There was no doubt if the Natchez law officers saw him now, they'd shoot to kill and ask questions later. And very possibly, they'd do the same thing to her.

The hall floor was chilly without her jacket, and she suddenly remembered the locket scraping along the floor with her. She was tempted to take it off. Were they listening to her every move? The horrible thought occurred to her that if they'd wanted her dead, she would be. She let the locket drop back beneath her blouse. They wanted her alive.

Had they been able to hear René's final whisper? "The clinic." Would they know better than she what it meant? Or were they already there, waiting for her to figure it out?

At the front door, she stopped to listen. The pounding of her heart blocked out all other noise. She forced herself to calm down. Outside she could hear the chir of the crickets, the rustle of leaves against a screened window as a gentle spring breeze undulated the limbs.

The smell of wisteria was woven into the night and she was reminded of David's plunge into the river. He'd escaped unscathed, and he would survive this, too. The fragrance of the small flower bolstered her courage and she maneuvered out the front door, keeping as low as possible.

She kept her body from freezing up with fear by keeping her mind busy. René's last words puzzled her. What was a bitter irony? And he'd clearly said "the clinic" twice.

She was creeping down the steps when it dawned on her that perhaps René had been answering her question. It would be a bitter irony if David had been secreted and held prisoner in the very clinic he'd helped build.

Her next thought made her stumble on the last step and she almost fell. Only the handrail saved her as she grabbed it and clung. Did Alan Smith know David was at the clinic? Was he part of this nightmare?

She remembered the doctor's kind eyes, his gentle touch, and his obvious regard for David. It wasn't possible.

The only way to find out was to go to the clinic and look. And for that, she didn't need an audience.

Lauren didn't hesitate once her mind was made up. Reaching beneath her blouse, she found the locket and snapped it open. With deliberate care she placed the small bug on the bottom step. The sense of satisfaction she felt as she crushed it beneath her heel was tremendous. Mistake or not, it was done.

Darting across the lawn, she cut through the redtops that marked the boundary. The clinic was several miles away, but she would be far more elusive on foot than in a car. Natchez was an easy town to traverse. The river bordered one side and the town extended, almost like a coastal town, along it. If she kept the river to her right, she'd end up close to the clinic. With a bit of luck, she'd get there without being detected.

Lauren roused a few dogs as she slipped across the manicured lawns, but her fear for David was much greater than her fear of a confrontation with Fido. She moved in the shadows of trees and shrubs, using the streets for sprints whenever she felt there was no chance anyone would see her. It took nearly forty minutes, but she found herself across the street from the clinic, hiding behind an old Pontiac as she watched the house for signs of life.

The street was silent, and in Alan Smith's converted home, one light burned in an upstairs window. David. She visualized him standing in the light, watching for her. It was enough to spur her across the street and into the yard. Circling the house, she looked for an entrance. She had to be quiet. David's life—and her's—depended on her stealth and cunning.

Near the back of the house she found a garbage can that would give her access to a window. The old house was built almost three feet off the ground, and the windows were big and high. If she could push one open, she'd have no trouble getting in. Except for the screen. It took a few minutes for her to figure out her belt buckle was tough enough to penetrate the slightly rusted screen so that she could unlatch the hook. Once that was accomplished, she lifted the screen from the hooks and let it slide gently to the ground. Old and heavy, the window balked as she attempted to raise it. Her perch on the garbage can was precarious, but she managed to inch the window up little by little. With a hefty jump, she was sprawled on the windowsill on her belly. She wiggled into the room and dropped limply to the floor.

She'd managed to enter the dining room. Even at a passing glance she took in the curved oak china cabinet and heavy furniture. Alan Smith had maintained many gracious touches in his clinic-home. At David's expense? She didn't have time to lay blame or accusations now. She had to get up the stairs and find David, if he was in the house.

The sensible thing to do was to check the darkened first floor. She moved quietly through the rooms. This was Smith's basic living quarters, and there was no sign of life. If David was upstairs, then in all likelihood, Smith was with him. And she had no weapon but a flashlight.

She stopped in the kitchen long enough to arm herself with a wicked-looking knife. Could she use it? For David she could. Without compunction.

Her most vulnerable point would be on the stairs as she ascended. She opted for speed and hurried up on tiptoe. Heart racing from exertion and fear, she made her way slowly to the room where a thin sliver of light sifted under the door.

She was almost at the door, knife lifted high and flashlight at her side when it opened. Alan Smith was framed in this light, his body stooped with fatigue.

"Lauren?" He was obviously shocked to see her. "What ... ?" His voice drifted off as he saw the knife.

"Where's David?" She'd hoped to search the house, find David and get out before confronting anyone.

"You'd better leave here at once," Smith said. "You have no idea how unsafe you are. They'll kill you."

"And David? I suppose they're holding him for a tea party?" She could hear the nervous quiver in her voice, but she hoped Smith could not. "I'm not leaving without him."

"Lauren, leave now. You don't understand." Smith took a step toward her.

She brought the knife down to waist level, the point aimed directly at his breastbone. "Where's David?"

Smith stepped back into the lighted room, allowing her a view in the door. David's prone figure was on a bed. One hand was cuffed to the hospital bed rail. A drip was attached to that same arm, clear bubbles rising steadily from the bottle.

"What have you done to him?" Lauren's control almost snapped. She bolted into the room, and then remembered Smith. He was making an evasive move toward the door.

"Stop!" she ordered. The doctor stopped in his tracks. "What are you giving him?"

"Glucose and a mild sedative. It was better for him if he remained calm." Smith didn't meet her eyes. "I wanted no part of this, but for David's sake, I had to."

"Stop that thing." She motioned to the intravenous tubing with the knife. "Stop it and give him something to wake him up. We're getting out of here."

"There isn't time," Smith said, finally looking at her. "They'll be back for him. My only hope was to pretend that he had a severe concussion. So they couldn't make him talk. If he couldn't answer their questions, they had to keep him alive."

There was an edge of truth in Smith's voice and eyes. Lauren felt her determination falter. Could she trust him? The answer was an absolute no. Trust was something she, not David, could afford at this time. If she got David out of the clinic, with her, he'd be safe. To leave him sedated was to leave him at the mercy of... who?

"Stop the drip. Now!" Lauren brandished the knife in what she hoped was a semblance of toughness. "Wake him up. Is he hurt?"

"A slight concussion, three cracked ribs, his face has been cut."

Lauren hurried to the bed. David's breathing was regular, his eyes closed peacefully. But a huge discoloration was on the right side of his face and a cut that had been neatly stitched. She watched carefully as Smith drew the needle from David's arm. He turned back to the medicine cabinet in the room and located a syringe and a small vial of clear fluid.

"If you hurt him..." Lauren couldn't finish the threat. She'd do whatever she had to.

"You'll never believe me, but I wouldn't hurt David."

"Yeah, I can tell." Fury gripped her and she wanted to lash out. "He saves your practice and your reputation and you repay him by holding him prisoner. But you'd never hurt him."

"I had no choice. When David asked me to detain you here, it was for your own safety. The circumstances are similar."

"Who brought him here?"

"René." Smith didn't hesitate. "David was unconscious. René was afraid he'd been injured. There was no place else he could take him. The hospital would have meant instant arrest. So René brought him here and handcuffed him. He said it was to protect him. He also said that if anyone came to talk with David to say that he was unconscious due to a head injury and that he couldn't talk." Smith looked over at his patient. "I got the impression that René saved his life."

"René is dead." Lauren watched as shock touched the old doctor's features.

"I never trusted him, but I never wished him harm. I remember him as a boy. He and David, so different, and always together."

Sympathy for the doctor tried to surface, but Lauren ignored it. "The key to the handcuffs, where is it?"

"A moment, please." Smith eased the needle into David's arm. The plunger pushed the antidote to the sedative in slowly. David's eyelids didn't flutter, and Lauren's chest contracted with fear. She'd just vowed not to trust anyone, and she'd allowed Alan Smith to inject something into David's artery.

"He should start to come around soon. The sedative was mild, and by putting it in the glucose, it was a very minute but steady dosage. This will be much quicker."

"The cuffs," Lauren reminded him. She had the sense that she had to grab David and get out. As soon as he could stand, they'd have to escape. "Do you have a car?" Damn her decision to travel around on foot. David was in no condition to scamper around town.

"Old but reliable."

He removed a key from his pocket and unlocked the handcuffs. "Let's get him up and moving. If you're going to attempt this, you have to go now."

Slipping David's arm over her shoulder to assist him up, she suddenly looked at Smith. "What about you? If David escapes, what will happen to you?"

"René is dead, as you say. It all depends on who was behind him."

"You don't know?"

"I can guess Nicole. A woman I've never admired." He lifted his hands, palm up. "I'm not afraid of Nicole."

"If she's behind this, she killed Bedford Tanner and René."

"At the moment, my concern is David's safety. Now, on a count of three. One, two, three..."

IT HAD BEEN TOO easy. Lauren cruised down the back streets of Natchez. David was waking up. Or at least trying. Should she head for Jackson, maybe make an attempt to get some federal law officers to intervene? The first thing they'd do would be to arrest the two of them. Jason Amberly was no fool. If he was the mastermind behind all of this, he'd have alerted the feds to the possibility of such a tactic. He knew the system, and he knew that she did, too.

"David?"

"Where are we?"

She told him as well as she could.

"What happened at High Knoll?"

She explained the sequence of events slowly as she took another right turn and made sure she drove the speed limit. There was little traffic around, and she was headed away from the river, away from town.

"I searched the antique beds. All of them in the house. If there's some spring or lever, I missed it."

"It was a wild chance, anyway." David pushed himself up in the seat and looked around. He ran his hand over the side of his face where he'd been struck and cut. "Stitches?"

"Compliments of Dr. Smith." Since he didn't remember his captivity, Lauren didn't want to bring it up, at least not right away. There was something else she had to tell David. Something much harder.

"When I was trying to set up your abductors, I went to your Aunt Em's house. David . . ." she faltered, "René arrived there, too. He's dead."

David didn't move. He continued to look out the passenger window of the car. "How?" he finally asked.

"He was shot. With an arrow. Before he died, he told me where you were. That's how I found you."

"And where was I?"

She swallowed. How much could he take at once? "At Alan's clinic."

"I see."

Defeat was in those two small words.

"He claimed he was trying to help you. He could be telling the truth."

"And we're no closer to finding the key to the map. Before this is over, I'll discover that there's not a single person in the world worth trusting." He finally looked at her. "Except for you, Lauren. You risked your life to help me."

She swallowed. "Don't make it sound so noble. I didn't have a choice, David. My heart was running the show."

He grazed her cheek with his knuckles. "When I should be the most disillusioned, you've given me a reason to believe. When I lost faith with the system, I think I also lost the ability to trust anyone, or anything. Now I find that I can trust someone, a woman I've known so briefly. What you've given me is impossible to define."

"I love you, David." Though her impulse was to put on the brakes and stop the car, she kept steady on the accelerator. There were plenty of things she wanted to tell him. Complex things that would take time to explain. Maybe it was all a notion she'd derived from a book, but she didn't care. What she felt for the man sitting beside her was bigger, and more important, than anything else she'd ever known in her life.

He leaned across the seat and brushed her cheek with his lips. "You've saved my life, and my soul. You deserve more than a declaration of love when we're being pursued by killers. Have no doubt what I feel for you. I won't say it, though, until you're safe from harm. Until I can show you what it means to me.''

Lauren's eyes misted over, but she blinked them dry. "Where to, Robin?"

"I hate to say it, but Aunt Em's."

Lauren thought about René's body. It was a sight she'd spare David if she could. "Are you sure?"

"When you thought that I'd searched everywhere for the key but the most obvious place, you might have been right. I never thought of Em's, but where else would be more logical. Darcy could have slipped it to her when she visited him in jail. Money was never important to Em. If it would have brought Darcy and Sarah back, she'd have turned over heaven and earth to get it. But as things stood, she, too, might have felt the treasure was tainted and better left hidden.''

"I looked through the house. Not thoroughly, of course, but just a cursory search."

"I lived there. I knew Aunt Em pretty well. If it's hidden, it won't be hard to find. It would be among the things of value to her."

Lauren headed the car back to the south side of Natchez. "We'll have to sneak in. No telling who's around there by now. Maybe even the police."

"Don't count on that. If you didn't report René's murder, no one else did."

She didn't question his statement. René was the last thing she wanted to think about as she pulled the car to the curb several streets over. "Can you make it?"

"Better every minute." He signaled them both out, and they began to glide down the street, ducking from shadow to shadow.

With all of his injuries, David was amazingly fit and graceful. Lauren knew he had cracked ribs and multiple cuts and bruises, yet he moved as if his bones were made of springs. She struggled to keep up with him, her own aches and bruises too apparent to her.

As he paused by an oleander that marked the corner of Em's property, David reached back for her hand. He drew her to him, caressing her with a controlled fierceness that made Lauren weak. "Stay here," he said. "Wait for me."

"Not on your life. I've come this far, I'm going the rest of the way."

"Anyone could be in that house." David looked across the lawn. The windows were dead blanks. "Lauren, they might have a gun."

"All the more reason for me to go. It evens the odds for my team."

"If I told you to stay here . . ."

"I'd follow you, so don't waste your breath."

"Stay behind me. As close as you can. If I duck, go with me."

She nodded her understanding and crouched beside him, heart hammering.

They moved as one across the open stretch of grass and onto the porch. The front door was open as Lauren had left it. Inside, they stopped and listened. There wasn't a sound, except the ticking of the old clock.

"The living room?"

Lauren whispered yes against his shoulder. She wanted to add, "Be careful," but there was no need. Together they crept into the room. Lauren dropped to her knees and moved toward René's body. She didn't want David to have to stumble over his friend. Whatever René had become in the last few years, he'd once been special to David. Her hand found her bloodstained jacket and she crawled forward. Searching the floor, she found nothing.

"David!" she whispered.

He was beside her. "What?"

"René is gone." She could feel the tension jolt through his body beside her. "No, he was dead. I'm positive. It wasn't a trick."

"Then where is he?"

"I don't know."

"Wait here."

David didn't give her a chance to argue. He disappeared from her side. She followed his progress through the house with a few telltale tinkles of china and creaky floorboards. He was searching the house. Lauren moved around the room. Where could a dead man have gone?

When the lamp beside her blazed into light, she almost screamed. David's solid footfalls on the floor reassured her.

"The place is empty. Someone had thrown the breaker, so I turned the lights back on." As he talked, David searched the room. The bloodstain on the carpet was undeniable. It was large, and ominous. But there was no body, only the jacket Lauren held in her hands.

"What are we going to do?" Lauren asked.

"Find the key and get out of here. Before whoever took the body decides to return."

Chapter Seventeen

David avoided the blood on the carpet as he brought the jewelry box to Lauren. Placing it on her lap, he opened it. "Aunt Em kept all of her most precious things here," he said. "I'd never thought to look before."

"I almost forgot." Lauren drew the locket from beneath her blouse. She slipped the chain over her head and dropped it into David's hand. "Nicole asked me to return this—after she and Jason put a micro, wireless listening device in it. She said you set great store by the necklace."

David held the delicate locket as if it might be deadly. "It was Aunt Em's favorite piece. Uncle Brett gave it to her on their wedding day. She wore it everyday, for as long as I can remember." His fingers closed around it. "I thought she wore it the day she was buried. I have no idea how Nicole wound up with it."

"She implied that you'd given it to her as a gesture of your affections. It was symbolic that she gave it to me." Lauren blew out her breath in self-deprecation. "Of course, I took it to mean she was yielding her claim to you and giving me her blessings. If I were any dumber I'd have to wear a name tag to remember who I am."

"Not everyone is as devious as Nicole." David reached down and picked up her hand. He held it gently in his, palm up. "I never gave Nicole anything, except money when she needed it. The idea of giving her any piece of Em's jewelry never crossed my mind. It would take a very special person to wear anything of my aunt's. A person I admired and respected. That's why I want you to have this." He transferred the chain and locket to Lauren's hand. "Until I find a more suitable piece of jewelry for you."

Lauren opened her hand and looked again at the expert craftsmanship of the locket. It was exquisite. But the fact that it belonged to someone David loved made it invaluable. She looped the chain around her neck and let the locket fall between her breasts. Catching his hand, she drew him down for a kiss. "Thanks," she murmured, afraid to say more because there was too much to say. He had implied so much—everything she'd ever dreamed about.

"Business before pleasure," he said, his gaze lingering on her lips. He took the jewelry box. Together they went through it piece by piece. They tested for false drawers in the old wooden box. After half an hour, they'd found nothing.

Lauren didn't have to check her watch. The grandfather clock chimed each quarter hour. The night was disappearing, and with it their chances of success. Whatever tale Alan Smith concocted, it wouldn't keep David's enemies at bay for much longer. Eventually Jason and Nicole would come back to Aunt Em's looking for him. At least now Lauren knew her opponents—now she knew how to fight.

"What else would be of value?" she asked when it was obvious the jewelry box would yield nothing. "Family papers, photographs." She reached for the album that was still on the floor where she'd dropped it earlier. "I was looking at this picture of Sarah Malachi-Lee. It looked like the one your Great-Uncle Darcy took to jail with him." She flipped through the pages as she talked. "Here."

She turned the book around for David to look. The sad-eyed woman stared back at them. Her hair was arranged in a soft bun that accented her slender neck and large eyes.

"She looks so sad," Lauren said. "I hope she had happy days with Darcy before she was killed."

"From the family stories I've been told, Sarah enjoyed life until her parents died. Then it was several years later that she changed. It was almost as if she'd learned something horrible about her own family, or maybe her mind snapped. She suddenly denied the Malachi fortune and moved to the slave quarters with Darcy. No one ever knew why. After that, she became more and more eccentric. Today, she'd probably be institutionalized. Back then, the fact that she allowed goats to roam freely through her home was cause for gossip but not action. She used to tell people that a herd of goats had more integrity than anyone in Natchez and that's why the goats were welcome in her home and no one else except Darcy was.''

"What could have driven her to such a point?" Lauren touched the edge of the photo. "She looks completely normal."

"Maybe that's the question we should have been concentrating on all along." David pulled the photo album into his lap as he settled on the floor beside Lauren's chair. "Look. The picture of Sarah is out of sequence. She's a 1930s member of the family, but it's here with the earlier family tintypes."

"I didn't notice her the first time I looked at the album. My eye was captured by that gruesome photo of the hanging." She pointed to the opposite page. "Doesn't he look as if he's daring the devil?" She singled out the outlaw.

"Or as if he doesn't expect it to happen."

"I read a quote in the newspaper that said Joshua Denton said on the gallows that he wanted his body given to your relative, James Malachi, the town physician. He made the statement that he thought the good doctor could bring him back from the dead."

"It isn't possible!" David's fingers began prying at the edge of the gallows picture. "I'd forgotten about that horrible family story, but it was one Aunt Em repeated to me often. She seemed fascinated by the past, especially that era. Before she died, she did extensive research on the period of Natchez history when the Trace was widely used and outlaws like Denton were the rule instead of a rarity."

"The Trace was as famous in its own way as the Chisholm Trail." Lauren had done a bit of reading herself. Not always in nonfiction books, but the novels she'd read contained a great deal of research. "Because of the mild climate down here, the Trace was popular with travelers and highwaymen."

David's chuckle was appreciative. "You're going to make a better Mississippian than anyone native-born." He was busily at work edging the old gallows picture from the page. "Got the one of Sarah free?"

The photo slipped out into her hand and she flipped it over to see if the back was dated. The words "Death is the Lord's avenging angel. Even the innocent must pay. Darcy Woodson" were written on the back in a shaky hand. Lauren couldn't stop the tears that formed in her eyes. Darcy Woodson had written the message on the back of the picture that was his only comfort in his last days.

David had a more difficult time extracting the gallows picture, but he had it out and turned it over. "'Marshall Malachi, 1829-1859. More than family,'" he read aloud.

Lauren handed him Sarah's picture and he read it aloud, too. He looked at her. "There was never a Marshall Malachi in our family that I know of. And as far as I can remember, Darcy and Sarah were crazy as loons, but they didn't have a religious turn. He'd never believe that Sarah's murder was an act of the Lord. He knew very well she was murdered, and that he'd been framed and would likely die, too."

"'More than family,'" Lauren repeated the phrase. "The Malachi in the photo is the doctor, a legitimate family member, James. So why is the name Marshall written on the back?" She pondered the questions aloud. "'Death is the Lord's avenging angel.'"

A flash of memory came to her. Lauren grabbed David's shoulder, her fingers digging in as the fragment came clearer and stronger. "The family cemetery at River Bluff. There's a tomb with an angel swooping down. I remember it very well because one of the angel's arms had been severed. I saw it the day I met René on the bluffs."

"I haven't looked at the cemetery in years," David said. "Now that you mention it, though, it was always Aunt Em who tended it. She wouldn't allow the gardeners to enter, and my mother never cared to work outside. So Em did it. Every week."

"We have to see if that's Marshall Malachi's grave," Lauren said, excitement building so that she moved to the edge of her chair.

"And if it is?" David had his own ideas, but he wanted to see what Lauren was thinking.

"Maybe it's a false grave. Maybe that's where the treasure is. Or at least the key."

"That's exactly what I was thinking." David checked his watch. "It's five. We have maybe an hour of darkness left."

"Get a shovel," Lauren responded. "Make that two."

"Gruesome little thing, aren't you?" David enfolded her in his arms. "I never realized you had a macabre side."

"There are things about me that will curl your hair," Lauren whispered into his neck. "And that's a promise."

"With just a little more practice, I think you're going to have that drawl down to perfection." He was about to capture her lips for a kiss.

Lauren squeezed him tightly, knowing that once he kissed her, she had no intention of stopping there. It would have to wait. "Get those shovels, sir. We've work to do."

DAWN TINGED THE EDGES of the night with grayness as David led Lauren through the woods that surrounded River Bluff. Adventuring as a young boy, he'd learned every nook and hill beneath the thick underbrush, and now he unerringly led them to the ornate railing that marked the boundaries of the family plot.

The white marble of the angel, right hand missing as if it had been severed by a mighty blade, was cold and intimidating to Lauren as she paused at the gate.

"It's funny, but she dominates the plot, doesn't she?" David said. The gate moaned on rusty hinges as he swung it open, sounding like the wail of a mourner. "I don't remember her, but I never spent a lot of time here. Aunt Em, though, said coming here made her feel as if she'd paid her respects."

Lauren handed David a shovel and she took a stance at what would be the foot of the grave. Beneath the angel, the headstone read Marshall Malachi, 1829-1859.

"You're certain Marshall wasn't a family member. Not a cousin thrice removed or a great-great-uncle's nephew?"

"One thing about the Malachi family and Natchez, we know our relatives. Those born on the right and wrong side of the sheet. Marshall Malachi never existed. Not in that time or not in any time. He's an imposter."

"Then let's hope this isn't a grave but a treasure site," Lauren said as she sank her spade into the rich sod.

David matched her two strokes to one as she worked at removing the dirt. As the sky began to pinken with dawn, David was up to his shoulders. He threw out a shovelful of dirt, then the shovel, and finally climbed out to dangle his feet over the side of the grave.

"It's empty," he said. "No bones, no casket, no hidden chest."

Groaning, Lauren dragged herself out of the grave, too. She sat down, leaning back against the tombstone that marked an empty plot of dirt and the dissolution of all of their hopes. The night was over.

"We've got to find that key," David said.

In the top of a Japanese magnolia a mockingbird set up a raucous scolding. Lauren looked up to find the small creature set in black against the vivid pink sky. Her gaze was directed through the open arms of the angel. Clutched in the white marble hand was a round object that she hadn't noticed from a straight-on view.

Curious, she sat up and reached to touch it. The marble was cool, and the object distinctly egg-shaped. It appeared as if the angel was half concealing the object.

"David, come here." She spoke softly, belying the rapid beating of her heart. Her slender fingers probed the surface. The egg slipped slightly in the clutch of the marble hand. "David!"

He knelt beside her. "Let me see." His stronger fingers worked the rounded marble carefully back and forth. "It unscrews," he said, amazement in each word. "Lauren, this could be something important."

When he had the egg worked loose, Lauren inserted her slender fingers into the secret compartment. With a cry of success, she drew out a roll of paper.

The sun nicked the horizon with a golden edge as Lauren unfolded the scroll. Written in the same crabbed hand as the map was a long letter. Together, David and Lauren sank to the ground, using the tombstone as a backrest as David read aloud.

"I have been accused of a terrible crime, the murder of the only woman who ever touched my life, my dearest Sarah. Her father denied me her hand in marriage. Though it broke both of our hearts, Sarah would not go against his wishes. She would not elope with me. Malachis did not sneak off into the night, she told me.

"At her father's insistence, she married a gentleman, Jackson Lee. She remained with him three years and returned home to River Bluff without any explanation for the absence of her husband. She said simply she did not love him and refused to live with him any longer. She had given it a try, and it was over. Her father had been wrong on all points.

"I had waited, knowing that she would return. Though we would never be husband and wife, we were each other's constant companion. Even better, we became best friends.

"In these last years of our lives, we have lived happily as brother and sister. She is of more value to me than anything on this earth. Now that she is gone, my desire to remain here fades with each hour. It is because death is not something that frightens or upsets me that I can face the ordeal ahead with calm and, I hope, dignity.

"I am an innocent man accused of a heinous crime.

I will be convicted, and more than likely executed in a fashion that will sate the bloodlust of my neighbors. How strange it is that both Sarah and I have become objects of contempt because we chose to live in a humble way. When we flaunted the Malachi fortune, those less fortunate loved us because of our wealth, while at the same time hating us for that very same reason. When we denounced the fortune, it was as if we'd denied everyone in town.

"We often spoke of this strange phenomena. To deny the value of Sarah's family money is an insult that people cannot take. They mean to punish me. How silly not to know that by taking Sarah, they have stolen my soul. Let them do their worst, I have no feelings left.

"There is the matter of the money, though. Whenever Sarah and I discussed what would become of River Bluff and the attached monies and investments, we never considered that both of us might die so close together, or so young. At the age of fifty-four, I do not feel that it is time to die, but with Sarah gone on ahead to show the way, I have no quarrel with following. It would seem, though, that so much has been left undone. Unsaid.

"Sarah's brother's family will reside in River Bluff. They will be good for the estate, and it for them. I am pleased by this decision. It is a house for family, with children running down the porches and playing on the lawns. They will give it new life, and perhaps a new soul. It is desperately in need of one.

"Sarah and I have acquired a small fortune in investments and trinkets, which we have decided to hide. We view this money as separate and distinct from the family money Sarah inherited, though it cannot be denied that it is a part of the Malachi inheritance. It is how this money came to be in the family that is the source of Sarah's denouncement of her family wealth. It is a shameful story that has touched many of the prominent families in Natchez.

"This is the money we feel was given to our relative, Dr. James Malachi, by the man labeled as an outlaw, Joshua Denton. We, Sarah and I, believe that Mr. Denton was not guilty of the crimes with which he was charged. Unfortunately, our relative, James Malachi, a man who'd taken a oath to heal others, was. We have come to believe that he was a cold-blooded murderer who rode with a gang of outlaws composed of other prominent Natchez residents—names you will readily recognize as forebearers of the men selected to serve as 'the jury of my peers.'

"Our forebear, James Malachi, and these others forced hapless travelers caught in the web of the gang to tell where money and valuables were hidden. Then the gang would go to those homes and rob them, killing women and children if necessary.

"Mr. Denton was hung at high noon in the Natchez square for the crimes of robbery, murder, arson, torture and kidnapping. We believe he was innocent of all charges, and that he stepped to the gallows believing that our relative would be able to bring him back from the dead, unscathed. He was a foolish man, a scapegoat used by men of superior intelligence—and superior evil.

"While all parties to these crimes deserved the utmost punishment, it was James Malachi, a doctor, who most betrayed his calling and his human spirit. Sarah found this fact a constant source of shame and degradation. The family she'd honored and respected was based on a man who stooped to any means for money. It was a blow that almost unsettled her sanity.

"But now she is at rest. The Malachi holdings are too vast for me to attempt to dismantle, and under the criminal charges of the law, I have no legal rights. Sarah and I took the precaution of hoarding away as much money and jewels as possible, without destroying the Malachi homesite. For you see, though Sarah abhorred her ancestors, she could never stop loving

River Bluff.

"This letter of explanation has been hidden with the key to the map. Should both map and key be found, then the riddle of the treasure will be solved—and the horrors of the past will be reopened. Perhaps when I am judged guilty and punished, it will be enough, for I am indeed an innocent man. My death may absolve my forefathers of their sins. I pray that justice will be served—a higher justice.

"Darcy Woodson."

David put his arm around Lauren and held her for a long moment. They were both moved by the words of a man dead for sixty years.

"There's something about you Malachi men," Lauren said, her voice roughened by emotion, "Y'all have a real passion for justice."

"Darcy Woodson was executed for something he didn't do. Even worse, it was made to appear like suicide. Why didn't he tell anyone about this?"

"Because of Sarah," Lauren answered. She understood. "Sarah suffered from the guilt and shame, and Darcy did whatever he had to do to make her happy. He must have loved her tremendously. He couldn't tell the secret, because it would have hurt Sarah, even though she was dead. It would have hurt the Malachi name. Her family name."

"This letter, then, was intended to be found years later."

"Exactly as it's happening." David held Lauren closer. "That poor soul standing on the gallows. No wonder he looks as if he doesn't fear death. He honestly believed my great-great-uncle could bring him back from the dead."

"He was a fool, but the men responsible for his death are fiends."

"So, Sarah's denouncement of the Malachi money is finally explained. She wasn't crazy, she simply had a code of honor. And she had family pride. Caught between the two, she did the best she knew how."

"For all of Dr. Malachi's evilness, there were so many other members of your family to admire. Poor Sarah."

David unrolled the letter that had reverted back to a scroll. Beneath it was another sheet of paper. This was blank with small holes cut in it at random.

"The key," he said. He chuckled with little mirth. "A child's answer. The holes highlight certain letters or symbols that tell where the treasure is hidden. Any child could have devised such a key."

"Yet it's stumped a handful of very intelligent people for several weeks."

"Too bad René couldn't see this." David's voice held grief, and anger. "He would throw a fit. He was expecting something that would require decoding by the FBI."

"I would have said Nicole was capable of anything—except killing René."

"I would have agreed."

"Too bad you didn't see who clobbered you on the head at High Knoll. Too bad I didn't see who got me." Lauren shifted her weight. It was full light, and she could sense that time was running out for them. "Where's the copy of the map you took from René's."

"At the clinic." He sighed. "How is it that Alan betrayed me, too? Is that going to be my fate, that everyone I love and trust betrays me?"

"Not everyone," Lauren reminded him with a kiss. "Maybe there's an explanation. And we'd better get there and do some asking."

David looked at the hole they'd dug in front of the tombstone. "I'll come back later and take care of this. For Aunt Em."

"She must have known about the treasure."

"Perhaps Darcy told her. She was old enough, I suppose."

"I'll bet he did," Lauren said, excitement rising. "I'll bet she hid everything for him. After all, he was in jail."

"You're probably right." David picked up both spades. "How shall we travel, by foot or chariot?"

"Let's get a car," Lauren said, "my dogs are killing me."

"Dogs, dogs," David mumbled. "Midwestern, I believe."

"Very funny," Lauren said as she fell into step behind him.

"THE CLINIC LOOKS closed," David said. They were sitting down the block in Lauren's rental car. "I would have thought Jason would have called in the marines by now. It's bound to be a trap."

"Let me go there," Lauren said, grasping the handle of the door. "I'll check it out."

"Are you sure?"

"If they arrest me, you can find the treasure. Once you have that, I think you'll have what Jason and Nicole want. The money is legally yours. They'll know the show is over. I don't think they'll give up, but maybe they'll make a run for it. At any rate, I don't think Jason would hurt me."

"I don't know." David grabbed her wrist and held her as she started out of the car. "I love you, Lauren."

"And I love you. When your name is cleared and life has resumed a normal pace, I'm going to hold you to that promise you made—time for us."

"You've got it." He released her arm.

Lauren walked down the block to the old house, up the steps and to the front door. She knocked with boldness. To her surprise, she heard someone scurrying around inside, as if they were hiding. Since the door wasn't locked, she entered.

"Alan?" she called out. "Alan, it's me, Lauren."

There was no answer. Had Jason and Nicole hurt the old man?

"Alan?" She hurried through the downstairs rooms, finding nothing. Upstairs, she paused. The door to the room where David had been held prisoner was ajar. She could see a body tied in a chair, the head slumped forward.

She knew he was dead. She could tell by the way the body slumped, and by the pool of blood on the floor.

"Dr. Smith!" She rushed into the room and stopped abruptly. There was nothing she could do. Running to the upstairs window, she opened it and waved frantically for David. He saw her immediately and began running toward the house.

A noise in the hall made her whirl around. Footsteps pounded toward her, too soon to be David's. Wyatt Reed burst into the room. "Lauren..." He stopped at the sight of the doctor. "What in the hell happened here?"

"They killed him." Lauren had seen too much of death in the past few hours. Her control was as fragile as a silk thread. Her eyes widened as she realized that Wyatt held a gun.

"Hey!" He pushed the gun into a shoulder holster. "I'm not going to hurt you." He went to Smith's body and checked for a pulse. He shook his head. "Looks like he was shot through the heart."

The sound of David's running footsteps echoed on the stairs. He rushed into the room and to Lauren's side. The look he cast Wyatt was wary.

"I've been tailing Jason all night," Wyatt explained in answer to David's unasked questions. "I've been just three steps behind him." He nodded toward the doctor. "Too late to prevent this."

"Why?" David asked. He went to his friend and put a gentle hand on Smith's shoulder.

"I'd think you'd have a better answer than me." Wyatt made a sweeping gesture with his arm. "This whole mess has centered around you, Malachi. If you'd stayed in jail where you belonged, none of this would ever have happened."

"Bedford Tanner wouldn't have died?" David asked.

"I can't say that for certain." Wyatt began to pace. "But the way I see it now is that when you escaped, you pushed Jason to the point of no return. He had to act. He had to do something to keep you locked away. Tanner was an inconvenience. He wouldn't play along with Jason."

"How do you know so much?" Lauren interrupted. "How?"

"Jason knew ⬛ in Natchez has hea⬛ really believed the⬛ map." Wyatt pushed⬛ couldn't wait to tell ⬛ spiring, as thick as thi⬛

"An accurate descrip⬛

"Anyway, Nicole got⬛ Jason." He shrugged and⬛ and I heard them talking ⬛ portunity and took a look a⬛ ⬛ of sense to either of us."

"If you knew Jason was ⬛ ⬛ing, it was your duty to stop him," David said⬛ ⬛ grown rigid with anger. "This man is dead, and so is René Devereau and Bedford Tanner."

"What was I going to do, charge the county D.A. with treasure hunting?" Wyatt replied heatedly. "I suspected him. I had no proof. If you'll recall, it was your arrow that killed Tanner, and likely Devereau. Your fingerprints were all over High Knoll. Not Jason's. You're a lawyer, David, you know you can't arrest someone on suspicion."

"Jason wasn't going to arrest David, he was going to kill him," Lauren added bitterly.

"I don't know about that, but he was obsessed. Burt and I have been doing everything in our power to stay close to him. I'm only hoping Burt's with him now."

"And Nicole?"

Wyatt's eyes narrowed. "She left town last night."

"Before or after René was murdered?"

"After."

"How do you know that?" David asked.

"Jason killed René. The way I'm thinking it happened was that René was a third party who wasn't really wanted anyway. Especially by Jason. He'd be just one more person to share the wealth with. When Lauren made them believe the key to the map was at David's aunt's house, they sent

René to take it from you—and to⬛
"And Nicole?"
"I'd say shu⬛
Lauren shu⬛
"He wa⬛
"Wha⬛
to get rid of him?"
go⬛
234

...son saw a perfect opportunity ...ok it."

...omewhere now getting rid of the body." ...dered. "And where's Jason?" ...s here." Wyatt nodded at Alan Smith's body. ...ever he wanted from the old man, he more than likely ...

"Alan didn't know anything." David's voice was rough with grief.

"He helped you escape, didn't he?"

"And he also held David prisoner," Lauren added.

"Jason had something on him. Something from a long time back. You see, Jason has a lot of power, but even more than that, he has a lot of information. That's why we can't simply call the police and say, 'Arrest him.' We're going to have to take him ourselves." Wyatt looked around the room. "He's consumed by greed and ambition. If we play it smart, we can capture him."

"I'm listening," David said.

"If we could find the treasure, that would be the perfect bait. And we have—" Lauren stopped herself and looked at David. They had the key, but could they really trust Wyatt Reed.

"At this point in time, I think David would be better bait," Wyatt said, his gaze resting on David. "The perfect bait. You've given him so much trouble, he wants you dead. If he thought he had a chance of getting to you, one on one, he'd be willing to risk everything for it."

"Nicole isn't that stupid," Lauren said. She didn't like the idea of David as the human sacrifice. "They'll go for the treasure. Let's use that instead."

The two men stared at each other, one testing the other. "Jason put that arrow in René's heart?" David asked.

"I was fifteen minutes behind him. I didn't see. By the time I got there, René was dead and Lauren gone. But if he didn't, Nicole did."

"I've considered that," David said slowly.

"As much as Jason wants you dead, Nicole has even more reason."

"David never did anything but try to help Nicole." Lauren had had enough. "She's insane."

"And insanely jealous," Wyatt replied. "David treated her with kindness, but he didn't want her. She can't take that kind of rejection. If he'd hated her and scorned her, she'd have understood. But he befriended her. That was beyond her ability to accept."

"Let's go, and we're not taking any chances. We'll offer Jason and Nicole the treasure and me." David smiled slightly. "I want this ended for once and for all."

"Sounds good to me. Where? When? What should I do?" Wyatt asked.

David put his arm tightly around Lauren. "Protect her. I can take care of myself. And as for when and where. Now, and in a moment we'll know where." He strode out of the room and reappeared a moment later with the copy of the map. Very carefully he anchored it to the bed. Then he took the key he'd placed inside his shirt and unrolled it, placing it over the map. The cutouts in the key revealed the letters and symbols that were easily read.

Like all good tales of treasure, this one has a well.
Midway down there's a red rock.
Remove it and indulge your fantasies.
Just remember that with such wealth comes a tragic past.
Use it wisely to redress the wrongs of society.

"So simple," Lauren said in awe, "and so much like Darcy Woodson."

"Old Darcy hid the treasure in the same well Sarah's body was dumped in," Wyatt said. "I heard a lot about his case. Seems he was innocent."

"Something I intend to prove," David said, and Lauren knew the words were a vow.

"The answer to 'where' is River Bluff, at the well." Wyatt looked from David to Lauren. "I'll get Burton and some backup."

"No!" David was adamant. "Jason isn't stupid, and we have no idea who might warn him. We can handle it. We'll retrieve the treasure, and then set the trap. All you have to do, Wyatt, is contact Jason and get him to River Bluff in about half an hour."

"What about the tours?" Lauren asked. "It's the middle of the Spring Pilgrimage tours."

"Even better," David said slowly. "The well is behind the slave quarters. No one will see us. It will make Jason feel even safer—and the idea of capturing the notorious Robin Hood Robber in front of a clutch of history-seeking tourists will appeal to him like a drug."

"David..." Lauren started to protest. "He'll kill you if he can."

"Wyatt, take Lauren to River Bluff, after you call Jason. I'll meet you there. I have to get some rope and a winch." He eyed the assistant prosecutor with a speculative glance. "If anything happens to Lauren, I'm holding you responsible."

Chapter Eighteen

Lauren took one last look at Alan Smith before she followed Wyatt out of the room. He paused downstairs and used the telephone to call the D.A.'s office. Jason wasn't in, no surprise to Lauren, but Wyatt left a message to meet him at River Bluff in exactly an hour. At nine o'clock. It would be slightly before the plantation house opened for tours, but it would work out fine, David had assured her.

"Ready?" Wyatt asked as he started toward the front door.

"I'm dead on my feet. I hope everyone else is as tired."

"Lauren, I've always admired your courage, and never more than now." Wyatt put his hand between her shoulder blades as he eased her out the front door. "David Malachi's a lucky man to have someone like you care about him as much as you obviously do."

"He's an innocent man caught up in a web of terrible events."

"You put yourself on the line for him."

"You'd do the same, Wyatt. You *are* doing the same." She gave him a tired smile. "On to River Bluff."

"One thing about working in a prosecutor's office. Many times the guilty go free and the innocent suffer. I'm glad to be able to change that, even if it is just one case."

They made the drive in virtual silence. Wyatt reached under his coat once, and Lauren knew he was checking his weapon. It would be a nice feeling if she had a gun, too. As soon as the thought came, so did the shock. She had never been one to approve of weapons.

Wyatt parked the car away from the main house. Several cars belonging to tour personnel were already there. He gave Lauren a reassuring smile. "Jason won't notice my car, I guarantee."

The old slave quarters were to the east of the main house. Lauren cast a surreptitious glance at the family cemetery. The mound of dirt they'd shoveled up was still there, clay red in the morning light. She followed Jason back to the cabins, now painted a picturesque white. There was still evidence of the fire that had nearly killed Sarah and Darcy. A fireplace stood among burned timbers and weeds, the only unkept spot on the entire grounds, a reminder of the tragedy. Lauren and Wyatt walked past the ruins and found a series of fifteen small cabins. Moving behind them, they found David rigging up a winch and rope at an old well.

"How about the main house?" Wyatt asked. "Wouldn't Darcy have put the goods in that well?"

"That well was sealed when the pump was put in. That's how I knew it was here." He tested the winch to see if it would hold his weight. "I'll go down in the well. Can you pull me out?"

Wyatt nodded.

"That's crazy," Lauren said quickly. "I'm the lightest. Let me go. Then the two of you can pull me out without any trouble."

"Anything could be down there." David shook his head. "I've heard of snakes moving into abandoned wells. No, Lauren, you stay here. Wyatt can manage me, or I'll let him down. Darcy's directions are so clear, it can't be hard to find." He pulled a flashlight from his back pocket.

"You two buffoons are going to have to listen to reason." Lauren picked up the rope and began to make a girdle for her hips. "I'm going down. I'll be out in no time and we can end this. David, if you or Wyatt get stuck, then Jason will have us at a disadvantage."

"She's right," Wyatt said slowly. "We can have her down and out in a few minutes."

David tested the line again, making sure the timber above the well would support the winch, line, and Lauren's weight.

Maneuvering so that she sat on the lip of the well, Lauren looked down. It was bottomless, a trip into darkness. She held out her hand for the flashlight. "Don't forget to bring me back up," she said, and knew her voice cracked a little. She hated heights, and she hated the dark. The well was intimidating, but it would only be for a few moments.

David's hands grasped her waist as he eased her over the side. He held her for as long as possible while Wyatt fed the rope slowly to the winch. Foot by foot, Lauren descended into darkness until the only light was a small circle above. David's anxious face grew smaller and smaller.

"I'll drop a rock to see how far to the bottom," David said. He slipped a small pebble over the edge. Lauren heard it hit water at what sounded like twenty or thirty feet below her. "Slow down," she called up, turning on the flashlight so she could see the walls. She had only to locate a brick that had been painted red. How hard could it be? She spun on the rope, and in the darkness she had a dizzying sense of vertigo that almost made her cry out to be lifted back to the world of light. Instead she let them ease her down the well as she moved the light beam carefully over every inch.

She found the red brick without trouble. It protruded slightly from the others, and when she reached out to touch it, it moved easily. "I've got it. Just hold me here."

Extracting the brick took more strength than she'd anticipated. It was firmly wedged in place. When she finally had it free, she was tempted to drop it into the water, but thought better of waking any sleeping demons that might have nodded off.

Clutching the brick to her chest with the arm that held her rope, she reached her right hand into the dark hole. She was afraid, of ridiculous things such as snakes and spiders and ooze. Her fingertips touched something smooth and stiff and she pulled it toward her as carefully as possible. It took her a few seconds to realize she had a leather pouch. Chances were that the stitching had dry rotted, so she moved it with great care.

She felt her excitement build as she realized how heavy the pouch was. When it came to a choice, she finally had to drop the brick and the flashlight to get the heavy pouch into her arms.

"Lauren!" David heard the splash and almost panicked.

"Bring me up! I've got it!" Success at last, she wanted to laugh as she was lifted back to the sun and sky and David.

As her head cleared the well, she took a deep breath of sweet air. David was hauling at the rope, and Wyatt stepped forward to relieve her of the heavy pouch. Using great care, he put the heavy bundle on the ground at his feet.

"What's in it?" he asked.

"I can't wait to find out." Lauren stretched her hand to him. She was hanging precariously over the well, and David was busy holding the rope. "How about a hand?" she asked Wyatt.

Wyatt's hand slipped beneath his coat and came out with the gun. The deadly looking weapon was pointed directly at David. He glanced at Lauren, registering the sudden fear in her eyes. Rope in hand, David froze. Only his muscle held Lauren above the well. "Hey, you guys," he said as he put the Browning 9 mm beside the well, "the gun was in my way." He leaned forward and drew Lauren into his arms, pulling her to safety.

"You scared me for a minute," Lauren said. She could see the tension still on David's face. Wyatt had frightened her. Now she felt slightly silly.

"I wouldn't hurt you." Wyatt shook his head as he picked up the pouch. "The stock was digging into my arm. I was afraid I'd drop you. We prosecutors don't normally wear guns, you know. I don't think the holster fits right."

Lauren took the pouch from his hands and dumped the contents on the ground. One ruby necklace sparkled into the grass along with several brilliant sapphires. Gold coins were mingled in with pearls and other items of very expensive jewelry. A portfolio, carefully sealed, tumbled out with the jewels.

David picked it up and broke the seal. With great care, he unwrapped the papers. "Well, I'll be." He held them down for Wyatt and Lauren to see. "Coca-Cola stock. Darcy and Sarah were eccentrics. Coca-Cola was a risky business back then. Now this must be worth a fortune. Not to mention the jewels."

"It's a massive stash," Wyatt said. "There's enough money here for everyone." He dumped more jewels onto the grass. The colored gems caught the early morning light in a burst of brilliance.

Lauren shook the pouch to make sure everything was out. The old leather seemed to disintegrate in her hands.

"I have an old sack in my car," Wyatt offered. He tossed her the keys. "If you'll get it, we can package this stuff up and get ready for Jason's arrival. I told him you and the treasure would be here. He won't be able to resist."

"Better hurry," David said to Lauren as he began to coil the rope. "I'm thinking the best place to take him on, without involving our friendly tourists, would be the bluff over the river. We'll have the woods as a cover, and I know them well. I want you and Lauren to take most of the jewels—we'll leave one or two here to convince Jason we have the treasure. I'll stay behind so that Jason can actually see me, and then I'll lead him to the woods."

"That sounds like a sensible plan. He won't expect me to be hiding. He'll think you've already dispatched me." Wyatt fingered several pieces of jewelry. "I've never seen anything like these."

"Some of them are antiques, Wyatt. I suspect they go back to the times when the Trace Outlaw Gang robbed travelers."

"Do you think?" Wyatt turned up an excited face. "How did old Darcy come by them? And why did he keep them?"

"It's a long story. Not a pleasant one. Darcy and Sarah were trying to undo something in the past, and I guess if there's any lesson to be learned from all of this, it's that the past can't be changed or mended. It's best learned from and left alone."

"It's the future I'm interested in," Lauren said as she gave David a meaningful look. "I'll be back in a minute."

She sprinted toward Wyatt's car, always careful to keep an eye out for Jason or Nicole. At the bluffs, David would have an advantage. She didn't want to mess up his plan.

Slinking over to Wyatt's car, she put the key in the trunk and popped it open. It occurred to her that the cloth sack was probably in the back seat, and she stepped around the car to look for it. A thorough search under the seat yielded nothing and she returned to the trunk. It was open several inches, and she lifted it up. Jason Amberly's dead eyes gazed back at her.

Lauren's hand froze on the trunk. She stared at Jason's sightless eyes and refused to register what she saw. Jason couldn't be dead. He was the one who'd killed René and Alan Smith. He was the person who'd tried to kill her and David. He couldn't be dead, because if he was, then whoever had set out to destroy David was still alive.

"No!" She stepped back from the trunk. "No!" She turned to run back toward the cabins—and David. She forced herself to stop, to think a minute before she simply reacted blindly.

If Jason was dead—and he was—then Wyatt had killed him and stuffed his body in the trunk. Wyatt had deliberately sent her to his car to find the body. Why? As his last little joke. He intended to kill David and then her.

Reaching beside the dead body, she pulled out a tire iron. It was the only weapon she could think of. A cold sweat touched her forehead as she realized that she'd left David, unsuspecting, alone with Wyatt. And Wyatt had a gun.

As she turned to run back to David, she heard a shot followed closely by two more.

Wyatt was killing David!

She ran with speed she never knew she possessed. Skittering around the corner of one of the cabins, she saw David leaning against the well. Blood trickled down his arm, and the expression on his face showed pain.

Wyatt Reed was scrabbling in the grass, dragging up strings of jewels, which he was stuffing into his pockets and inside his shirt.

"Jason is dead, Malachi. He caught me when I killed Devereau. I was dragging René's body into the shrubs by the house when he sneaked up on me. Crafty bastard. He almost got me. But it surprised him when he saw my face, and I had a chance to kill him before he could get me."

"Take all the jewels and the stocks, Wyatt, but leave Lauren alone."

"And you?" Wyatt looked at him long enough to gloat. "I suppose you want me to let you live, too."

"I don't care what you do to me as long as you let Lauren live."

"Noble gesture, Mr. Robin Hood, but it won't work. Lauren knows too much. I'm sure she's found her boss in the trunk." He smiled. "No, Malachi, Ms. Sanders is too big a liability. Besides, she wouldn't want you to get lonely down in that old well. First you, then her. And I'll have the treasure. Justice will be served at last."

"It's a strange justice you're talking about, Wyatt. Those jewels belong to the people of Natchez. They were stolen from travelers by a gang of outlaws."

"You don't think I know about these jewels!" Wyatt held up a fistful and let them rain down on his face. "My great-great-grandfather died for these jewels. He believed in a Malachi! He believed your great-great-grandfather could actually bring him back from the dead." Wyatt laughed. "That's rich, isn't it? He trusted your great-great-grandfather so much that he allowed the people of Natchez to hang him publicly. He took the rap as a terrible outlaw, because he was asked by James Malachi. Now that's a history lesson for you, isn't it?"

"Wyatt, that's the past. You can't change it and neither can I." David pressed his hand to his shoulder in an attempt to stop the flow of blood.

Lauren watched from the corner of the cabin. She didn't know what to do. She had no gun, only the tire iron. If she excited Wyatt, he could step around the well and blast David to bits—and she knew he'd do it with the least provocation.

No help was coming. Wyatt had not called anyone. He'd talked into a dead telephone, playing along with the charade that Jason was behind everything. As difficult as it was to believe, everyone who might have helped her was dead.

Hefting the tire iron, Lauren charted a course that would bring her up behind Wyatt. If he kept on ranting at David, she might be able to sneak up behind him and take him. Not likely, but it was the only chance she could see. She stepped away from the cabin, just enough so that David could see her. Panic crossed his face and he tried to struggle to his feet. Lauren signaled him back. If he tried any heroics, he'd get himself killed for sure, and very possibly her. Surprise was the only thing she had going in her favor.

Sweat burned her eyes and she pushed her glasses back up on her nose. When this was finally over, she was getting contact lenses, no matter how much they irritated her eyes.

She moved back, away from the well. She'd circle down about five cabins and cut back, hoping to approach Wyatt from his blind side. He must know by now that she'd discovered Jason. He'd sent her to the car deliberately. Wanting her to know there was no one to help her.

She had one last thought about rushing up to River Bluff and getting the tour guides to help, but even to her the ladies in their crinolines with pastel ruffles and hoops were useless. She'd never have time to call the police, either. Any second Wyatt could decide to move in for the kill.

At the third cabin she moved around to the back. She was twenty-five yards behind Wyatt. He was still wielding the gun, talking about the injustice of the past. David was reasoning with him, or trying to. He was telling Wyatt about Darcy's and Sarah's attempts to make amends for the past, how they'd found the jewels and begun to understand where they'd come from.

"Why didn't they tell the truth?" Wyatt asked. "If they were so noble, why didn't they simply tell the truth."

"Because it didn't matter," David said tiredly. "Don't you see? No one cared about that anymore. Darcy Woodson lost the only person he ever loved, and then he lost his life. Isn't that payment enough, Wyatt?"

"Maybe for you, but not for me. Never for me. My father was born here. From the first day of school until he ran away at twelve, he was humiliated and ridiculed by the other children. Folks around here were never willing to let him forget. So he ran away, changed his name and decided to start a new life. That's what you advocate, isn't it, Malachi? A new life. Can't undo the past so upgrade the future? Well, he tried. But a funny thing happened. He didn't need the folks around here to ridicule him. He'd learned how to do it himself. He was so damn good at it that he did it to his kids and his wife and to everyone who came into his life."

Lauren wanted to put her hands over her ears. Even an amateur psychologist could see the anguish that Wyatt Reed had lived with—a suffering deep and intense that had grown from a wound simmering for generations.

The past was simply an excuse for his father's fears and conduct. But it was the force that had shaped Wyatt. He believed if he could avenge the past he could correct the future.

If she'd had time, plenty of long hours to spend with him, she knew she could help him. But too much had happened. Three people were dead. And Wyatt intended to make it four.

She darted from the cabin to an old chinaberry tree, then on to a Japanese persimmon rich with dark green leaves. So far, she'd closed the gap by five yards. His back was still turned to her, and if she moved quickly enough, she might be able to take him by surprise.

"Talk to him, David," she whispered under her breath. "Talk to him and keep him busy."

"I'm not to blame for what my ancestors did." David spoke up as if he'd read Lauren's mind. "Neither are you, Wyatt."

"Forget it, Malachi. I've killed already. One more won't make the death sentence any less electrifying." He laughed. "If they catch me I'm a dead man."

"Take the jewels and get out of here," David said. "Take all of them. I'll never mention they were found. Just go and leave me and Lauren alone."

Lauren moved to an old oak. The rest of the way was in the open. She'd have to dash for it and bring the tire iron down with enough force to stun him. Her hand was clammy on the iron so she wiped it on her shirt and got a better grip. She psyched herself up with one last vision of Scarlett on the stairs of Tara facing down a Yankee soldier. Scarlett had shot the man in the face. All she had to do was deliver a bump on the noggin with a tire iron.

Arm held over her head, she ran out from behind the tree directly at Wyatt.

Something alerted him to her charge and he turned, gun pointed directly at her. David leapt to his feet and charged from the opposite side. Wyatt aimed the pistol at Lauren. He hesitated for a moment, and in that split second David launched himself for one final effort to knock Wyatt off target. The sound of a gun cracked the morning air again.

Lauren fully expected to feel the bullet ripping into her body. Instead she felt nothing. She ran on toward Wyatt. David struck him behind the knees and the two men fell together.

It was all slow motion. Lauren tried to run but her legs seemed made of heavy, heavy rubber. They bent and shook, but they didn't move. David and Wyatt rolled in the grass. She saw the Browning fall, and neither man made a grab for it. Wyatt fell on top of David, but that position was quickly reversed.

David gained the upper hand and sat on Wyatt, his fist drawn back for a punch. Slowly he lowered his hand. He looked up quickly at Lauren, who stood only feet away. The tire iron was still arched above her head.

"He's been shot," David said. He grabbed Lauren and pulled her down beside him. Protecting her as well as he could, he looked around the slave quarters. By the edge of one of the cabins a raven-haired woman in a peach-colored antebellum gown stood holding a gun. She sauntered toward them.

"Nicole!" Lauren couldn't believe it. Nicole Sterling looked as if she'd stepped out of the page of *Southern Living*. Not a frill or ruffle on her frothy dress and hat was out of order. Only the pistol she held with such casual familiarity was out of place.

"Only a fool from Kansas would try to kill a man with a tire iron," she drawled as she stopped at Lauren's feet. "Mississippi women know that when a man needs killin', you use a gun."

The tire iron still clasped in her hand, Lauren slowly got to her feet. On closer inspection, she could see that Nicole's eyes were red-rimmed. Her porcelain beauty was marked by grief carefully hidden under bravado.

Nicole dropped the gun at David's knee. "He killed René. He promised me no one would get hurt. He killed René." She sank to the ground, dress puffing out like a deflating hot-air balloon.

"Nicole! Nicole!" The worried voice of an older woman called from behind the cabins. "Did you find those awful boys shooting back here. Those kids don't have any respect for the Pilgrimage or hunting season. They're going to kill a tourist one day and then..." A gray-haired woman dressed in the full regalia of a Southern plantation owner's wife halted at the edge of the clearing. "What on earth?"

Lauren dropped the tire iron and bent down to David. The bleeding had almost stopped. As David sat up, Lauren looked over at Wyatt. He was still breathing. Nicole's bullet had gone in his chest, but Lauren couldn't determine the damage. She turned to the older woman. "Get an ambulance. Fast!"

"Stay right here," the woman directed as she backed away with quick steps. "I'll make the call. Just don't come up to the house. The guests would just die! It would be the scandal that ended the Pilgrimage. I mean, just when you think River Bluff is going to turn into a respectable home to show you people do something crazy again!" She turned and ran, her slate-blue gown swaying behind her.

Nicole nudged the gun with her foot. "I should shoot her too," she said calmly, looking after the retreating figure.

David knelt over Wyatt. He checked the wound carefully before he sat down beside Lauren. "I think he's going to live. There's nothing I can do for him. The paramedics will be here soon."

"What about the treasure?" Nicole suddenly asked. "Did it ever even exist?"

David held up a diamond necklace that had fallen from Wyatt's pocket into the grass. Nicole didn't even reach for it. "There was a time when the treasure was important. Then it became more of a game for me and René. It wasn't finding it, it was tricking you, David. You'd always gotten everything you ever wanted. René struggled so, and the good things of life just dropped in your lap." Her voice nearly broke but she straightened her back and continued. "We never meant to harm you. Never. We wanted the money, but we never killed anyone. When Bedford Tanner was killed we realized that another person was involved. We didn't know who, not until Wyatt came to us yesterday afternoon. He talked René into following Lauren to Aunt Em's."

"And Jason? Where did he fit in?"

Nicole shook her head. "Nowhere. He was never a part of anything, just a man driven to succeed."

"So much tragedy, and for what? A past long dead and never able to be changed."

Wyatt groaned and David returned to him to see if he could offer any assistance. In the distance there was the wail of sirens.

"What's going to happen to us?" Nicole asked.

"I don't know," David answered. "You'd better wish for a miracle, Nicole."

Lauren forced herself to her feet. A few pieces of jewelry were still scattered on the ground, and she knew she should pick them up before the vehicles came and crushed them. A ruby pin caught her eye and she bent down to retrieve it. "Like Dorothy's slippers," she whispered. "I want to go home. Back to Kansas where things like this don't happen. At least not to me." She pushed her glasses up on her nose and realized they were filled with tears.

"Things like this happen everywhere, Lauren." David struggled to his feet. His uninjured arm went around her shoulders. "But if it's Kansas you want, then you'll have it. I promise. A few weeks at home with your folks is exactly what you need." He kissed her hair, then her cheek, and finally nudged her chin up so that her tear-blurred eyes met his. "But then you have to come back here. There are a few loose ends we have to tie up."

TWO WEEKS IN KANSAS had done Lauren a world of good. She'd finally managed to stop the nightmares that had nearly driven her to the brink. She'd cried and cried on her mother's shoulder. At last the tears had dried. She hadn't wanted to come back to Natchez. Only David's insistence had convinced her that it was something she had to do. Besides, Wyatt Reed's arraignment was due the next day. Strangely enough, she was to testify regarding his mental stability.

On the flight back to Natchez, Lauren had tried to decide what she would say. Once again she'd stand before Judge Clinton. Even though she'd resigned her duties in the Adams County District Attorney's Office, the judge had asked her to testify. He'd made a good case for the fact that she'd seen Wyatt under stress and had a better insight into his emotional status. It was also unfair in one way—she'd almost lost her life, and her love, to his twisted view of reality. She sighed. That was it, then. Wyatt Reed didn't have a real grip on the world around him. She'd have to state what she believed.

And she had one small roll of microfiche to return to the newspaper. She'd almost mailed it back, but she wanted to apologize and make sure it arrived safely.

When the small plane touched down at the Natchez airport, Lauren almost refused to disembark. Looking out the small round window, she caught sight of a tall man in a conservative charcoal gray suit. For a moment she didn't think it was David, but then she knew. All thoughts of turning back fled. She'd never imagined how much she wanted to see him, to feel his arms around her and his lips on hers. She was out of the plane and down the metal steps in a flash.

"Lauren!" David opened his arms.

She rushed into them, knowing suddenly a tremendous truth. "I thought when I went to Kansas I'd gone home. But I hadn't. I'm home now, with you."

RIVER BLUFF was magnificent in the full bloom of a Southern spring. Lauren took in everything as David drove up the long drive to the stately old house.

"What are we doing here? I thought you were living at Aunt Em's?"

"I am, but there's something we have to finish here," David said.

"I don't want to go back to the...place where Wyatt was shot."

"You don't have to." David took her hand and held it.

"And Nicole? How is she?"

"Mending. She's with her sister in Shreveport, Louisiana. I don't think there will be any charges against her. As far as anyone has been able to determine, she and René injured no one."

"Except you," Lauren said.

"Not physically. Not really."

"In the worst way. They wounded your belief."

"And you restored it, Lauren." David stopped the car at the front door. He pulled her across the car seat and out the driver's side with him. As he walked up the steps, he picked up a bow and quiver.

"What are you up to now?" She felt a chill of apprehension. Nothing about that bow looked good to her.

"Trust me," David said. He grabbed her hand and led her into the house, up the stairs and out a bedroom to the second-floor balcony.

"What do you see?" he asked.

Lauren surveyed the beautiful lawn. The second-floor vantage point allowed a grand view of the gardens. There were roses and all types of blooming plants she'd never be able to name. There was also a fountain she'd never noticed before, and to the extreme right, the cemetery. The red earth had been replaced and new sod laid down. The marble figure of the angel was still standing, but Marshall Malachi's headstone was gone.

"Had to make room for future Malachis. Real ones," David said.

"Not any time soon?" Lauren asked.

"Remember the legend of Robin Hood? How it ends?"

Lauren looked at him. He was so solemn. Panic struck at her heart. Was something wrong with him? "At the end, Robin is dying and Little John holds him up at a window so he can shoot an arrow." She watched in fascination as David fitted the arrow to the string and began to draw back.

"Go on," David prodded.

"Wherever the arrow landed, Robin wanted to be buried there." She felt her throat closing. David drew back with all of his strength and let the arrow fly. It seemed to sail forever in the blue sky, lacing through the trees until it disappeared, only to reappear as it stabbed into the ground near a circle of ancient oaks draped in Spanish moss.

"David, the feathers aren't white. They're green." She looked at him.

"I know. It's a very special arrow. My last."

"Your last?"

"I'm retiring as Robin Hood. I've turned over the jewels to the director of a local halfway house. The funds will be used to build an orphanage, something that's needed here in Natchez. Strangely enough, all the charges against me have been dropped. The people I robbed have decided to 'donate' their stolen goods to the service of the community." He shrugged. "I've done everything I could do to redress the wrongs my family did. I think we've paid enough. Darcy, Sarah, Aunt Em and me. I'm done with it all. I want to lead a normal life with the woman I love."

"And the arrow?"

"I thought perhaps a new tradition was in store. A happy ending. Where the arrow has landed, that's where we'll be married. Unless, of course, you'd prefer an indoor wedding."

"And miss all of this beauty?" Lauren moved into his arms. "Not for anything."

"Then we'd better make it fast. Spring is but a brief respite between winter and summer. The blood tests can be back in three days."

"A bit impetuous, isn't it?"

"I've been thinking about it since I've known you."

"And I thought you only wanted a partner in crime?" Lauren dared a look up at him. "I'm as happy as a hog in a mud waller."

"Is that a yes?"

"Does possum taste better the second day?"

David groaned. "Where do you hear those corny phrases?" He swept her up into his arms. "Never mind, don't answer. Just give me a kiss."

**Relive the romance...
Harlequin and Silhouette
are proud to present**

by Request

A program of collections of three complete novels by the most
requested authors with the most requested themes. Be sure to
look for one volume each month with three complete novels by
top name authors.

In June: **NINE MONTHS** Penny Jordan
Stella Cameron
Janice Kaiser

**Three women pregnant and alone. But a lot can
happen in nine months!**

In July: **DADDY'S
HOME** Kristin James
Naomi Horton
Mary Lynn Baxter

**Daddy's Home... and his presence is long
overdue!**

In August: **FORGOTTEN
PAST** Barbara Kaye
Pamela Browning
Nancy Martin

**Do you dare to create a future if you've forgotten
the past?**

Available at your favorite retail outlet.

HARLEQUIN®

INTRIGUE®

Hop into a pink Cadillac with the King of Rock 'n' Roll for the hottest—most mysterious—August of 1993 ever!

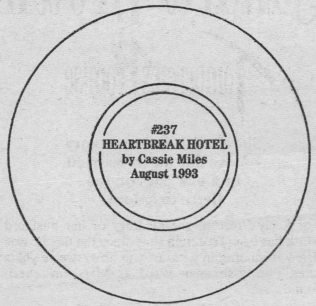

**#237
HEARTBREAK HOTEL
by Cassie Miles
August 1993**

All Susan Quentin wanted was a quiet birthday, but she got lots more: sexy greetings over the radio, deejay Johnny Swift himself—and a dead Elvis impersonator outside her door. Armed with only sunglasses and a pink Cadillac, could they find the disguised "King" killer amid a convention of impersonators at the Heartbreak Hotel?

Don't be cruel! Come along for the ride of your life when Johnny tries to convince Susan to love him tender!

ELVIS